MW01223710

BETWEEN BODIES LIE

a novel

H. M. BLANC

authorHOUSE®

AuthorHouse™
1663 Liberty Drive
Bloomington, IN 47403
www.authorhouse.com
Phone: 1-800-839-8640

Published by AuthorHouse   03/12/2013

ISBN: 978-1-4772-6911-4 (sc)
ISBN: 978-1-4772-6912-1 (e)

Library of Congress Control Number: 2012917133

BETWEEN
BODIES LIE

Prologue

Between bodies of land, across bodies of water, between our bodies, these sheets stretched the distance of oceans, folds like white-crested waves . . . They carry us on tides almost meeting in the touch of flesh, then carried away and set adrift.

—

Some mysteries are solvable, some truths knowable. Other truths shift like the surface of the water, depthless and laced with quicksilver where she stands knee-deep, her skirt hem clenched in her hands, looking back to the shore where he sits rooted and unable to follow.

Stories must have shape. His must be sold. So he takes the shapeless, the formless, in his own way falsifying the truth, in his own way making it more real. He binds it to his own myth, like the person we present to others, sowing sorrow to reap he knows not what.

He writes: *We are stories we tell to others, subtly crafted, to make ourselves more interesting. We must give shape and form to what is shapeless, formless. In the end the truth becomes blurred.*

Is it any mystery that we never fully know one another?

One

Porter is drunk.

"I'm leaving tomorrow," he says.

He holds the phone, black framed by the corner of his mouth, speaking perhaps to his agent, but then again, perhaps it is to someone else on the other end of the line. These things do not matter, only that he is departing in a day's time.

"Are you sure you won't reconsider?" His mouth is still against the well of the receiver, but he addresses a third party in the shadows of the room. A light goes on somewhere in the distance, pulling the last remnants of his focus out of that world at the other end of the wire.

Her mind is a wonder that rewards exploration . . . Or is it 'exploitation'? Is it plunder that will make her yield? Need she be sacked to gain her accolades?

His mind absently scribbles its invisible prose.

She is from some Eastern European country, something with a 'v' or a 'z' in the title. He cannot remember now which one. Not now, with his mind thick diluted and polluted, washed with gold liquor. Would it make a difference if he could recall, could learn her culture and heritage? To then have to sift through: what she accepted and rejected, what she assimilated, what she rebelled against, what she treasured and what despised. Perhaps she despises him. Is it because of her culture, or perhaps because of his?

And yet he has always felt so distant from any idea of his own culture. He is washed clean of country, detached from history, all of them only environments to observe. He comes away from tradition as a piece of art someone else has created, a painting he would not see without its frame, bound in on four sides and kept separate from his present. Or so he tells himself.

Her hair is almost black, her eyes almost black and both glossed and shimmer. He thinks of a black animal's pelt. Those eyes look at him now where he slouches on the sofa, her lips parted over sharp teeth about to speak. There is something of the predator stalking another predator. He would be the wounded.

"Are you packed?" she asks with her Slavic accent. She moves towards him, comes to stand between his knees, shedding her dress that falls like snakeskin, and she climbs over him and he sees only images.

Images and frames.

—

A bird flies from the wire, it travels continents, traverses oceans but cannot bound the distance between you and me

—

There is a crossing — a crossing and a cross — something meditatively unreal, a weight to carry like a dream within a dream, as elusive as his hope. He sits by the window and his hand caresses the armrest as the plane banks.

I am a writer but I spend more time thinking, looking out of windows. Wasted ink blots my mind and runs the pages rampant.

As the plane descends, he looks through the clouds, through the canopy of leaves wondering what he will find down there.

There was a call — taken place before; before the plane ride, before the alcohol and making love on the sofa, her eyes like a predator's — a conversation with the black plastic handset that caused a guide to be arranged from another part of the world.

"You need to do something," his agent had pleaded.

"When I come back, Peter, I will have something." A story to sell, he added silently.

"God, I hope so, Tobey . . . for your sake."

Tobey, a schoolboy's shortening for his name: *Cristobal.*

Cristobal, a good Spanish name for such a poor Englishman.

I am Cristobal, on my birth certificate, on my deathbed. A word given me for convenience, and I have attached stigmas of loss, loneliness, ambition and failure to it, so many false fruit stuck clumsily by the mind to this title, by others also.

He said nothing in response to Peter, shielded himself with silence and then the weak dismissive, "I'll see you when I get back, Peter. Don't worry."

He steps from the plane and the air currents slide over him, like a warm towel over his head and under his collar, and the sweat comes immediately, oiling all angles. "I will meet you there," said the girl with the eyes of a predator. "I will find you." He remembers it now that he sees where 'there' is, has an image of where he is to be found.

He collects his luggage, the carousel moving in a slow mesmeric jounce, loose tiles swinging. One can almost picture the bicycle chain beneath, the man behind the curtain of plastic strips, pedalling to nowhere. *Wizard, grant me some courage, a heart.* An overweight duffle-bag worms its way out instead, followed by a worn Samsonite. He heaves them off of the carousel and abandons the makeshift Oz.

The walls are freshly painted white. There are modern looking stores with show-windows and lit signs and bored looking attendants dolled up for some misguided pageant; Miss Information, Miss Direction, they compete in indifference. Customers move towards them and the attendants look annoyed, the tourists oblivious. They look down on each other in turn. It all smells of disinfectant. He moves slowly through the haphazard line through customs and out onto the street where Joseph immediately spots him.

Joseph is what he would expect an island guide to be. Joseph's skin is muddy, his hair extremely short and greying, and eyes claiming a glimpse of Filipino. He looks like he would belong amidst the locals, bustling aimlessly, except for the Bermuda shorts and bright polo shirt which set him apart and bridge the gap to the tourist. His manner is openly friendly, without the suspicious reserve, shyness or zoological curiosity of the other locals' looks.

"Hello, Mr. Porter," he smiles with surprisingly perfect teeth, his narrow eyes narrowing further, radiating friendly wrinkles. He reaches out his hand and

7

Porter shakes it. Joseph's hand is thick, firm and feels of dried leather. His eyes are dark irises surrounded by yellowed whites, as if stained by nicotine. Porter also notices a glassy shine and thinks of a reservation Indian he once knew.

There is a car and a drive. Joseph does not stop talking for the entire trip to the hotel, but Porter is too tired to absorb much. He sits low in the backseat watching the faded green fields go by on the side of the highway. The highway dips and rolls as Joseph drives over it, the sprawling hollow beast of the rusted Cadillac gliding and bobbing like Jim's raft and he Huck at the stern. *Mississippi Asphalt.*

Bits of Joseph's ramble get through: "African, Indian — East Indian mind you, not American Indian — and Chi-nee mostly . . . a slave heritage, although the Chi-nee came as labourers, so technically they weren't slaves . . . most now are mixed though . . . everybody sleepin' with everybody . . . if local sex was politics there would be peace on earth," he laughs, ". . . used to be a British colony, then a Spanish colony . . . the French try their hand too, but it didn't take . . . America practically own the place too during the war . . . life here is peaceful . . . very laid back, very laid back . . ."

Porter lays back, takes in the slate blue sky and smoked clouds, the fields and shanty towns that drift by between the snatches of red sunspots that flash behind his eyelids. They bounce, crude cradle rocker this Cadillac — Porter in the belly of a tin whale. They pass under a flyover and then Porter can see the city beyond the dashboard, slowly at first, the buildings seem to gather and rise at the speed Joseph drives. There would appear to be no planning; cement buildings cobbled together around colonial style houses, squeezing them until some burst their seams, popping paintjobs and spilling splintered wood from their shells. Some have done what they could to conform, playing up their bright quaintness because people can't crush something so quaint, so "cute" — ask the dolphin, ask the tuna.

They reach the guest house, a small bare affair. Whitewashed walls peeling on the outside, retreating from tiny rivers and tributaries that run through plaster. Plants; fanning fronds and palm leaves, yellowed and sagging, drooping shrubbery, all near the failing end of rustic charm. A low wall surrounds the meagre yard and supports long iron bars connected across the top to form its fence (a style he associates, not unpleasantly, with cemeteries). They walk up the short path, the bare concrete stairs three steps up and inside.

There are a couple of flies and a lazy revolving fan that rocks from where it is suspended from the ceiling. The floor is tiled, a clay Aztec pattern, the walls a pale yellow, the thinnest coat over bare concrete. Joseph escorts him to the small check-in counter and the girl, attractive and dark-skinned in a loose dress. Joseph speaks to her in a quick jabbering that Porter can make little of in his numbed state but recognizes as a Patois, a broken cocktail of French, Spanish, English and Portuguese.

Joseph laughs. The woman looks at Joseph with mild hostility then smiles at Porter and proffers a key with a credit-card-sized rectangular keychain. "Mister Porter, welcome. I hope you enjoy your stay," she parrots in heavily-accented English.

Porter smiles back and her eyes soften slightly. He has that effect; something seemingly sophisticated about his looks and non-threatening in his physicality, its show of age suggesting that, while he can still get it up, sex is not the first thing on his mind. She must be in her thirties — older than Nadia — not thin but with soft curves hinted at beneath the jersey fabric. He takes the key, noting the shine of her skin, something warm and sexual in her scent, and makes his way up the narrow wooden staircase to his room on the third floor. He tries to take his two cases but Joseph insists on toting them, although he grunts and jostles them against the walls at each landing.

The room looks more comfortable than he would have expected from the lobby; not large, but open, a queen-sized bed centred against one wall, an old wooden wardrobe and straight ahead two wooden French-doors. A fan spins lazily overhead, more firmly secured than the one in the lobby. Porter checks the washroom; white tiled shower-stall, a toilet that flushes and running water in the basin. He splashes some water on his face while Joseph drops the bags clumsily beside the bed.

Porter comes out and sees Joseph standing near the door waiting. "Thank you," Porter says.

Joseph smiles, waves a hand as if to say it was nothing. Uncertainly, Porter removes some bills from his wallet and offers them, but Joseph holds up his hands and shakes his head chuckling. Joseph pulls out his own wallet and removes a card, "This is the number to reach me at. You call me anytime you need to go anywhere — middle of the night, no worries." He hands Porter the card. Porter takes it with his free hand and in the same movement, like an exchange, he feels Joseph take the money gently from his other hand. Porter looks up. Joseph smiles, shakes the money once, "Thank you, Mr. Porter," and he begins to leave. "Remember, you call anytime, that number there." He closes the door behind him and Porter is left alone with the ticking of the fan.

He walks to the French-doors and swings them open. There is the swell of light traffic and people moving about, voices calling in the sing-song local dialect. He feels a warm breeze and he can see the rooftops of concrete buildings and galvanize, electric wires sagging from pole to pole. The air is just short of clean, and imbued with dust and salt from the ocean, like a light sweat — the scent of living.

He rests his bags upon the bed and begins the process of unpacking, laying out items in a ritual of materialization. He claims his new dwelling with items from his suitcase and bags. Piece by piece — a toothbrush, a comb, shirts placed on hangers — all serve to imprint his existence upon his physical surroundings, to signal who he is and call himself into being.

When he is done, he surveys the room from the corner of the bed and it still feels empty, his meagre items swallowed by the bare white walls and warm air. The bed feels equally empty, not yet claimed by nights of sleep or explored in lovemaking. He slides his hand across the bare surface with its hollow spring.

He hefts his camera and goes out onto the balcony and snaps a couple of random shots of the street below, the rooftops and sky. There is the sense of discovery awaiting him, followed immediately by the fear of failure. Officially, he is here to do research for his latest novel. In truth, he is hoping to find the story here, for in his mind he has nothing, not even a beginning.

He goes back into the room and pulls a notebook and pen from his travel bag. It is easier for him to order his thoughts with pen and paper, quicker than the agonized stagger of his two-fingered typing on his laptop, while peering at letters past his glasses which he would have to don for the task. This way his hand can keep up with his thoughts. And he even prefers to have the reference of lines crossed out, those inked scars a record of the mistakes made to arrive at any truth he may reach.

—

I am the outsider, everywhere I go. I come to this country and become a stranger in a strange land, because it is all I can do to make my state seem more natural — for it is unnatural to be a stranger in one's own house. And so geography changes while I remain the stranger.

—

The phone line crackles occasionally with static. He holds the receiver close in the dark. The sun has gone down but the wind has died and he sits on the mattress in his room sweating.

"So you are coming?"

"Yes, yes, I told you, as soon as I am finished here." He is pleased to hear the smile in her voice, can even miss her in a way. In the heat he can imagine her thin body beneath the sheer-dress she shed like snake-skin. "You give me the address," she says.

"Yes, I left all the information there. But tell me when you're coming. I'll pick you up at the airport."

A laugh. "No, I told you, I will find you. What, are you afraid I will catch you with one of the local girls?"

"Nadia," he says reproachfully, but he smiles because she is laughing, flirting with him. This is what it takes, a million miles to rekindle some kind of closeness, this distance to bond.

"Are the local girls pretty? I hear they are very pretty."

He thinks of the girl at the check-in counter, attractive dark skin, a primal stir in him. "I don't know," he says, "I haven't been out yet. Just got in this afternoon and I'm exhausted. Only person I've met is my guide, Joseph."

"Joseph? Is he handsome?" She is teasing again. He can hear her grin, pictures her sharp teeth, dark bangs, finger toying in the phone line.

He thinks of Joseph, wrinkles and leather, the full paunch. "He just may be your Adonis."

She laughs, "Sounds lovely."

"I'm going to go. I'm exhausted."

"Okay. No girls for you tonight. Just do it yourself and think of me."

"And will you think of me, when you are?"

She giggles. "No, I will think of Joseph, the Adonis." More laughter. "I am serious now, think of me when you do it."

"Nadia," again he admonishes, but he does, he thinks of her.

—

In his sleep he dreams of her, bathed in sweat and tangled in the sheets, but at some point she becomes the dark-skinned girl from downstairs, or at least an approximation of, since he finds it difficult to recall her clearly. It is involuntary, but in the movement of his dream it does not seem unnatural, and she holds on to him as though to comfort him, as though to console him for something. He wakes up aroused but feeling uncomfortable, troubled by an aching loneliness and the closeness he felt to that stranger in his dream, tenderness he did not feel when it was Nadia.

The room is hot and stifling even with the windows open as they are now. He digs out his cigarettes and lighter from the travel bag and lights up, hoping the smoke will dispel the few mosquitoes and calm his insides. There is occasional noise from the street outside, a car running past, the splintering of a bottle, the call of a dog some distance off, all brief and barren. There is enough light that he can see the room clearly, as though it is not shrouded in night but only a shadow. He looks out of the doors at the navy sky, wondering at the conspiracies that shape a life to bring him here, so far out of his element. How he struggles to learn human nature, but cannot begin to master his own.

In this setting the question gnaws at his extremities: "Who are you?" and it carries none of the weight of deep philosophy, but a certain simplicity that makes him feel a fool for lacking the inkling of a response.

Two

He wakes to what sounds like the blaring of a horn strapped to a loose motor rattling. Then there is an acrid scent of chemical. By the time he looks out from the balcony he can barely make-out the back of the truck through the cloud of smoke issuing behind it. He closes the doors and goes inside, taking refuge in the shower.

Washed and dressed, he thinks to call Joseph but decides instead to do a quick survey of the area on foot. Downstairs there is no one at the counter and he is a bit relieved. He steps out into the warm air of the street, looks left, then right and begins to walk towards what looks like the main avenue.

There is a difference in the colours here. At home everything is grey and beige, here there are oranges, pinks, the buildings and the people, but they are not the vibrant colours depicted in the brochures and television adverts, these have been washed and faded by weather and detergents, so that even these colours tend towards a spectrum more earthen.

He attracts looks as he passes the stalls of fruits and vegetables. He does not smile, only perhaps the fleeting corner of his narrow lips tweaking at a few, a curt nod of acknowledgement and a casual, "Good morning," in response. He does not smile because he has travelled enough to know that a stranger walking down the sidewalk smiling at everyone announces himself as a foreigner. Only a tourist, a man on vacation and financially comfortable has no worries in a place like this. And to announce himself as such is to announce himself a potential target. So his face remains for the most part serious. He is watchful, he observes, which is what he is here to do anyway.

He sees an awning with two plastic tables and chairs squat beneath and he ducks into the small shop before he is absolutely certain it is what he is looking for. Inside is small and warm, a narrow strip divided by a dimly lit display case full of pastries and bread. The air is musty. A fan hums somewhere, unseen and unfelt. A dark and elderly East Indian woman, the kind who is all sinew and bone and will live forever, stands behind the case and smiles at him. "May I help you?" she asks in a voice that sounds surprisingly English.

He allows himself a smile in return. "Do you have coffee?"

"Yes. How would you like it?" she immediately turns to a counter behind her and pours and mixes.

"Black, one sugar. And, um, two of these."

She hands him the coffee and the two pastries resembling squared croissants and waits patiently as he fumbles through the foreign money, eventually handing her exact. She smiles and nods as he heads outside, seats himself at one of the tables and watches the crowds move by. He sips the coffee which is rich and bitter, and decides this will be his morning ritual even before he bites into the flaky pastry.

—

In the back of Joseph's Cadillac he watches the downtown streets stroll by, populated with a variety of colours and coloured people. He can count the whites on his finger if he was so inclined and it toys with concepts of minority outside of economic bounds. What impact does that have; a financially influential minority? He thinks of the uprising which occurred here on this island and tries to picture violence on these streets.

He asks Joseph for his thoughts on the coup, but Joseph sighs dismissively. "To be honest, Mr. Porter, it doesn't make much difference to the common working man. We are a friendly people. Politicians are crooks the world over, we just accept that. The average man here concerns himself with putting food on his plate and enjoying any spare time he can manage. You can't change them greedy politicians." He is quiet for a moment as his words hang in the humidity and the car pulls up to a modern building of glass framed by solid concrete. "Though maybe now and then it's a good idea for somebody to shake them up, let them know there's only so much thieving they can thief." Porter cannot help a smile and Joseph looks over his beefy shoulder smiling too. "Here you go, Mr. Porter. I'll wait here for you."

Porter enters the building of clean white walls and glass where the local offices of the UN are housed. At the security desk he asks for Jack Kaplan. A phone call is made and a brief elevator ride later Porter is introducing himself.

"Jack." It is the quintessential American name and Jack Kaplan is quintessentially American. Perhaps a bit more suave than the average, but every bit as self-assured and commanding as one would expect from the movies; dark eyes, square jaw (only just beginning to soften with age) and his quickly assessing stare, he is a leader and a survivor. Porter shakes Kaplan's hand and immediately feels dominated by the man — the Kaplans of the world who conquer, while the Porters watch passively and are conquered. He looks Porter over once gripping firmly, recognizes Porter as unthreatening and so welcomes him.

"Nice to meet you, Chris," he immediately claims the right of familiarity — a first act of occupation. "Walk with me, will ya." Kaplan walks brusquely, with Porter trying to keep up, a too-old-lackey in tow. "Things are always crazy here before a long weekend, and it seems like every other weekend is a long one. It's amazing how many holidays these people have. Still, we get the time off too, so it's not so bad."

He follows Kaplan down a hall where the American sticks his head into a couple of offices, calling a quick word before marching off. Eventually they reach an office with an outer room, an attractive local sitting at a desk, Kaplan's secretary. Porter sees Kaplan's manner shift slightly as he leans close over the girl's shoulder, a light smile on his face. "Are these the faxes from Nigeria?" he asks, stretching down to lift the corner of pages in front of her, his arm against her shoulder. His face is close beside hers, although he appears to be absorbed in scanning the documents. Porter can read no blush in her coffee complexion. She looks at Porter from behind dark-framed glasses quickly and he smiles, and she looks back down and Porter is uncertain whether her discomfort is a result of Kaplan's proximity or simply Porter's observation of it. He wonders if they are lovers, the display for Porter's benefit, Kaplan marking his territory, a dance of virility to discourage Porter and enforce the status of Alpha male. Kaplan straightens up then gestures Porter into the beige office where Porter in his beige suit can blend into even further obscurity.

"I over-exaggerate it, really," Kaplan says as he drops into his padded seat behind the broad desk from where he commands. "Truth is, nothing of real urgency happens here. And thank God for that, because the locals would have no idea how to function in an emergency. There's no such thing as expedience here. Two speeds: slow and stop. Still we try not to fall into bad habits, so we treat everything as urgent. The result is we end up with a lot of free time." He smiles. He is charismatic, has a heavy charm of his own. "That's how we have time to entertain people like you. You know; writers and such. An integral part of our job really is socializing, entertaining. And there is an art to it."

Porter smiles back, fears it looks ingenuous, "I believe it. It's something I've never had a knack for though. Peter would always tell me I should learn to be more social, for the sake of sales."

Kaplan chuckles. "That sounds like Peter. How is the old dog?" He does not wait for a response, "He called me and told me you were coming down, but he didn't give me much details. Just said he had a really great writer wanted to do some work down here, could I introduce him around. Of course I said, no problem — known Peter for years." He begins to scratch at pages with a ballpoint pen as he speaks. "He mentioned your book, but I'd never heard of it." He does not look up, does not break stride. "Course, I don't get much time to do much reading . . . well, recreational reading that is." He finally looks up at Porter and grins. Porter smiles back. Kaplan pushes the pages away and rocks back in his seat looking at Porter more casually now. "So, can you tell me what you're working on, or is there some sort of superstition — like, you can't discuss it till it's done, type of thing, or it won't get written?"

"No, nothing like that. The thing is, I don't really have it fully, I guess 'solidified' is the word, as yet," Porter says. Then, feeling something more is required, "It's about people reassembling the wreckage of their lives after a traumatic event. I thought it would be interesting to try to examine the culture here, see how people were affected by the coup."

Kaplan chuckles and shakes his head, "Well, I wish you luck with that. But between you and me, I think you came to the wrong place. People here don't mull things over. You want to see people dealing with after-effects you should've visited a shelter back home. People here are different. They accept everything. They're upset for a little while, they react emotionally right after an event, but then they shake their heads, cluck their tongues and move on. Water off a duck's back. You wait and you'll see. Nothing was changed here by the coup. People just went back to their lives and forgot all about it. No one was punished and the dead stayed dead. C'est La Vie, the living have to live. That's the way it goes here."

He stands up and comes around the desk, signalling a close to the meeting. Porter rises. "But don't let me discourage you. You'll see. I'll introduce you around and while you do your research you may just have a little fun too." Kaplan ushers him out the door past the secretary and they walk down to the lobby. "I'll give you a call. There's supposed to be a function tomorrow, some local artist or something. I'll let you know. You can mingle a bit with the island's upper-crust, I'll introduce you to the wife, it'll be fun."

Porter thanks him as Kaplan holds the front door for him. "Oh, and Chris," Kaplan leans out and Porter looks back expectant, "don't worry, I won't tell Peter that his writer doesn't know what he's writing yet." Kaplan grins and winks, then disappears back inside and Porter walks to the waiting car.

—

Joseph takes him for lunch, a small shop on an avenue. They step out of the bright sun into the shade of the shop where they encounter another type of heat, sweating bodies crammed close in the small space. There is no line, just a press of bodies to the counter and a bovine kind of eternal patience on the faces of the crowd. Two men talk loudly in a corner. The woman in front of Porter mutters complaints under her breath. A couple beside her laugh and the man keeps rocking back and forth, oblivious of his jostling of the two men behind him, who glare occasionally but say nothing.

Joseph casually shoulders his way through the crowd and Porter follows him, keeping close. The guide orders, hissing and cooing at the three women behind the counter, repeating his order with sprinkled endearments to the fat Indian woman, her dress spotted with grease, who writes it down. The woman's face is a series of bulbs: goggle-eyes, nose, lips — and Porter thinks that Joseph's endearments know no discrimination. Porter dutifully pays while Joseph stares at the woman's ample and bulbous breasts. They are given a slip of paper, which is entrusted to Porter as his reward for paying, and they shift back slightly and wait. It takes him a while to figure out that there is a system. Items are slid out and the women call out numbers and the customers push forward to collect. He quickly realises that the numbers are not being called in order, so there is no way to gauge how many people have come before them, or how long their wait will be. Still surprisingly soon their number is called and Porter and Joseph move forward again.

A door swings open and a girl enters from the kitchen. There is something about her that draws Porter's eye. Even in these surroundings she appears as something purely natural. She cannot be older than seventeen. He sees her hands move, supple curves of her wrists and tapered fingers, delicate and deft at the same time. There is a look of American Indian, as though she were descended from those native settlers who inspired Thanksgiving, her straight black hair tied in a thick plait that hangs down her back. She wraps the package and hands it to him and he receives it as a settler's gift, stammering, "Thank you."

She looks at him fully and smiles, holding his eyes as no animal in the wild would. There is an acknowledgement there, a mutual curiosity. His admiration so far is for an object of beauty, an ancient artefact rooted from the ground. It is not desire he feels, other than the desire to observe her, to study her movements. He is not aroused but enthralled. She studies him briefly, bestows the hint of a smile. He can only wonder what interest she could find in him, a man three decades her senior.

He takes the package startled, but Joseph is already guiding him by the arm back through the crowd and the girl has turned back to her work. Porter feels somehow cheated by Joseph's failure, alongside the world's, to realize that something of import has occurred, at the same time feeling a greedy privilege at having the discovery to himself. The feeling subsides quickly once they are back out on the street and reality sinks back into his bones and he feels foolish even as he eats his roti, curry running over his fingers and pleasantly singeing his mouth, and talks with Joseph, thinking of the shop girl the entire time, trying to cement her image in his mind.

—

He has Joseph take him to a grocery to get a few essentials, then back to the guest house. He will begin the serious work tomorrow. Outside the guest house a small mongrel eyes him curiously from where she reclines beside the stoop. She has short brown fur with a black muzzle and black smudges around golden-brown eyes. Her oversized ears, two triangles perched precariously on top of her narrow skull, tilt forward as though waiting for someone's summons.

He comes back into his room which has already begun its job of becoming familiar, taking him in slowly and becoming his. He discovers a spider's web in one corner that bellies like a ship's sail against the breeze. The spider is small, with thin sharp legs. He leaves it, going to the small kitchen to put away his

23

items. It takes him a while to light the gas burner, which eventually emits the satisfying 'whump', and he places water to boil for instant coffee. He craves coffee even though he is slick with sweat, and the lie of the spider's web flickering in the breeze is that the air seems humid and stagnant.

He takes out his notebook.

First impressions; there is something innocent about this place, as I thought there would be, but it is tempered with something else. One does not call Nature 'innocent', and here the air is rife with those things in the animal kingdom — everything breathes a casual air of sex, of struggle and (one can easily imagine) of violence.

He pauses for a moment then thinks to write something about Kaplan, before stopping to fill his cup and shut off the flame. He stirs the cup, blinks in the steam and inhales the scent. He takes that first sip which scalds the tip of his tongue before sitting and writing about the girl in the shop. It is a long drawn out description filled with speculation, twists in thought and random guesses at her nature. By the time he is done writing, his coffee is fit to drink and he sips steadily, reading back and then scratching out the entire bit about the girl, leaving only a couple of lines.

Grace. Something connected to nature, so that it appeals directly to the instinct, bypassing any reasoning or question of why. She is Pocahontas, the hope of the New World, wise with all of the kindness and knowledge of the things we have forgotten. She is Promise.

—

Snapshots of Time's Passage:

1. He flips channels on the television as the light fades beyond the French doors. It is difficult to find any local programming and when he finally does he finds the information hard to follow. There are so many languages here, he wonders how they communicate. When he finds a news programme in English he listens for a while, but the newscaster's clipped over-pronunciation annoys him. The stories are all crimes of passion, robberies, a couple of kidnappings.

2. It is dark out, his room quietly invaded with the sounds of passing cars and street voices, the lights down. He holds the phone receiver and listens to the ring on the other side, imagines it echo through the empty apartment, the sound drowned out for Nadia as she dips her head below the shower jet. Or perhaps she is out. She would not sit and wait for him or his call. Perhaps she is on a date, in a fancy restaurant. Perhaps she will bring her date back to the empty apartment, lay him down on the sofa while she stands barefooted on the soft carpet and peels away her dress, watching with the eyes of a predator . . .

   The ring carries on unanswered and he places the receiver back in its cradle.

3. He is lying back in bed, one arm behind his head, watching the fan spin, his mind on Nadia, the bookstore where they met. He remembers it in tilted images, flashes that gather momentum before slowly solidifying into a moving picture: He reads. A polite smattering of applause. He answers questions, signs books, smiles, works on being

social (because Peter has asked him to, because it is good for sales). Then she approaches . . .

He had noticed her when she came in; young, beautiful, sharp features, dark hair and dark eyes. She came in late, causing some commotion, damp from the drizzle outside, in a leather jacket and jeans, a blue scarf, shouldering a backpack. She looked like a college student. The commotion was just a slight shouldering of a neighbour, but she was small, wanted to get to the front of the latecomers so she could see. She whispered apologies and he looked up from reading, only a moment and her eyes flashed as she smiled mischievously at him, there in front of everyone, a hand pushing back a lock of damp hair. He went back to reading trying not to betray an internal flutter.

Afterwards she approached him as he was signing books. He was seated and so he looked up at her. Her hair was tangled and damp, her pale face appearing devoid of make-up, thin lips pink. She was still beautiful. "I'm really looking forward to your book," she said, his first hint of her accent.

"Thank you. I hope you'll enjoy it," he tried to smile professionally.

"I liked the last one, Imperfect Symmetries," her eyes held him steadily, "although it was not as good as the one before."

He was taken aback, recovered quickly, polite smile in place, "Well, the critics agreed with you on that."

"Come to think of it, neither was that one as good as the first. I hope this new one doesn't continue the trend," she smiled again, dark slashes of her eyebrows pointed, still the hint of mischief.

He was thrown off guard by the assault, found himself looking at her as though he were a mongrel cornered. She bit her lip, still smiling, eyes still locked on him but he did not know what to make of the smile, could not tell if it were truly vindictive, but her eyes smouldered. They faced each other like that a moment and it was only when she spoke again that he realized the rest of the room had faded for a moment. "I actually don't have a copy yet for you to sign."

He tried to regain some of his composure. Still he slid a book from the pile beside him, "Well, here you go." He opened the cover, looked up at her with his pen poised, "I'll give you a copy, to make up for past transgressions. Just don't tell anyone."

"Nadia," she said, telling him what to write, "with an 'i'. Thank you." She regarded him with the same bemused look, then leaned in as though studying his penmanship as he wrote and spoke more quietly, yet it still was not a whisper, "Put your phone number. I should reimburse you for the book, for your lost earnings."

He looked up and her face was close to his. The mischievous smile appeared again and in her eyes, but this time it was complicit. He could feel cold air off of her from the moisture and it struck him suddenly that she must be freezing. He felt the tension then for the first time, but not the last, of the desire to take care of her while at the same time fearing her bite. But there was no denying her beauty, her features as delicate as her words were brash, and her smile softened and now he seemed to sense that there was a hint of nervousness behind the façade. The jumble of words that had come to mind bottled up instantly and he wrote the number on the page, quickly and hoping no one else had seen.

She took the book, ran her hand once over it in exploration. "Thanks." And then she was walking away, her backpack bobbing, as an elderly, pear-shaped woman leaned in towards him, offered three hardcover volumes and spoke emphatically, a never ending string of words of which he registered not one.

4. He dreams of Nadia with other men, their faceless bodies burrowing into her as she laughs with joy, laughs at him, mocks and disdains. He stands naked, his impotent member a sign of his indifference and the only emotion comes when the thought dawns that he is hollow as a belly starved. And then the emotion is but a twinge, a shrug for a missed chance already passed.

Three

He stops to buy a paper before his coffee and pastries, then sits beneath the awning on the sidewalk, crosses his legs, sips the coffee and unfolds the paper. He was awakened once again by the blaring of the truck and its spewing chemical smoke. "They spraying the area for mosquitoes," the woman in the lobby explained. "Two passes, now they done."

The morning is light, although grey clouds shade the distance and hover over the view of mountain range far beyond the rooftops. He sits peacefully as people move by, intermittent shadows fluttering across his table, until one shifts over and remains. He looks up, at first seeing only silhouette before the sunlight. Then she comes into view, standing erect as he looks up at her. He is a bit startled by her presence at first. She appears to be looking at her reflection in the shop window, then she glances across at him and smiles before moving closer to the glass, leaning over to peer in.

Out of the shop, in the open air, she looks more in her element. Her black hair is loose, falling dead straight and silken in the light. He watches her absently and at one point, still leaning towards the glass, she glances across at him again and he smiles. She smiles back, studies the window again. He senses her desire to speak to him, as he senses his own desire to make contact, as though he had arrived on the Pinta or Nina, as though he were Columbus trying to make contact with the natives — Cristobal Columbus with his pastries and his morning papers.

She straightens up and he feigns interest in his paper until she turns decidedly to him. "Hello," she says simply.

"Hello."

"You were at the shop yesterday?"

"Yes," he folds his paper to encourage the conversation, tries to think of more to say but fails. "Yes, I was."

She looks at him curiously but her face is difficult to read. "Where are you from?"

"London. England," he says. She nods slowly, appears to be waiting. "My name is Cristobal," he extends his hand.

She puts a foot forward, shakes his hand with a gentle grip then steps back. She hesitates a moment before offering, "I'm Coraline."

"Would you like to sit?"

"No, thank you, I can't. I have to get going." As though to reinforce her statement she takes a couple of steps back, raises a hand in farewell.

"Well, it was nice to meet you, Coraline." He tries to sound casual but suddenly is aware that their eyes have been locked the entire time.

She smiles as though deciding he is a child, "Nice to meet you too, Cristobal. Goodbye," and she turns and walks away, glancing back only once, but not at him, rather it seems only to allow him a glimpse of her profile.

———

I arrive here, my first instinct is to relate to these locals as youngsters, a third world people, but perhaps it is only because I envy their lightness, their freedom from the burdens we have foisted on ourselves. I admire their naturalness and, yes, even their ignorance in some cases.

These things seem natural, and yet this country is a third-world nation, there is squalor, corruption and tremendous crime. It makes me wonder, when I look at my own country: is this the price of civilization — the repression of our natural drives? Perhaps we are not the social creatures we think. Perhaps we are not meant to find common ground, to seek ourselves in the other but only to take what we can, survival of the fittest, both physically and emotionally.

———

He cannot help but wonder if Kaplan is right. As he talks to the islanders he sees their vagueness about the past, about their own personal history. He wanted to believe that Kaplan simply could not see behind the facade, did not possess a keen enough perception to read between the lines and find true emotional depth. But the more he speaks to these people the more he is confronted with a disassociation taken place. The same phrases repeat themselves from different mouths, like taglines from movies or headlines from articles written and ingested by people a million miles away. "It was really bad," several of them say, "the shooting and the looting. Anyone with a store in town lost a lot a lot of money." And this seems to be the extent of the residual damage, the financial loss, the damage to property, things which affected the daily work afterwards.

The outrage is only for these things, the interruption in daily life. There is no expression of any political outrage, not unless he inquires and then it seems forced, put on. There is a demonstration of a kind of passionate anger, laced with long impractical words, and he gets the distinct impression that they are mimicking a television politician in a secondary school play. He wonders had the bomb been dropped here would their comments have been limited to, "Hiroshima? Yes, what a mess, had to be sweeping the porch every single morning for weeks!"

He talks to one man, a friend of Joseph's, who lost a cousin in the violence during the coup, but the man talks about it as though it were an accident. He does not seem to hold anyone accountable, does not seem to expect any justice. He accepts. They all just accept. Porter finds himself disappointed with this handful he has met, but the disappointment spreads to the rest of the population as he looks about him. He wonders if he has made a mistake coming here, but somehow the image of Coraline comes to mind and a mystery, or at least a curiosity is reignited.

They travel choked streets into the heart of downtown, to a fifteen-storey office tower where he meets a local businessman. It is a meeting that Kaplan has arranged for him. "He's a good man to talk to," Kaplan had assured him. "Indicative of the type you'll find here, but on the better educated side. The business men are the ones who felt it, and they're the only group that really exert any sort of influence over government policies." Kaplan had sounded rushed but jovial on the phone. "Also I sent around an invite to your little lodgings there, so you can meet the missus and some of the art aristocrats of the island."

Porter had thanked him. Now he sat before the businessman in much the same attitude as he had sat before Kaplan. Phillip Kernahan's skin is pale with a slight ruddiness, hair tight white curls. The man seems intelligent and Porter gets a general overview of the coup.

The military group had invaded the parliament building, as well as the one local television station and two of the three radio stations. They demanded the government step-down and that a certain local politician instated as Prime Minister. The local politician in question disavowed any connections to the militant group and their intended coup, however he was suspiciously one of only two ministers absent from parliament at the time of the hostage taking.

A series of threats and negotiations took place during which the then Prime Minister was shot in the shoulder — he would forever lose full functionality of his left arm — and amnesty granted to the members of the militant group. During the five days of the hostage crisis there was extensive looting and violence by the local civilian populace. It is estimated that twenty-four deaths are a direct result of the militant action. Five deaths are attributed to "related" violence, with six more being suspicious borderline cases.

Five months after the event an election was called and the local politician, whom the militant group attempted to place in power, won the popular vote and became Prime Minister.

Porter listens as the man recites the story like a well-learned thesis paper, but then he hears more of the same lines as before, the detached, "It was a terrible thing." The loss is again broken down into dollars and cents for him, this time with an added allotment for the loss in foreign income since tourists, the businessman notes, were "frightened away from visiting our beautiful little island. It was a terrible shame, their action," he condemns the militant uprising.

In a sort of frustration Porter calmly asks the businessman before leaving who he voted for in the election. The man's body language shifts becoming for the first time a bit defensive. "Well the truth is," he explains, "that the government at the time really wasn't looking out for the common man. They were bourgeoisie. My argument was not with the uprising's message, but with their means. We are a peaceful and democratic people. The next election should have been waited for and change would have been made just the same. Time heals all wounds. There was no need for violence."

Porter thanks him for his time and meets Joseph back out in the sun-baked street.

—

He makes two more visits, conducts two more interviews with similar results. Then relief eventually comes in the form of Doctor Lillian Mungroo, a small half-Indian half-Latin woman with large almond eyes and a small neatly shaped mouth that resembles a flower. Dr. Mungroo speaks passionately and Porter quickly notes the woman as an exception. She was here during the coup, she explains and treated a number of victims of the resulting violence. "There was never an accurate body count given. Do you know that there was no inquiry held by the government after? I mean, how ridiculous is that? And they want to talk and dream of being a first-world country."

She talks about the turn of personality, the change in people; those you never thought capable of violence were suddenly found looting and even killing. She seems to have a good grasp of human nature and speaks of a general tendency for locals to not consider outcomes. "They don't think ahead," she says. "They indulge themselves and listen mostly to whatever it is the gut tells them to do. It can be the source of some hilarious satire, but it is mostly dangerous and more and more it is becoming destructive. There's no sense of responsibility for actions."

She speaks thoughtfully but there is something of the foreigner about her. She refers to 'these people' as though she were not one of them. When questioned he finds that she is in fact a local, although she studied abroad for several years in Canada. She wants to go back, she admits, but first she will serve her time. "It's terrible, I know," she says. "I'm as guilty as the rest of them. I complain, but then I feel the task of changing anything is so beyond me and so I just opt to run away . . . save myself." She smiles a bit sadly and Porter wonders if he is meant to offer words of condolence to her, to make her feel better about her decision.

He cannot think of any words of comfort although he does not mean to condemn her by his silence. For his own part he can understand her feelings of helplessness, that feeling of being unable to change the world around you, far less save it. Some of us can't even save ourselves. He thinks this as he shakes her clean almost perfect hand at the door and thanks her for her time. She tucks a lock of her shoulder-length brown hair behind her ear and he notes the shape of her face and that she is in fact, even without make-up, a very beautiful woman. He leaves her alone in her stark office, feeling as though he has added to the starkness of those bare walls somehow and heads down the narrow flight of stairs.

Four

There are canvas rectangles and squares filled with vibrant colours, oranges and yellows, heavily laden to create textures. The work is skilled, engaging but not challenging. One is not forced into political or philosophical thought. The paintings are well composed and decorative. Porter stands before one picture which depicts a young black schoolboy kneeling to tie his shoelace. The boy kneels below a large window divided into four panes and through the window both sunlight and rain seem to diffuse in a surreal swirl of lights and blue and orange, creating a rippled stain-glass effect. Porter stands, staring out of this window trying to see beyond the glass when Kaplan appears beside him.

"Not bad, huh?" Kaplan drains the watery remains of his drink. He wears a replica of the same dark suit and appears to have come straight from the office. "Come," he says. "Come, meet the wife." And so Porter follows him through the well-dressed backs of the art gallery crowd, lamb to the slaughter, to meet Kaplan's wife.

They move through backs draped in fine materials, hands poised with fluted glasses, and approach one such back, a form in a shimmering burgundy dress, sandy-brown hair laced with gold falling almost to her waist, well-tanned shoulders, full hips. "Ana," Kaplan comes up beside her, ignoring the couple she is listening to, "I'd like you to meet Chris. Chris Porter."

She turns partly to Kaplan, then follows his arm with its renewed drink, turning to face Porter on her other side, causing a slight flick of her hair. "Chris, this is my wife, Ana."

She smiles, sizing him up with hazel eyes. She does not offer her hand but a tilt of her head to the side. "Chris, it's very nice to meet you," she says.

For his part he gives a slight bow, "Likewise."

"So you're one of Peter's?"

"Yes," he sips his drink, a little uncomfortable under her gaze, which is present, focused on him and not drifting or searching as people's eyes usually are at these events. He immediately finds her interesting, as well as attractive. "Yes, I'm one of his stable, as the saying goes. Though my days as a prize stallion are behind me I'm afraid."

She smiles politely with somewhat broad lips beneath a delicately pointed nose. Her eyebrows furrow a moment in contemplation, "I believe I read one of your books."

"Really," he cannot deny a certain disappointment.

"Really?" Kaplan pipes in. "I had to tell him honestly I'd never even heard of him."

Ana glances at her husband, just a flicker, but then she is studying Porter again, her head tilted, as though the answer were written on his face, as though he would conceal it from her, and he grows increasingly uneasy beneath her stare. Eventually her eyebrows relax, head straightens, "The Sceptic's Banquet," she says, pointing a finger, having caught him out.

"That's right," he admits with a guilty smile and hides behind a mouthful of alcohol.

He does not ask what she thought of it, is happy to let the matter drop, but she continues. "I quite liked it," and there is a look in her eyes, an awareness of his unease and she seems to be taking a playful enjoyment in her effect on him.

"When did you read that?" Kaplan asks distractedly, gulping his drink and looking around the room.

She barely turns to him. "Months ago," she says, and there is a brief surge of annoyance in her voice which she quickly subdues behind playfulness, "I tried to get you to read it." Then back to Porter, "But he's always way too busy. Those golf balls won't whack themselves, you know."

She smiles behind her glass and Porter smiles as well. Kaplan is less amused, still looking distracted. "Look," he suddenly says, "I've left some papers at the office. I need to run get them." He is already fishing for his keys in his pocket as though to underscore the urgency of his mission. "Porter you don't mind looking after Ana for me till I come back, do you?"

"Of course," Porter says, but his acceptance is assumed.

Ana seems less pleased with the arrangement. Porter catches a flash of anger directed at Kaplan which she quickly masks behind a formal looking smile. "Jack?"

"I won't be long, honey, an hour at the most. If you get sick of here just head over to the Coliseum and I'll meet you there. Okay?" He kisses her on the forehead, slaps Porter on the shoulder, "Thanks, sport. I'll see you guys in five for dinner," and he heads out the door.

Ana stares after her husband crossly, but aware of Porter's attention on her, she looks back shaking her head as much to say, 'these kids!' Then she looks down at her drink and there is an almost audible sigh to her shoulders, he can feel her collecting herself, just a brief moment before she looks up, a plastic smile pinned in place and eyes now dull, the shutters drawn. "Jack's always running around for work," she says and her mouth tweaks at the choice of words. "So, how is Peter?"

No, he thinks and the urge comes over him to shake her by the shoulders, slap her or kiss the smile away from her lips, anything to reawaken her, to do away with the social dummy that has taken her place, the wooden conversation and empty stare. *Break down and cry*, he wants to tell her. *It's alright. I'll understand.*

"He's well," he says instead and they drone on about Peter for a while.

"What have you done here so far?" she asks.

"Not much. I like to take the first week or so to really just absorb the atmosphere." He does not want to mention the people he has spoken to so far. "I find it helpful towards having a better context for relating."

"As opposed to doing it the other way around."

"Well, Peter would prefer that. Get the information first, you can fill in the context later, I think he would say."

"Does sound like something Peter would say." A little light has returned to her eyes, maybe it is the wine, but she looks around the room now, no longer present, no longer with him in the moment, and he is not surprised when she says, "Let me introduce you to some people. Have you met the artist?"

—

Voices in hollow wombs. The people she introduces him to cannot pull him from her. She takes him around and he follows dutifully, smiles politely and takes their questions. However he is more interested in her; her actions, her expressions, the modulations of her voice. Somehow he knows something about her already. She is not the spoilt neglected society wife. In a way she would probably welcome that role. It would be an escape from that thing that draws him. Even when she excuses herself, abandons him momentarily to the artist, a well-travelled, well-spoken African, Porter listens as attentively as he can, eyes fixed. But part of his mind wanders with her through the crowd, attached by a ghostly filament, that common bond that he has already recognized even if she has not — the depth of their loneliness.

She hides. Even before when they spoke she was hiding; her pleasure in his discomfort, a playful distraction from her own ill-ease. He sees the hints more and more as she takes him around, eager to allow him the lead, to avoid attention herself. He tries to be the magician and offers his tricks; rehashed lines from eons of cocktail gatherings, slogan art critiques, bite-sized wit, philosophical hors d'oeuvres. She is thankful, until she sees that he is aware of what he is doing, that he has guessed her secret. He delivers a particularly saucy line, with all the relish of the society gossip and as the small group all laugh, his eyes meet hers askance of their wine glasses and she sees through him, as clearly as he has seen her. She sees the entertainer's mask and then the hollowness beneath it.

—

They finish their drinks, their smiles, their performances, bow and leave the stage. She does not mention what she has seen, nor does he. For these are the things we do not speak of, but only learn and hope the other forgets.

—

It has begun to drizzle and the raindrops on the window diffuse the streetlights into amber stars beyond her profile. He tries to stare ahead and she drives them to the restaurant, the Coliseum. "Jack will meet us there," she says needlessly. "Thank you for keeping me company. Jack will look for any excuse to duck out of those things. I don't know why I keep dragging him. He really has very little interest in art."

"Well it was my pleasure," he says. They form the words to fill the silence because that is what they were raised to do, to fill the negative space. "You were a very gracious host, and there were really some interesting people there. It'll prove invaluable material I'm sure."

She smiles tightly and they fall quiet. He has perhaps gone too far, the words emptier than the silence, but he would be content to roll along, to sit beside her in silence with only the slosh of the tires and the groan of the wiper blades bowing back and forth, to sit saying nothing and drive into the night until they run out of highway.

"So, may I ask what your new book will be about?"

He finds himself relating abstract ideas, speaking of love and loss, missed connections and damaged souls. It is not what people want to hear, they want a solid plot, a hero, a villain, a quest and triumph. He feels foolish after only a moment as he always does but has committed course and every attempt to try to make his ideas more palatable only serves to make them more mundane. Still he talks, only working out his unformed ideas as he speaks, giving them even more of a sense of rambling.

But she listens and smiles, happy for the distraction, interjecting a question occasionally so he realises that she is enjoying losing herself in the abstract themes, general concepts that take her away from the specificity of her present. Porter finds himself grateful that he sent Joseph home under Ana's assurances that they would get him back, for it has afforded him this time.

The ride to the restaurant is not long and as they enter Kaplan is waiting for them. He already has a drink and stands to greet them.

"Did you get your papers?" Ana ask a bit too pointedly.

"Yes, yes," Kaplan ushers them to sit, kisses Ana heavily on the temple. "Terribly sorry about that, Chris, goddamn work never stops," he gives Porter a wink, stretching his arm across the back of Ana's chair. "Even when I'm out, people still look at me and see my title. Don't get me wrong, it has its advantages. But it can get very tiring."

"No problem at all. We had a lovely time. Your wife introduced me to some very interesting people." A waiter comes and they order drinks.

Kaplan waits until the drinks are brought before he continues speaking, punctuating with a jerk of his glass. "Oh that artsy-fartsy crowd? Don't get me wrong, I mean I know you're a writer and everything and you probably see your share of these events. Still the majority of that crowd tonight haven't got a clue, just a bunch of pretentious snobs with too much money and too much time on their hands."

"Jack," Ana is glaring at him.

"What, Ana?" he looks back at her steadily and she turns to her menu.

"Can we just have a pleasant dinner, at least?"

Kaplan looks at her a moment longer, purses his lips then slugs from his glass before looking back to Porter. "Sorry, I guess I'm not much one for 'culture'. But let's eat. If it's one thing these people can do it's cook."

"Of course everything is fattening," Ana says smiling over her menu.

Kaplan grins, "That's how you know it's good."

They are all friendly again, all on good terms, the hosts and the hosted, everyone plays their role excellently. The food is brought and it is rich and flavourful. He does not try to catch Ana's eyes, does not scrutinize her movements. He focuses mainly on Kaplan who does most of the talking. They laugh, they are entertained and they genuinely enjoy themselves, all three.

A pleasant dinner.

—

Ana leaves them and Kaplan drives him home. At the guest house, as Porter pushes open the door of the dark sedan, Kaplan studies him a moment.

"You married, Chris?"

Cold thoughts suddenly seep into Porter from a continent, miles away. "No," he says. He does not elaborate and Kaplan does not seem to note that he has become sober.

"Good for you," Kaplan says distractedly, looking ahead. "You know for some situations it's necessary. But it's not natural. It's not a natural state for a man to be in." He looks up and smiles suddenly, "Especially for a writer," he says more festively. "A writer needs to experience the world. Sample everything. So many different types of love, so many women, shapes and forms. There are some beautiful women here, I'll tell you that. But you'll see for yourself, I'm sure." He winks and waves.

"Goodnight," Porter smiles and closes the door.

He watches from the steps as the car pulls away then makes his way into the guest house and up the dark corridor to his room. As he closes the door behind him he is suddenly aware that he is not alone. He walks softly, giving his eyes time to adjust to the moonlit darkness. The room is occupied, he can sense a presence and then a scent seems to trigger something. He sees her form on the bed before he notices the cases against one wall. She lies on her side and as he approaches she shifts, turning her upper half, twisting towards him. He kisses her forehead and eases onto the bed beside her.

She blinks groggily, "Where were you?"

"The Consul and his wife, they took me to an art show and then to dinner. You should have told me you were coming."

Her dark eyes focus on him and she smiles. "Then it wouldn't have been a surprise." She stretches and he moves into her outspread arms, kisses her and she pulls him to her.

"How did you get in?"

45

"I have my secrets," she teases, rising, easing him back, removing his tie. She kisses his neck, his chest, begins removing his clothes.

"I missed you," he says and immediately wonders why. It is only convention to say it. His body responds faithfully but inside is left cold from his insincerity.

She moves, her body still sleepy, "I know," she says, easing over him, taking him over. "I will make you miss me more."

—

A few days after the book reading Nadia did call him. He was surprised by her accented voice on the receiver. She spoke naturally as though they were close friends, "Come have a coffee with me," the first thing she said, not even confirming it was him.

"Who is this?" he asked, but he knew, had thought about her eyes, the moisture caught in her hair and the bemused smile.

She laughed lightly as though reading his thoughts. "Nadia, from the book signing. Nadia with an 'i'. Come, have a coffee with me, I will buy — payment for the book."

"Well, Nadia, I'm not sure . . ."

"Not sure? Let me decide for you then; yes, you should come." She rattled off the address of the cafe.

He could not help but laugh at her cheerful optimism. "Well, ok then."

She gave him no time for second thoughts, "Good, you should come quickly though," she said playfully. "There are some men here and I don't trust how they are looking at me. Ciao." She had rung off.

He had examined himself in the mirror, the slacks and buttoned long-sleeved shirts he always wore, giving him a sense of elegance, or maybe it was only formality, either way he had wondered if they spoke more of age now. He briefly considered changing, but decided against it, and left the apartment in a state of mild agitation.

He spotted her immediately, thanks to the same blue scarf, which she wore now open at her neck. They sat and spoke and she made everything easy for him with the exception of her age. She was seventeen years his junior, a number which he would establish much later, but could have guessed at on their meeting. She was intelligent, charming and vivacious and he felt his pulse quicken with her, but he also worried, felt himself foolish when she found excuse to grip his hand, when she did not release it though the exclamation was complete and his mind focused there with a heady sense of drunkenness. For that was it, she was intoxicating. She was intoxicating and he was intoxicated, an old drunk. She made him feel older. Too old to be suddenly getting it into his head to seek new adventures and throw caution to the wind.

Months later she would pull him to dance in the rain with her, and though he wanted to be like her, throw his head back ecstatically, eyes closed and soak in the elements, his mind could not help but acknowledge what the crowd would think: look at this girl, vivacious, free-spirited! Now look at this old fool, this poor old fool has probably lost his mind.

That first date he had a sense of unease in the back of his enjoyment, like a popcorn kernel stuck in the teeth that did not dislodge until they had reached back to his apartment. It was by her request and he was still confused, still in doubt that she could want him. She was seeking only literary discourse, he told himself, her flimsy excuses to view his books were genuine. Even as he put the key in the door he worried that his hand would shake and so he was focused intently on driving the key firmly home when he was suddenly aware of her shadow shift close and her mouth against the side of his neck. His mind flooded with relief even as he kissed her, stumbling through the door.

He would get used to the looks, the admiring and the disapproving. In the literary crowds they would gossip, it was all the talk for a while, the cocktail gossip, but he knew behind the whispers and the sideways glances they were thankful he had provided them with copy, and in the end to them he was "an artist" and allowed the eccentricities this implied. Closer friends forgave him, glad to see him move on from being the morose widower. She was good for him, they would reason, she was full of life, what he needed after his association with death, and there was therefore the added implication that it was just a phase. She was too young and they would grow apart.

They did, but it was not their age he felt that had done them in, but their natures. Nadia was ambitious. She wanted success, wanted admiration. She spoke to him that first date as a struggling writer. She told him that she wanted to write novels, but she always put off showing him her work and he never saw her write. The few times they had stayed at her place, a small room in a boarding house, he had seen a stack of journals. Her "work" she had referred to them at the time, but he was never permitted to read them, and over time she spoke less and less of her writing, of her novel, and when she eventually moved in with him the notebooks did not appear to make the transition.

"Your first books were great," she told him early on. "True art," she had called them. "But you seem to have lost your way." He had listened intently, studied her lips. "Perhaps you need a muse." And that was the key to what Nadia had wanted. She could not be a great writer, but she could be great by proxy. She would inspire him, be his muse and thus immortalized.

When his next book failed it was the beginning of the end for them. She continued to enjoy her status in literary circles, but he knew she was disappointed that she had not moved him to greatness. His failure was hers and she was no longer as flamboyant as before, became somewhat more subdued. She traded on her sex instead. Whereas before she had opinions for every occasion, acted as the philosophical centre of every discussion, now her circle grew smaller and she would mingle in gatherings, inevitably commanding a small circle of males who would stand listening and taking her in with their eyes.

They continued on, falling into habit, neither one willing to let go of the dream, the image of the writer and his muse. And so on a small island in a half-rate guesthouse they find themselves, the mediocre writer, his failed muse, and disappointment, inextricably tangled in the bed sheets together.

Five

Shadows flash across his table at the café. He tries to read the paper but glances up at every other figure in expectation. He smokes a cigarette and drinks his coffee, the pastries in a brown paper bag spotted with oil on the table in front of him — two extra for Nadia. He drains his cup without having absorbed anything from the paper which he folds and puts under his arm and he walks back to the lodgings.

—

"It is so hot here," she says.

She is standing by the French doors, her arms spread, hands pressed against the jambs. She wears a light dress, almost transparent and her body looks pubescent.

He makes a cup of coffee for her and puts it to rest on the desk and sits on the edge of the bed. She picks up the coffee without a word and looks at him through the steam. "Why can't you write something about Paris, or Italy?"

"Maybe next time."

"And this hotel. If you can call it that. It is barely a hotel."

"It's a rooming house really," he says.

She looks at him irritated, "A rooming house." She turns away from him, looks out the window again. "You know if you act like you are a nobody everyone else will eventually assume that is what you are."

They have been here before and he lowers his head and sighs. "What's that supposed to mean?"

She turns back to study him. "I mean that they can put you up somewhere better than this. Peter knows what a great writer you are. You've made so much money for him and he puts you here, in this . . ." she searches the room contemptuously for the word, "hovel."

"How much money I've made for Peter, I think any profit I may have brought him I must've burned through on the last couple of books." He does not worry to tell her that he is the one who wanted this place, who asked to avoid the Hiltons and the Marriotts.

"You shouldn't talk like that, you sound . . ."

"What, Nadia, 'Old'? I am old."

"You defeat yourself with that talk." She turns away again, leans against the doorway looking out at the bleached blue sky, the terraced hills in the distance.

Is she wrong? Probably not. But she does not understand, he thinks. She cannot begin to understand him. They do not argue, only because he lacks the requisite passion to do so. If they could argue, if he could get angry, shout and rail as he used to, equal her with curses and accusations until she would eventually break something. If he could do that as he used to then it would be alright. She could smash the lamp and then they would subside into silence and slowly make their way back to each other, slowly and plaintively at first, bodies only touching, brushing, then fever rising until they bit and thrust, the final stages of the battle fought in the act of reconciliation. He looks at her form leaned against the sill, the curve of her hip jutting, buttocks formed through the light fabric, wants to feel close to her, or at least longing or desire, but he feels nothing. Her back seems cold and it is the backs of all of those in his literary world, the back of the world turned on him.

—

They stroll through the market, makeshift stalls of wood and galvanized sheeting, dusty looking vegetables and the bright plastic colours of peppers red, yellow and green, like crayons. They stroll absently, having come here from a sense of obligation to view the local scenery. Nadia strolls ahead of him, Joseph somewhere behind. Joseph, whose eyes lit up at the sight of Nadia, took her in blatantly from head to toe before smiling at Porter like a proud father.

Nadia takes pictures, approaches stalls and smiles before raising the camera leaning forward and snapping a shot. She can bring that lens into two inches of a vendor's face and they don't seem to mind. He wonders where that ability comes from, to be so casual about that intrusion into another's space. How people seem to accept it. He would feel affronted but, as he has learned, he would smile and accept it as well. She likes to take pictures of him, he provides, "instant-melancholia," she says with a laugh. "Don't smile," she directs, "just look around you. Now look at me." She has a good eye. And she directs him well.

Nadia took up photography four months after his last book was published. It was her consolation, one of several things she tried in order to reinstate her grasp on the artistic. Unlike the other attempts, she had a knack for photography and she began to work small jobs here and there. It gave her a new sense of independence. She had recently got a job assisting a fashion photographer, an attractive young man she had met at one of their literary functions. She spoke most of the night with the man before he had invited her to visit his studio the next day. She had returned from the studio to the apartment with a flush of triumph, announcing her new job to Porter. He had tried to be happy for her, but already sensed wariness in his gut. Porter suspected she was sleeping with the photographer before the first week was up.

He never confirmed this because part of him sees every interaction of Nadia's take on a sexual connotation. Every man she speaks with at a party Porter sees as her potential lover. Even inanimate objects become phallic when caressed by her hands. She cannot bite into an apple without him wondering if she has ever been with a woman. Sex emanates from her and as she moves through the market he almost fears for her safety. No, part of him knows that he suspects Nadia of betraying him in collusion with the entire world, and so he has never confirmed whether the fashion photographer is her lover. But it is also because a part of him almost does not care, would be relieved. Leave, he thinks, so I may die in peace.

They walk from the market along a trail of beaten grass, to the edge of a wide murky lagoon. He follows her, aware that he is following. She snaps pictures. He stands back and observes her from behind. "My sister would have liked it here," Nadia says. The shutter snaps. He cannot see her face, only wisps of dark hair and a slice of her cheekbone and jaw. "She likes the heat," again the shutter snaps, hums, "and nature."

He stands watching her, his hands in his pockets, observing her as though she were a local he had just met, a stranger not a lover, someone not yet beyond necessitating politeness. She rarely talks of her family. He has heard only passing references to her sister. He believes there is a brother as well, but that he and Nadia are not close. She is closer to the sister, a competitive closeness that sisters can share, each understanding and consoling the others failures while absently contributing to them.

Or so he imagines it to be with Nadia and her sister. The truth is that he has not met any of them, has not even seen a picture. Perhaps the sister is no longer alive, or perhaps she did not exist in the first place, simply some extension of Nadia herself. Any of these things are possible, he thinks, as he watches her. Neither has she asked him about his family. He has never spoken to her of his wife. She showed no curiosity in his history — again that word. He looks at her and wonders who she is, whom she thinks he is. What one exchanges in the intimacy of lovers, is it always so little?

They make their way back to the car and back to the room, travelling in calm relative silence and he is surprised when back in the room she kisses him, draws him quietly with her to the shower.

—

A PICTURE entitled "A Man In Exile":
A man stands in beige slacks, a white shIrt, sleeves rolled to his elbows. He is tall, slim, with brown hair that is streaked with silver. His eyes are lined, dark and deep-set — sad eyes, he will later be told, the source of his instant-melancholia. He stands sweating, his head bowed, examining some green peppers with no real intent to purchase. It is apparent by his look, by the posture of his body, that he has no real purpose to be here in this foreign market, where he so obviously does not belong. The light is somehow warm and foggy at the same time, a bright sun partially obscured by passing rainclouds.

—

Towels lie twisted and he sits and stares out of the doors into the dying evening, eyes catching brake lights glowing red in the distance then blinking out. She is asleep across the bed and he sits trying to write, trying to formulate ideas that fail to come. He thinks he should simply write an adventure, create something for Hollywood — a hero with a drinking problem, a villain with a penchant for fine cuisine, they can do battle on the Eiffel tower, and Nadia can have her Paris vacation. Happily Ever After.

But nothing is ever so simple. Why can't he let it be? No, the hero with the drinking problem lacks the will to care whether the villain with the penchant for fine cuisine is brought to justice. It will not bring his wife back and so let the world be blown to bits, let others partake in his pain. Besides, the villain is only manifesting his own loss as well and so they are both on the same path, indulging some form of revenge — how can one's be more right than the other's? And isn't any action a form of revenge, every action driven by a need to counter some loss or feared lack? Mankind creates life to counter its own mortality, a form of revenge against death. Porter sits before the laptop attempting to create in order to counter his own fear of emptiness, the fear that there is nothing in him worth expressing. For four books now, thousands of pages, he has been told, "No there is not." Once he had something to say, an idea to express, but no more. Now the critics agree: Cristobal Porter is creatively deceased.

The phone rings, a deep quick bell. Nadia squirms and groans. Porter crosses the room to answer it. It is Kaplan calling him, with an invitation to dinner.

—

"Porter! Glad you could make it. And this is your friend, Nadia? A pleasure to meet you, Nadia, absolutely charmed. Come, come, it's very crowded here tonight but Ana is just this way. She's holding the table for us. Excuse me. Watch your step," Kaplan pushes through the backs crowding on the open-aired veranda, clearing a space for Nadia to pass. Porter is left to hold his own but emerges not far behind them. Kaplan is making the introductions between Nadia and Ana.

Ana has an air of calm observation as she shakes Nadia's hand. Nadia appears unaware of her effect on Kaplan thus far — she is the only one who does not notice. Porter notices Kaplan's heightened attention, the touch of nervous energy and the boosted desire to engage, to host thoroughly. Porter is certain that Ana is aware of it too, even as Kaplan turns to him with a re-evaluating eye and Ana leans in to converse with Nadia. Porter sits with his back to the crowd, looking out to sea as he sips his whiskey, his tie feeling a little tight in the evening breeze, but never mind he will loosen that later. "Hope you don't mind, Chris," Kaplan is saying, "but we've got a few more friends coming down."

"Of course not." A tilt of the glass. "The more the merrier."

The conversation between Ana and Nadia has fallen away. A few courteous remarks exchanged, but neither is willing to feign interest in the other to any great degree. Nadia is a number of years Ana's junior and would rather have the attention of the men. For her part Ana does not seem interested in any attention. Porter feels that rare sensation of embarrassment when Ana looks at him briefly and smiles and he feels a sudden desperation, wishes he had not brought Nadia here for what Kaplan's wife must think of him. There is a desire to explain himself that leaves him feeling lesser.

"You are a diplomat?" Nadia asks Kaplan and he smiles eagerly.

"Yes, that's correct. It's really not much of a job in a place like this though," his eyes pierce and penetrate her, even as he raises his glass to his lips, then tilts back breaking contact. He follows his drink with his eyes and glances across at Ana, "We enjoy certain perks, certain benefits," he smiles, then glances back to Nadia. "For example we have a boat."

"Oh I love boats," Nadia leans forward slightly, finding Porter's hand as her piece in the game they are playing. She glances across at Ana, "You must go out to sea all of the time, that's why you're such a lovely colour," endearing, social. Ana smiles barely. "I want to be that colour: Golden," she giggles.

"Golden-bronze, like burnt honey," Porter suggests.

"Like pancake syrup," Kaplan says.

"All over," Nadia grins.

"Oh, I'm lucky when I don't come out looking like burnt toast," Ana smiles.

"It's perfect though," Kaplan says, "we were going to invite you out anyways. We're taking a couple of days. We have a little house on one of the coastal islands. I figured we could take the long way around the island, show you guys around, then stay over at the house a couple nights. Sound good?"

"Oh lovely!" Nadia exclaims. "Isn't that lovely, Chris?"

"Lovely," he smiles genuinely, feeling the first sedations of his drinking. "Sounds like a wonderful opportunity to see the lay of the land."

"It will be," Kaplan assures, casting a smile at Nadia before knocking back the last mouthful of his drink.

"There really are some beautiful spots on the island," Ana says.

There is a sudden commotion as two other couples burst out of the crowd and Porter finds himself introduced, but missing names — a businessman and another diplomat. They are shuffled around in seats and Porter finds himself beside Ana to his right and the business man on his left. On the other side of Ana is the diplomat, then his wife beside Nadia and then Kaplan.

Comments are being made and Porter finds himself momentarily lost in the mix. Nadia laughs at something Kaplan says and the businessman leans across his wife to apparently add to Kaplan's anecdote. Ana suddenly speaks on Porter's right, "I pulled out your book again. Your name is published as Cristobal?"

He turns to her and the general merriment at the table suddenly has its volume turned down in his ears. "Yes. That's actually my name: Cristobal. Quite ridiculous, I know."

She smiles, lightly a spark glints in her eye and he has a feeling suddenly of the conspirator. She leans in and he is aware of her proximity. "Well actually," she says, "my given name is Anais." He studies her eyes. "On my birth certificate, I swear," her hand squeezes his in brief reassurance. Her hand is warm. "Oh, everyone calls me Ana, but technically my name is Anais. It's funny because I'm pretty certain my parents never read a word of hers. Still, what's in a name?" She grins, her eyes still studying him before eventually she looks away. Porter as well considers her a moment longer and then the merriment comes back into focus; an uproar, the businessman's wife smiling lost, while the businessman leans forward over the table, almost out of his seat guffawing, Nadia laughing against Kaplan's shoulder. Kaplan arms open across the backs of the chairs to either side, nods towards the diplomat at the centre of the fun, the diplomat making mock-stern denials while his attractive wife drapes herself over his shoulder like a fox shawl.

Porter smiles into his drink, steals a glance across at Ana. He sees her watch the others, smile pinned in place, sees her observe casually, take note of all that passes, saying nothing as Porter himself says nothing, as though blind to the sexual current that passes in flashes and sparks between Kaplan and Nadia; the trailing of a hand across the forearm, palm on a bare shoulder, whispered exchange of breath and the angled flick of the iris from the corner of the eye coupled with the corner of a smile. These tiny flirtations, so minute they are not considered indiscretions. They cannot be called 'infidelity'. But then still, what is in a name?

They drink, talk, laugh, drink more, this small group of expatriates. The businessman takes his wife around the dance floor. They come back sweating and breathing heavily as though from a bout of love-making. The businessman's wife flops down in her chair with a gasp, but her husband wants more and Nadia takes very little persuading. At some point they all watch Nadia, the men admiringly, the businessman's wife wistfully, the diplomat's wife challengingly. He is not sure what Ana's look conveys. It is a passive aggression, a mild distaste for the inevitable without blame. It is defeat, he realises, behind a mask of living.

Kaplan watches Nadia twist with relish. The band has become louder and so they each feel secured in their silence. Kaplan leans across the table, whispers something to Ana in a moderate shout impossible for anyone outside to understand. She smiles, that slightly bitter smile that Porter has seen before, her eyes on Kaplan as she shakes her head. Her eyes communicating everything to him, that she knows where his energies pull him, what his real purpose is. He does not hear a word her eyes say, waves her off and leans in to the diplomat and his wife. Before long the diplomat's wife is rising, dark and lithe and she is making her way out with Kaplan onto the floor to join pulses with the drums and do battle with the other couples.

Porter stands and walks to the edge of the deck leaning against the railing, now turns to look out to sea as he pulls the pack of cigarettes from his pocket, shakes one out. The water is dark and lights glisten from the masts of boats anchored just far enough out to be phantoms.

Ana appears beside him, cradling her drink in her hands. "Could you spare one?"

He shakes one out for her and lights it for her, then lights his own. She blows a stream of smoke out to the night. "Jack doesn't approve," she smiles momentarily and they are conspiring once again. "So Nadia seems like a very nice girl."

"Does she now?" Porter is aware of the play in Ana's voice.

"Where did you meet?"

"A book reading," he says.

"Really?" she is toying, something bitter beneath the play. "And you asked out one of your fans?"

"She asked me out actually."

"I see."

"Do you?"

"A very modern, progressive woman, I guess. Men like that."

"Some men," he does not know what she is driving at. She is taking out her frustration on him. "And how did you meet Jack?"

She seems to stop, arms folded she exhales again over the sea and her face softens. "I'm sorry, I'm a little out of sorts tonight."

"We've all had a few to drink."

She smiles back at him and it is more genuine, even grateful. She turns her head to look to the dance floor where Kaplan and Nadia hold each other.

Now these things cross the mind, in retrospect we thought them, we knew and it seems so obvious now, but at the time we let them go, pretended to ourselves that our imaginations were only fuelled by our unhappiness.

Ana's hand rests a moment on Porter's arm, "We weren't always so unhappy," she says. She is referring to herself and Kaplan but she may as well be speaking for him, Porter thinks, for them all, for the entire world at this morbid carnival. "But it's likely we never really knew each other." She looks searchingly into Porter's eyes, her eyebrows drawn, "Sounds so cliché. I don't know why I'm telling you this," she suddenly smiles, laughs it off.

"It's the alcohol," he concedes her shelter.

"Do you dance?" she asks.

"Very poorly."

"Well it seems the only thing to do. Shall we try?"

He holds her on the dance floor, the music having turned slower as they sway in each other's arms. He tries not to hold her too close, rails against this instinct. He can feel her softness, not the taut sinew of Nadia, but a fuller curve and flow of flesh over bone. He feels sweat run against his temple, catches sight of the perspiration beaded at her neck just at the hairline and again the sound of the crowd is drowned by a drone within him and the only few sounds remaining — his pulse, the rustle of her dress, the parting of her lips and their breathing — are amplified to drown him. And the scent of her, the scent of her salted skin.

After a long while Kaplan cuts in and Porter is a man woken from a slumber. He pretends it is the alcohol that has him sleepy as Nadia slips into his arms and they continue their slow drift on the floor. And strangely Nadia's body now seems foreign — small, light and unreal, insubstantial — as though it does not fit the mould of his arms. He glances at Ana with Kaplan, but she seems at peace, unaffected by the change of partners, as though nothing could please her nor make her discontent. Nadia burrows against him and he looks again out to the black water laying under the night and those burning orbs that would take him, if he only could, out to sea.

—

Back in their room he and Nadia make love — though 'love,' he thinks is the wrong word, nor do the terms 'have sex,' nor 'intercourse' seem to do it justice. It is love in a sense only if one implies some sort of narcissism, an act of self-aggrandizement. She stands before the mirror removing her earrings when she glimpses him sitting on the edge of the bed, drunk and worn, watching her. There is only animal attraction now, the physical, as she holds his reflection in the mirror with her eyes. She opens her dress, eases it aside and he is risen with the falling veil, his arm around her as he bites down on her shoulder and she grips the back of his head, eyes on the mirror even as her breathing quickens, her head tilting back and eyelids lowering. But her eyes still hold the image fiercely, her pleasure there in the reflection.

Six

He sits in his café and smokes a cigarette, wearing shades against the clear morning sun, and tries to make his way through the local paper.

"Good morning," she says, her voice clear as a mountain stream. He is a bit startled to see her standing there smiling over the edge of his paper.

"Good morning, Coraline."

She tilts her head bemused, "Cristobal," and he almost thinks she curtsies.

"Can you sit this morning?" he asks, folding away the paper. She does not speak but takes the seat opposite him. "And how're you this morning?"

"I'm well, thank you," she says. She smiles and studies his face, eyes moving up and down and he once again has the sense of being a representative of a foreign tribe, as though they have been thrust here to make communication. "You come here every morning?"

"So far," he removes his shades, "since I've been here. I like routines — possibly a British trait."

He wins a smile, "From London?"

"Yes."

"Oh. I've been to London."

"Really? How did you like it?" he asks.

Their civility is practiced, formalities of first contact that must be gone through. He feels a touch uneasy sitting here with this girl less than half his age. His curiosity about her is instinctual, sensing something about her nature that he wishes to delve into, to learn how the mind behind those eyes works. He feels that she is curious about him in a similar manner, a most straightforward interest in what type of person he is and what makes him so. Simple curiosity, yet this very direct exchange of interest is allowed to have nothing straightforward about it.

"It was very cold when I went," she gives an illustrative shudder.

"Well, it's always very cold," he assures her.

"I was also young, maybe twelve. But I liked it very much. Is this your first time here?"

"Yes, it is. Let me get you something. A coffee, pastry?"

She accepts nodding with a smile and he goes inside and returns with his offering, setting it before her and she studies him as she sits with perfect posture, light breeze swirling steam and fanning strands of her dark hair. She thanks him, takes a quick sip of coffee. She clamps down on her lips to sooth the burn.

"Sorry, I wasn't sure how you like it, so I just got regular."

She gives a quick nod and a smile, lips still clamped.

"And what brings you here?" she asks eventually. She has a way of tilting her head with each question that brings back his impression of a deer or wild creature, although there is the corner of a smile that suggests a waning absence of nervousness.

"I'm doing research for a novel," he says. "I came to get some background on the coup."

"I see." She looks into her coffee a moment. "Well, I'm afraid I would be no help with that. I only remember staying home, playing cards for three weeks until they said I had to go to school again," she smiles broadly. "I was actually disappointed when it ended. Of course I had no idea what was going on, or at least very little. It wasn't until after when stories were told in school . . . One of my friends lived downtown and said she heard shooting every day. There were bullet holes in the street signs near her home. And then there was a child a couple of years below us. Her father was killed. I'm still not sure of the full story though. I was just aware at the time that her father was killed, everyone whispered it, but no one really talked about it. I believe he was a member of the uprising."

"Do you remember if there were sentiments in the household, one way or the other, for or against the uprising?"

"My family thought it was wrong. My uncle said there was no basis for it, it was pure bullying. The government was elected democratically, he said. He said, you can't point a gun at someone's head because you don't like the outcome of a democratic election and tell them 'Vote again'. He said it was corruption to do so. I think he was very disappointed in the country when the next election was held."

She seems to drift and he thinks that she is somewhere in the past. "Because it vindicated the uprising?" he asks.

"Yes," she comes back to him, smiles. "But I don't know much about it myself, as I say."

"No, this is very helpful. It's more important to me with what I'm trying to find out. I'm not so interested in the politics as much as the human element. How people were affected personally."

"It's all politics of one form or the other, isn't it?"

He studies her as there is a dawning of understanding and a smile spreads across his face. "You're a writer as well," he accuses and she laughs, an earthy bubble somewhere between a woman and a girl.

"I write," she says. "It's not the same as being a writer. I mean, I've never sold my writing."

"Well that's not the distinction," he says. "You can be a great writer and never get paid."

She looks at him curiously, then raises her coffee, still studying him over the rim. "Well, I'm not sure yet. I will let you know when I figure it out."

—

His talk with Coraline is pleasant but brief. She excuses herself saying that she will pass again, she knows where to find him now. He goes back to the hotel where Nadia is frustrated with him. He cannot be bothered to appease her.

"Fine," she says. "Go to your interviews and I will find some way to amuse myself. Probably I will just sit in the bar downstairs and get drunk."

"It's work," he says feebly.

"So is getting drunk alone," she says, but now even she knows she is being difficult and he is allowed to kiss the back of her lowered head before going out. At the door she calls out to him from in the bathroom, "The foot tap in the shower is leaking. Tell downstairs to send someone to fix it."

—

Joseph awaits him in the lobby and there is no one else around. Porter makes a mental note to tell them about the shower when he returns. The Cadillac is preheated as usual when he gets in. They travel into downtown to the Library there. Porter can make out Kaplan's offices a few blocks away. The library is under renovation and they are directed to a side entrance. The building appears to be an old fort, with thick squat walls of beige, the kind that seem to forever hold moisture. The result is that it is a pleasant temperature inside even if the air is a bit musty.

The hallway opens out into a hangar-sized room with open terrazzo floors and fans hanging midway down from long stems. There are two levels lined with books and pamphlets. He is shown the bank of computers by one of the librarians, an attractive and fashionable young woman in a tailored work suit who smiles with gloss-red painted lips. He watches her as she walks back to her counter, playing in his mind a brief image of kissing her dark cheek, before forcing his mind back to his present task.

The newspaper articles offer little more information than what he has already uncovered here and in his research before coming. He follows a trail of articles on the coup leader, Abdul Kadeem. The man is referred to as a "charismatic speaker" repeatedly in articles but there appear to be no traces of any of his speeches. Son of a labourer, he was raised and educated locally. There is little that appears exceptional about him, except that a man who appears so unexceptional could lead one hundred and thirty men in an uprising against a government.

The trail grows sparse after the coup, with the exception of articles on the ensuing legal battles for reparation. There are speculations of Kadeem running for government office himself, rumours which do not materialize, and then one brief article about a land quarrel where the sect leader expresses a disappointment with the government he took up arms to promote.

It is all peripheral to Porter's aim. He is aware that he is grasping blindly for inspiration. The lack of information is more eye-opening; the failure of any substantial probing by the government or media, details missing from the public eye of causes, the why and how. He thinks of Dr. Mungroo, her suggestion that the people balk at the notions of responsibility, of consequences.

He leans back in his chair, pushes his glasses up on his head and rubs his nose bridge. It can sometimes seem an alluring concept, to be removed from facing consequences. It can be a way of cutting one's self free from the past, of attaining freedom. But what is good for one must be good for all, and in that scenario one must wonder what becomes of morality and who is to be its watchman.

—

When he returns to the apartment there is no sign of Nadia. On the kitchen counter there are a pair of earrings, silver with blue beads. Beneath them is a piece of paper torn from one of his notebooks. She has scrawled a message in her childish script: 'Gone out with the Kaplans.' He wonders if she called Kaplan or if he called her, decides it does not matter. Then he wonders if Ana is with them. He doubts it, but for the brief moment he considers it he feels a touch of jealousy.

He decides to walk the streets, familiarizing himself with the surrounding areas. He finds a narrow avenue a couple of blocks down that appears to be a miniature market; a flower shop, wooden stalls with second-hand books, a shop window filled with kitchen utensils and a small store with old vinyl records that plays a strangely middle-eastern trumpet song. Inside the record store the young woman behind the counter glances up at him before going back to her writing. He flicks through the records, the scent of dried cardboard from their blistered sheaths. They are familiar American pop records; the Beach Boys, the Byrds. He comes across the Platters and the Mills Brothers as well, but the records all seem warped and water damaged and he wonders how they are able to sell anything.

Coming back onto the avenue he sees the mongrel from outside of the boarding house. As he lays eyes on the small mutt her ears raise again as though expecting his summons. She lowers her nose to inspect the ground accentuating her sharp shoulder blades but continues to regard him. They look at each other a moment before she is distracted by two small boys running into a nearby alley. Her face breaks into a smile and she lopes after them.

He enters another shop filled with an odd assortment of artefacts, items that have the feel of the discarded. Dolls and sculptures made from wood, steel, coconut husks and shells. The aisles are narrow, forcing one to invade the personal space of these relics; a raggedy-Andy or Rasta-doll with woollen hair teased and clipped, a wooden drummer with wind-chime arms, joints held by rubber bands. Porter looks into the painted eyes of a tribal mask, the empty eye-sockets of a fierce clown. There is something derelict and mysterious about this place, like the history found in attics. He drifts through curiously. He considers bringing Nadia here, but there is a pride in knowing of this secret place that he does not wish to share with her. The question arises unbidden as to whether Ana knows of this place. He pictures watching her move along the aisles, her ghost leaving ghosts of fingerprints in the dust. He decides that he will return at some point, will find a talisman to purchase, but not today.

Back in the street his brown mutt rushes out, tongue lolling. A pocket-watch sized stone hurls after her and glances across her thigh eliciting a soft whelp. Porter sees two young boys come to the mouth of the alley, stones in their hands. The small mongrel looks back at them, her ears tilt forward and she moves shyly a few steps towards her would-be playmates. Porter sees one of the boys raise his arm back and let loose. There is no playfulness in his eyes or his throw.

His aim is off and the little mongrel skips a few paces to the side as the stone skips along the asphalt. It rolls up close to Porter's foot and he stoops down and picks it up. The mongrel trots a little closer to the boys. The same one as before, raises his hand with another stone. The dog cowers slightly, seeming to accept her role in the game. But the boy seems more self-conscious under Porter's watch. Porter makes a show of examining his own stone, weighing it in his hand. The boys hesitate. Narrowing his eyes, Porter begins to gauge the distance between himself and the young truants. The boys make their decision and turn and run, disappearing down the alley. The mongrel starts in their direction but they are too far gone and she pauses to consider Porter.

"You have terrible taste in friends, my dear" Porter says. "The Gods seem to have played a trick on you." The mongrel smiles up at him. She looks back dotingly in the direction the boys have taken, her ears drooping a moment in disappointment, before following Porter a few paces back, back to the guesthouse.

—

The piano is old and wine brown. Porter slides a finger over a chewed key, slowly depresses it with an empty clunk.

He had a female friend, a Professor, whose husband beat her. "It's not his fault," she would say, "he was beaten as a child." She would make excuses for him. Until one day she ended up in the hospital. She divorced him, but never filed charges. What makes a person do these things? What makes one react with violence, what makes the other accept? The sum of these experiences that define who we are, at what point can we rally against them, defy them, chose to be other than who our experience has shaped us to be? Is it a matter of will inherent? Are we either born with the ability or not? Or do we all have it in us to reshape the clay which God has formed?

He had a friend, a writer, who was abused as a child. This friend was the nicest person one could ever hope to meet. Porter never suspected his friend's dark past, never would have, the man cast no shadows, until a night in a bar in Tangiers. "Porter," he said, having spilled his tale, both men rather drunk, "I could never do that to someone. I could never put them through what I went through."

Porter is not sure why he thinks of this as he sits at the piano in the small bar in the hotel, knocking back scotch on the rocks in isolation — Nadia was right, it is work.

When he had returned, Nadia had gone into a fury at his failure to have the shower fixed, another of his failures for her to notch on some invisible belt and tighten around his neck. He smiles at the ridiculousness of his self-pity and the act of smiling makes him feel better. That and the scotch poured into his skull.

He leans his head down against the warm grain of wood, closes his eyes a moment to solidify the fog. He senses her behind him even before he feels her fingers in his hair, her hips touch his back, her lips against his ear. He squeezes his eyes tight, depresses the key, tries to bury himself in the vibrating tone. Beneath the sweat his skin prickles. Coward, he thinks. This is the makeup, here it comes and he doesn't want it, but is too weak to deny it. Her arms slide down, around him and he turns, pressing his head against her chest, avoiding her eyes as she engulfs him.

She will lead him back to the room and he will follow as a lamb willingly slaughtered.

Seven

It is strange how we betray ourselves. We see ourselves through other's eyes.

He looks at Ana sitting there with her knees drawn up under her chin and wonders how she lives. Nothing too simple, nothing black and white, for everything in emotions is grey, one moment bleeding at the edges into another until we are uncertain as to where anything began. Nothing too simple; her posture, the way she holds her shoulders straight, head erect — yet nothing simpler.

She spends her days in vigilance. She is always watching him, the other. Half of the time she spends despising him, wondering where this traitor has come from. She watches to catch a glimpse of the man she married, even as she spends the other half of her vigil willing him to turn and face her, to ask her 'what's the matter,' to beg forgiveness for his treacheries. And these, her two purposes, overlap and dissolve into each other. In her mind he will turn to her unable to ignore the fire in her eyes that burns defiantly and then, in this same scenario, it is suddenly she who breaks down and begs his forgiveness for his unfaithfulness. It becomes unclear to her where guilt lies and who is to be judge.

Porter looks to the bow where Kaplan is speaking to Nadia. She holds her head low and looks up at him smiling, the tip of her tongue between her teeth. He holds something in his hand, a piece of string, and he leans in close, to speak past her shoulder. Their figures are superimposed on the eye by the white light and lies that burn away the horizon. The boat ploughs the sea leaving white foam like upturned earth, fading in the distance.

It seems obvious to Porter the game that they play, coy smiles exchanged with each other, and Porter tries to find it in himself to feel jealous or betrayed. But it is not there. He cannot summon indignation. His only emotion is a sad longing when he looks at Ana. He wonders if she can see the game, the courtship that her husband and Nadia goad each other into. He thinks she is aware, but she puts on a front, either because she is used to it and no longer cares or she feels helpless to do anything about it. They are all so distant; Nadia and Kaplan, offering false promises with their spoken words and silent insinuations, Ana and Porter, accomplices to their own betrayals by their silence.

Islands, he thinks. They are the four of them islands. Separate lands scattered on this boat and out at sea. Like so much ash.

—

This mask I wear has become me and the person I always felt I am grows smaller and smaller, dwindling behind the wall of my façade.

—

The boat makes its way along the coast. There are beaches where golden bathers lounge in the sun, stare fly-eyed from blacked-out sunglasses. There are areas of boggy marsh where the waters lap slow between roots standing like thick spider's legs from the water, shaggy headed trees borne on their backs. The wind whips all day from unexpected directions, warm in the morning and cooling by the evening until it is quite chill. For lunch they eat cold cuts of roast beef, salami and ham, olives and cocktail onions along with a potato and macaroni salad. Around two o'clock they anchor in a small deserted bay. Kaplan dives in robustly. Nadia stands in her bikini, her thin limbs already gathering colour. After a little while and some friendly taunting, she jumps from the boat and slices feet first into the water, coming to the surface giggling.

He watches Ana leaning back reading a book. She has positioned herself so that the wind does not blow her hair in her face, although the occasional renegade draft does send a lock of strands for her to remove. He looks at her and thinks that there is nothing particularly exceptional about her. Certain of her features are more caricature than sculpture — the lines beginning to become visible at the corners of her eyes, her shoulders are a bit too narrow, hips a bit too wide for her to be considered an image of some Vogue ideal. And yet as he looks at her he sees something both so simple and so complex that he feels drawn.

"Come on, Chris!" Nadia shouts. "The water is fantastic."

He smiles out at them and removes his shirt and his slacks, his suit already on beneath. "Are you coming in?" he asks Ana.

She looks up at him, squinting against the sun, a kind of smiling grimace, "Maybe in a bit."

He dives in and the water is at first surprisingly cold, but quickly warms to being very comfortable. Nadia darts above and below the surface of the water like a dolphin. Porter wades, does some laps and hovers. Kaplan does the same, although his manner is more playful. He calls to Ana and makes a joke of splashing water at her, although she is much too far to reach. He also chases at Nadia, pinches her heels below the water, and comes up laughing at her start, shaking water from his hair like a friendly wet dog. Ana eventually comes down wearing an attractive one piece and Porter watches her descend the ladder into the water. She lowers herself below the surface and comes up smoothing back her hair smiling and they all wade around like kids at a watering hole.

Later Porter and Kaplan explore inland playing briefly at *Robinson Crusoe*, bare-backed in the shrubbery. Porter examines fleshy green leaves and sodden bark, the elegant tree-skull of driftwood, while Kaplan stabs at the earth with a stick and talks about international banking and diplomacy. Nadia meanwhile hunts for seashells and Ana stands with the foam touching her feet, arms wrapped around herself and watching the sun's pale haze low on the horizon.

Their foray is not long before they are back on the boat and sailing again out of the bay with drinks in their hands, wind whipping them as the sun slowly blinks out. And the boat continues on eventually approaching another, larger bay, this one populated with three houses, one at each end of the bay mouth and the other nestled inside. Porter can see the wide wrap-around deck, with an awning lit with a string of bulbs, the second floor and balcony, large glass doors and drawn cream blinds behind them. A light winks near a jetty and he makes out a small boat, a pirogue, ploughing towards them. They load their bags with the help of the caretaker, Warren, who pilots the single-engine craft with all on board to land. They have a light dinner, drinks on the deck and then prepare for bed, all happily worn from the long day.

—

Porter is alone in his room, Nadia having disappeared somewhere into the belly of the large house. He is unpacking his bag when Ana knocks on the open door jamb.

"Hello," he says and she enters.

She presents him a lightly worn novel with a touch of awkwardness, trying to appear casual. "It's your book. I knew I had it still." She smiles at him then looks down at his toiletries and other belongings arranged like armies encamped on the mattress.

"I see," he says, examining it, uncertain of what is expected of him.

"Would you sign it?" she asks casually without looking up. She gingerly picks up his razor, old-fashioned with an ornate wooden handle and examines it smiling.

"Um, of course," he looks on the dresser for a pen, almost hesitant to leave her with his things. "Just my signature?"

He looks at her as she examines the razor, then she glances up and she smiles abashed. "Sorry, it reminds me of one my father had. Where did you get it?"

"It was a gift."

She traces a finger over the handle, "It makes me nostalgic." She grins that too-wide smile just a moment then quickly replaces the razor. "I'm sorry," she says turning to go. "Write me a little something. Just hold onto it until you think of something appropriate." She stops in the doorway, "I'll let you settle in." And she goes.

He lies awake in the night with Nadia beside him and he watches her back tinged red, a dandelion rash sprung around an insect bite on her shoulder and he tries to think of what to write to Ana in that opening leaf. In the morning he will shave and feel her finger-trace in the grains of the wood of the razor's handle.

Moments. A writer needs to create moments, but in reality moments create themselves, a sense of ease of being with someone without judgement, with a content acceptance. No words need pass, no particular action taken, a cold glass passed and the timing of a smile that puts you at ease. How we came to know each other, accepting that some things we would never know. An understanding that things could have been, perhaps in another life, but there are no other lives, only this one. And so we sigh in our souls and accept what chance would not permit, an idea we try not to follow to its conclusion for fear that either way it will disappoint — turn into the perfect thing we cannot have, or the imperfect thing that will tarnish hope, take the dream from our tragedy. There my Lady Ophelia, not yet drowned beneath the reeds. Here Cristobal Porter, an aging Prince of Denmark.

—

He leans back in a lounge chair writing notes in a leather-bound journal bought in Italy. Nearby on the porch Ana is stretched out in the hammock in a blue tie-dyed wrap, reading a novel. It is quiet, the sound of the surf and occasional bird chirp or cricket all a soothing whisper in the background, the reminder that you are not alone in the world. Ice shifts in his glass as he sips scotch then glances across at Ana, burnt honey skin glowing warm against sun streaked hair and eyes touched with amber. Something about her reminds him of the driftwood, worn smooth and sun-baked. And he makes a note of her in his book.

It is just after three. They all slept in late, then had a large brunch and continued in a lazy vein. Laughter sounds somewhere in the house's bowels, Nadia's laughter. He looks up but only to see Ana's reaction. She does nothing, only staring too intently at the page. He imagines Nadia laughing, Kaplan pressing close to her, the contact of their bodies, wonders if the thoughts cross Ana's mind. He suddenly feels saddened. He knows he is indifferent to the notion of Nadia having an affair, hopes only that it will provide an impetus for some change in their relationship, dissolution of it, but he realises now looking at Ana that her feelings towards her husband are not the same.

Is it marriage that makes the difference, he wonders. It is elusive to him, that type of emotional contract. He thinks of his own wife, of his troubled marriage and he is confronted with his own failures, his own lies. He wonders if Ana has it in her, those frailties, the ability to truly understand or even commit adultery. In the end, he thinks, anybody can break a promise, marriage only puts the rest of the world in the jury box beside the beloved.

There is a snap of the shutter and Porter looks up to see Nadia with her camera aimed at Ana. She lowers it and smiles and Ana smiles back a smile barely masked. Nadia turns the lens on him and he, used to the presence of her mechanical eye, resumes his writing. Kaplan comes out shortly after as Nadia sits on the armrest of Porter's chair and leans against his shoulder. Kaplan looks a bit flushed to Porter's eye, but it could easily be his imagination.

"Get you another drink, Chris?" Kaplan offers.

"Thank you."

"How 'bout you, Nadia, would you like something?"

"No thanks," she says. "I'd like to go out fishing," she beams. Nadia squeezes Porter's shoulder, tilts her head to rest against his affectionately. Porter feels he is being used, a show, a taunt for Kaplan. "Didn't you say you would take us fishing, Jack?"

Kaplan comes over, hands Porter his drink. "Ana?" Kaplan shakes a glass lightly at Ana who looks up from her book to the glass, shakes her head and resumes reading without meeting his eye. "Sure, we could do some fishing," he carries on.

"Great. Chris, you want to come fishing with me and Jack?"

She presses in close and he is still the cuckold though he knows it and he is tempted to say yes just to see if she will betray disappointment, to let her know that he is not a complete fool. "Actually, I was hoping to just unwind a bit and get some work done. You don't mind?" He looks up innocently and she gives him a quick peck on the lips.

"Oh you're so boring," she grins and ruffles his hair in her hand. "Still that's what you're here for. Write your masterpiece, make Peter proud."

Kaplan is leaning against the banister, the seascape and sun behind him. "I feel sorry for you, Chris," he says. "You're the only one here to work while the rest of us play."

Ana has looked up from her book. "But when the rest of us have gone the way of the dodo, Chris will still be around, his ideas and opinions still there for the world to hear." She smiles serenely at Porter.

"Yes, but what's the use of that when you're not around to enjoy it," Kaplan counters. "No offense, Chris."

"None taken. Actually, I'm afraid I'm inclined to agree with you. Only, well one has to make a living somehow".

Nadia jumps to her feet, "Ana, you will come won't you?"

"No, thank you. I'm afraid I really can't stand fishing."

"She thinks it's inhumane," Kaplan grins.

"It is," Ana says.

"They're fish."

"They're living creatures." She is not an activist, does not impose her will only refuses to take part. In fact, Porter observes, she does not seem to impose her will anywhere, seems to accept that her influence does not, cannot extend beyond herself.

They chat for a while back and forth then Kaplan prompts their departure. Porter goes down to the seaside to see them off. Warren ferries them to the boat and Porter strolls along the beach feeling the sand and stones beneath his bare feet. He makes his way back up to the porch and his journal and Ana who still sits reading.

—

Porter and Ana sit in a domesticated calm. Porter continues to write in his journal and sip scotch while Ana reads. He looks up to steal moments of perhaps his own minor adultery of ideas. For example, when she at one point pulls her hair to one side, inadvertently offering the exposed side of her neck to him, that sculpted arch of flesh that glistens momentarily with a bead of sweat that runs across her nape, he is transfixed.

Eventually she rises and stretches, muscles taut over bone, then she walks to the banister and looks out. For the first time he sees the trace of the scar above the bathing suit back — a line between her shoulder blades that disappears into the suit. He wonders how far it runs. She turns as though feeling his eyes on her and he smiles casually. Her eyes blaze a moment, as though he has said something harsh, then her head lowers and she smiles at him softly, recognizing the falsity of the accusation. "I was in a car crash. It was pretty bad. But, well, I'm still here." She studies him a moment and he waits in the silence for her to continue, but she smiles and looks back out to sea in the direction of her husband's disappearance. She seems to feel she has said enough.

—

On their way back to the mainland, Kaplan suggests they see the marshes on one of the small islands. They are all in semi-casual evening-wear, the intention being to go straight to a dinner function on their return. Porter and Kaplan are in slacks and shirts, the women in light dresses. The boat rests in the late-afternoon seascape.

They motor to shore in the boat's dingy and walk on the shores to the stagnant lagoons that waver beneath the roots of the trees. The sun is dying and the water turns dark and silver. Kaplan wants to take Nadia to the other side of this rock for her to take pictures. Ana does not want to go. It is her first real sign of protest and Porter feels that she has begun to suspect as he does. It suits Kaplan fine, her flat refusal. He and Nadia sail off. Porter agrees to keep Ana company until they return.

Porter has enjoyed his time, both relaxed and productive. He and Nadia have not made love. One night he made some advances but she claimed she was tired. He suspects that she and Kaplan have already begun an affair. He finds himself more intrigued by Ana and perhaps his suspicion is to pave the way for his own conscience. They have become friendlier, having established an easy familiarity, a comfort that settles in their silences.

The thin scar runs like melted wax from below the nape of her neck the length of the soft valley of her spine. He can see it here and again behind the crossing straps of the back of her dress. He wants to touch her chin, turn her face towards the setting sun. She rises and moves away. He sits and does nothing, again and again. She looks out at the subtly shifting water. Porter watches her from behind, the setting prime for a Greek tragedy. He can see her setting roots, body twist and transform to a tree or flower, the Anais blossom. He thinks of driftwood.

Her feet are bare on the sand and slowly she walks out into the water to stand calf-deep in the shallows among the moving reeds, holding up the hem of her dress, gathered in her fist just above her knees. She looks out like someone contemplating a journey or awaiting a sailor lover's return. He half-expects her to begin wading further out into the water towards the mouth of the river, to disappear into the sea. Something inside of him seems to sigh and ache at the thought of losing her to the water and he watches her form against the skyline with a pre-emptive sense of loss. Then she looks back over her shoulder at him, smiles sadly, as though he has guessed her intentions and by doing so has cancelled any hopes of their reality. They stare at each other that way for a long time, before she eventually seems to admit defeat. Slowly she wades back to the shore and him waiting.

The boat returns and they sail back to land, silence between the four of them in the encroaching dusk.

—

For who would cork his heart in a bottle and cast it out to sea?

Eight

The mongrel Porter has named Pasiphae has taken to trotting behind him as he exits the guest house. She follows him shyly at first then darts past him playfully, and then falls back again. Tongue-lolling in a hobo-grin, she seems thoroughly pleased simply not to be chased. As he sits at his cafe, he tries to ignore her and to read his paper, sip his coffee and eat his pastry, but her eyes are fixed on him awaiting a command or some expected entertainment and he can feel that he is watched. Each time he raises the pastry she becomes alert, ears forward, mouth tight, and her eyes sadden. It is an impressive performance and he eventually rewards it with the second half of his pastry — patron of the arts that he is. The dark proprietor scowls disapprovingly behind her shop glass. The mongrel snaps up the pastry in a few bites and watches raptly for more. Porter opens his paper and Pasiphae eventually hunkers down not far away, resting her chin between her paws, prepared to wait.

Coraline sits down with him taking passing note of his new friend. He is surprised but pleasantly so, his mind having been on loneliness, on the coldness which was the casual conversation in the apartment between himself and Nadia. Meaningless words saying nothing, merely meant to create a boundary between them, a buffer or a divider. Nadia's every comment was edged for aggression, the leaking faucet a cause to go to war, his inactivity in dealing with it a summation of his failure as a mate, as a lover, as a man. Even when he eventually picked up the phone and rang the front desk she was not satisfied. His demand was made too weakly, he deserved to be dismissed by them, should not have required her persuasion to act.

Now Coraline sits across from him, her face warm, encouraging, curious. There is no judgement there, no disapproval. She does not seem to demand anything, only waits like an anthropologist who will make a note of all of his movements. "And how have you been?" he asks after their hellos.

"Not bad. You haven't been to the shop?"

"No."

"Can't take the curry, too spicy?" she grins.

"No, it's not that. I've been with some friends to the small islands. I forget what the locals call them."

She laughs, "I don't even know their names myself. We just call it 'off coast'."

"Off coast?"

"Yes. 'We're going off coast', or 'You've been off coast'."

"Oh, ok. Well then, I have been off coast."

She laughs at how he says it and he does not mind. "So how did you like it?" she asks.

He has a sudden image of Ana in the water looking back at him. "It was very peaceful," he says.

"How is your research going?"

"Not so well, actually," he tells her honestly. "I find the people here have a very passive attitude to events. It's not what I expected."

"You are looking for the philosophers?" she smiles.

"I suppose so."

She studies him a moment and he feels highly aware, deliciously probed by those shining dark eyes. "I know someone you should meet," she says, sitting up and he wonders if she intends to take him immediately. "My uncle, Stellan. Give me your phone number. I'll call you when I can arrange it."

"He's a philosopher?" he smiles as he writes the room phone number on a journal page and rips it out for her.

Coraline smiles wide, her eyes narrowing, cheekbones rounding. "He believes so. He is a very interesting man though. You will like him, I promise."

"Thank you," he says.

She rises. "I will call you. Goodbye, Cristobal."

"Goodbye, Coraline."

—

Nadia rages. He knows that she is making excuses. He should get angry, accuse her, cast her out or at least make it difficult for her. He says little or nothing instead. Holds his head in his hand, mutters apologies while she throws her things in a suitcase screaming that she will not stay in this shithole hotel a moment longer, that if he feels this is where he belongs he should not drag her down with him. She will find a proper hotel, she shouts and he admires the passion in her acting, her face turns red, the veins in her neck standout as she screams at him to go to hell.

Perhaps her anger is real though, he thinks. Perhaps she has stored up her venom and now, finally at this parting she has spewed her hate, though the specifics are misaligned. Or maybe even there he is wrong. Perhaps the dripping foot-tap has somehow come to represent their entire relationship to her, that corrosive and mentally warring repetitive leak of his ambition, the deflation of a soul that would hiss quietly in her ear every night, a finger tap-tapping at the forehead, "tap-tap", every night, every day, minute after minute, hour after hour, soul draining away. And every day she would watch him go to the well, take his toilette, dispense his being to spill down the shower waste, to see him know that he is broken and continue to do nothing about it. Perhaps, he thinks, she does love him in a way. Or at least once did.

All of these thoughts run half-formed as he sits on the edge of the bed, head in his hands, fingers in his hair against the sweat soaked temples, while she rages and drags her suitcase to the door and slams it behind her. He does not get up, does not follow her, mostly because he cannot stand the thought of a scene in front of the other guests, or in the street. He knows too at that moment that he has no love left for her — for since when did love ever care whether it caused a scene. Love, he thinks, does as it pleases, "can cause a riot in a nunnery," and he smiles grimly to himself and immediately feels guilty, as though he has insulted Nadia's value. And why should he care? Far less for it being only a sin of thought known only to him, and yet still there is guilt — perhaps the price of a Catholic upbringing, or simply something innate, a burden; his empathy overly developed. How can he feel guilty for this slight when he has remained numb to so much else?

He sighs, pours himself a strong drink and stands on the balcony looking out at the night, listening to the sounds of the street. From somewhere comes a throbbing beat, like a quickening heart and he can feel the vibrations faintly through the walls. He closes his eyes a moment as a cool breeze floats over him, then throws back the balance of his drink. He looks up at the sky and can see stars and satellites. He suddenly feels unburdened. For the longest time, he realizes, he has been under the yoke of his inability to act, to do anything for Nadia. Now it is only him in the dark waters and he can finally drown in peace.

The pulse and the warmth and salt on the breeze which breathes of life conspire to urge him into a change of clothes and out the door in search of people and the living. He passes a thin dark man on the stairs who smiles and speaks to him just as he has passed.

"You are a guest here as well?" the thin man asks.

"Yes. On the top landing."

"Ah, you are British."

"Guilty," he smiles.

"I am just here on the second. My name is Martin." Porter shakes Martin's hand. "And your lady friend, she is not British though," he smiles with clean small teeth but his timing seems odd and Porter suspects he has overheard some of the argument between Nadia and himself.

"No," he says but does not offer more. Martin seems to wait for more but it is not coming and after this beat Porter smiles, "Well it was nice meeting you."

"Yes, I'm sure we'll see each other around."

"Good night." Porter continues down the stairs and to Joseph's car waiting.

The bar he finds himself in is an old colonial house converted. The downstairs has been opened out and a bar constructed in one corner. One walks through the front gateway and up the main path. Table and chairs are set up on the lawn at either side. He climbs the stairs to the wrap-around porch and through the door to the dimly lit interior. At the bar he orders a scotch for himself and one for Joseph who is his drinking companion tonight.

It is a middle-class bar and attracts a wide variety of customers; twenty and thirty-somethings mostly, better dressed than the older clientele and the foreigners who wear shorts and Hawaiian shirts. Porter has a couple of drinks smiling and nodding alongside some of Joseph's friends who talk about work, the government and sexy young girls all in a general mishmash that voices their frustration, annoyance and titillation respectively. Porter listens vaguely and observes the room. After a while he excuses himself to get some air.

Outside, he lights a cigarette, aware of the irony and looks around. An attractive woman stands talking to two men nearby. She is tall and slim, with dark straight hair, olive skin and a narrow face. She looks Spanish and their eyes meet and she smiles slightly before looking back to the man talking. After a while and a few exchanged looks she excuses herself from her party and comes over.

"Good night," he says.

"Hello." Her hands both hold the stem of her wine glass and she leans forward and presses her cheek to his. "It is customary for friends to kiss 'hello' on the cheek."

"Well, I'm glad to know we're friends," he says.

She glances over her shoulder at the two men watching then back at him. "It simplifies certain things to appear so," she says. She sips her drink and examines him over the lip. "I can see you're not from here. English?"

"That's right. And you? You're local?"

"Yes. My mother is Spanish, my father Italian, but I was born and raised here. You like it so far?"

A smirk escapes him. Emboldened by drink, he lets his eyes travel once over her and raises his eyebrows.

She laughs. "The island," she clarifies, "you are enjoying yourself?"

"Yes. I'm having quite an interesting time." It feels like a lie and Nadia has left him and although there is some deeper relief in that it is not a gratifying feeling. No, his experience has been disappointing, but you do not say that. Suddenly everyone in the country is his host and he a guest here. Make yourself at home, people say. But you never do. You do not insult your host, even with the truth, especially with the truth. All these white lies.

"My name's Chris."

"I am Monique." They don't shake hands for the sake of her guardians but study each other a moment with smiles.

"It is very nice to meet you, Monique."

Later he sits up in bed alone, fully dressed but for his bare feet. The doors are open to let in the night air and he is hot and shrouded in that fog that booze creates. He thinks of Monique, of their conversation, her eyes and light shine of perspiration on her collarbone. They talked for a while of mundane things, jobs and living and then she introduced him to a group of her friends that later included the two watchers. They all chatted and laughed. The majority of the conversation was beyond Porter, personal stories and gossip about people he was not familiar with. In the end there had been no tryst for he and Monique, not even an exchange of numbers. It had not bothered him, it was merely pleasant to have been included for the moment and they all made him feel included at the table. He was granted interest for his simply being from somewhere else, able to turn stories of minor functions into conversation imbued with the exotic of the foreign.

The apartment now feels empty, filled with only dead objects. This could all be buried, should be buried, he thinks, like the tenements of Pompeii, preserved and fossilized. The world has no more need of it. The fan spins and he stares out of blurry eyes unseeing.

Nine

The phone rings, pounding against his temples and pulling him from sleep as he pulls the receiver from its cradle squinting against the harsh sun. He is met by a dial tone, his caller having given up on him. He takes it as a sign and drags himself wearily from the bed. He is still dressed and he makes a cup of coffee and sits out on the small balcony, seating himself on the bare tiles and lights a cigarette.

It is already close to midday and the sun blazes and the air is stifling, like coming awake in a furnace. Yet still he needs his coffee and his cigarette, the routines that help him adjust and find his feet in the day. He inhales deeply, aware of white paper bleeding to ash, that cinder glow, neon-edging in geographic patterns, a dissolving shore. Smoke fills his lungs, reassuring, like closing your eyes (which he does) and sinking your head underwater. He thinks of the way that some acts can visit either extreme, be either soothing or terrifying, totally dependent on whether they are voluntary or imposed — the introduction of another's will altering our perception.

He finishes his cigarette and remains there for a while when the phone rings again. He is surprised to hear Coraline's voice, so young on the line without the intelligence of her eyes to give her age. She invites him to a family lunch and he suggests that he have Joseph drive them.

Coraline rents an apartment in a small two-storey building of fading blue paint. When he and Joseph arrive at the appointed hour she is on an enclosed balcony looking down and she jumps girlishly to her feet and trots down the stairs. Her hair is out, she does not appear to wear any make-up, nor is there the scent of perfume when she sits beside him in the car, only the mild fragrance of a scented soap.

They drive for almost an hour, pass open overgrown fields and travel down narrow crumbled streets with shoddy wooden houses where old women sit on porches and stare out with dark eyes from dark sun-leathered faces. They speak for the first half of the journey and travel in silence for the second, looking out of the windows as the salted wind blows against their faces.

Coraline's Uncle Stellan is the same height as she is and almost twice as wide. He greets them outside of his house which is a modest-sized, unpainted wooden structure on stilts in the middle of an undefined clearing with what appears to be a wild jungle of trees and bush sloping upwards at its back. He is short and thick, everything about his features broad and he is darker than Coraline. His hair is un-brushed and in peaks like a child-drawn rough sea and he wears dark shorts and a shirt unbuttoned halfway, revealing a large portion of his chest and beginnings of his belly. He welcomes them and introduces his family to Porter, his wife Sita, and their three children; a nine year old girl, four year old boy and an infant attached to Sita's hip. And then there is his grandmother, Coraline's great-grandmother, who sits stoically upon the porch like all of those other old ladies, her steel-coloured hair tied back in a tight bun from her dark lined face, wrinkles like a walnut's shell. One of her black eyes has the tarnished-marble shine of blindness. She has a high noble forehead and thick wide lips which she has passed in shade to her great-granddaughter.

They sit down to a sprawling dinner on a very plain stained-wood table. The food is by turns sweet, spicy, juicy and dry. There is nothing bland or plain, everything is immersed in pungent flavour. They talk about family matters as the children move seamlessly from chairs to laps to the floor. Granny says nothing but stares placidly at Porter as though observing his spirit.

After lunch they go outside and sit on chairs in the open yard. Porter and Stellan smoke while Coraline occasionally calls the young dogs to roll at her feet, scrubbing their heads, sides and bellies. Stellan's conversation is occasionally punctuated by a hacking cough.

"You see the thing is," Stellan says continuing their dialogue, "it comes back to standing on the shoulders of giants. These days everyone wants it easy. It is the falsity of the American market machine. Not the American Dream, mind you, as so many people are fond of saying, but the false marketing machine. That machine which suggests everything can be attained quick and easy." He snaps his fingers, "Now!

"It is what I like to call the Promethean curse," he continues. "Prometheus steals fire, gives it to man. But a price must be paid. Prometheus pays the price, has his liver pecked out for eternity by a pack of *corbeaux*. Unfortunately, man pays nothing for this and it is such that we continue. We want to be handed the flame but to have someone else pay the price. When you don't earn your way, you rarely appreciate what you get.

"For example, this country; we never had a fight for independence. There was no war, no major revolt or revolution that set us free from British rule. Truth is we just became too expensive a property to maintain, so they cut us free. That is before they discovered the oil, of course. But the result is for the people here, that they take their independence for granted. They assume their freedom and don't take the responsibility that comes with it. The government? Well, you want to read a book about our local politics? To really understand how it works, the best book for you to read is *Lord of the Flies* — children playing a dangerous game. And same thing with the coup — children playing war with real guns and real violence and no clue about consequences."

Stellan grows thoughtful a moment until his faraway eyes wander onto his niece. He suddenly changes mode, "Has Coraline told you about her book?"

Porter acts surprised, "Coraline has a book?" He looks at her and she smiles and looks away embarrassed.

"It's not finished," she says, narrowing her eyes on her Uncle. "And it's not really original."

Stellan smiles with obvious pride. He waves her comment aside, "Oh, no story is original," he says with authority. "They are all re-imaginings in some form or the other. Ask Porter, I'm sure he will tell you the same. The Greeks beat us to anything original. Heck, even Shakespeare wasn't original. It's not what you say, it's how you say it. Take classic themes and reinterpret them. All the same object of life, just show your view, bring your perspective to it. Right, Porter?"

Porter and Coraline smile at each other in a shared warmth towards her Uncle. "What's your book about?" he asks.

She hesitates a moment before telling him, "It's just a collection of local folklore tales."

"It started from a conversation we were having," Stellan interjects proudly. "You see, what we realized was that most nations have their morality tales, fairy tales really, to instruct people, to teach them. Here we have a mishmash of cultures but what has happened is that these characters have sprung up, cross-bred demons from different cultures, evil characters that take advantage of man's vices and in this way they are a threat to get you to remain virtuous. But they are characters without tales, without actual stories. It is only: 'don't engage a prostitute because she may be a la diablesse,' but no real story about the man who engaged the la diablesse, if you understand what I mean. They don't start, 'once upon a time' . . ."

"I want to put them into a collection that people all over can access," Coraline says. "Tell the fables in a classic story form."

"Sounds wonderful," he says.

"The Sister Grimm," Stellan says and laughs.

She scrubs the dog's ears as it rolls against her bare calves. He can see her beam behind her curtain of hair.

He is pecking at his laptop keyboard, frustrating himself with the clumsy clutter of words that are stuttering forth onto the page. He gets little farther than two sentences before holding down the delete button sweeping the page clean. He eventually decides to transpose some of his notes on his conversation with Stellan. He writes a brief paragraph then rises in frustration, lighting a cigarette and stalking onto the balcony. He paces back and forth breathing smoke quickly burning it down. He is about to drop the filtered stub when he hears shouting out in the street, a commotion that grows into a mob of voices arguing. He sees people running, turning towards the noise further up the road and he decides to take a look. He retrieves his camera and heads out.

There is a sense of anticipation as he strolls towards the sound, the tumult growing like an approaching heavy rain. Following the scattered watchers he rounds a corner and is afforded a view of a small square where a crowd has gathered. There seems to be a push of about twelve to fifteen men on one side. They are dressed alike in long white robes and knitted skullcaps. Three at the front of the group are arguing, all shouting at the same time while the others stand stern or angry behind them, tense as though prepared for action.

Their opponents are outnumbered, four men in grey short-sleeved suits. One of the grey men is shouting back at the white robes, while another tries to restrain him, to urge him away. The third grey suit stands sternly but seems aware of the odds. Porter takes several photos, already coloured black and white — white robes, grey suits, concrete buildings and slate sky.

A crowd of onlookers has gathered close as well and watch with anticipation, lick lips, rock back and forth like men on a starting line. The line between them all seems close to snapping. A siren gives a brief blare, a clearing of the throat to announce police presence. The onlookers come unplugged, charge dying as they back away, make space for the uniformed police officers who ease between the two groups. One officer seems to try to placate the white robes. He stands in front of them making calming gestures with open palms, while the other officer pulls the angry grey suit aside, berates him maintaining a grip on his arm.

"What happened?" Porter asks a young man close by.

The man seems to shrug his thin body indifferently.

"Who are the men in grey?" Porter tries a more specific line.

"Those the minister's men, Watch Guard."

"And the ones in white?"

The young man scratches his adolescent sketch of a moustache. "Those Kadeem men, nuh. Watch Guard used to be with Kadeem men. Now they just work for the Minster. Well, I mean, Kadeem used to be the Watch Guard. The Watch Guard, ya know?"

The crowd has been dispersed. The Minister's Watch Guards are walking swiftly away. The police get into their car. The white robed men, Kadeem's men, stand in the square. They turn in among themselves, making jokes to give themselves courage, a feigned casualness to show anyone watching that they have won the round. Porter snaps more pictures. He wants to venture closer but decides against it.

The young man is right beside him now. "Kadeem men shoulda beat them Watch Guard." He looks Porter over awkwardly, forces a chuckle. "They woulda kill them Watch Guard." He smiles again to show they are comrades.

Porter feels uncomfortable under the man's dull gaze. "Thanks," is all he can think to say, then excuses himself and walks away.

—

"Hello?"

"Tobey? Is that you? Peter here." Peter's voice is distant and tinny.

"Yes, Peter, it's me."

"Great. I tried calling earlier but I couldn't get through. How goes the research?"

"Good. Very good," he lies.

"And Nadia's not distracting you too much, I hope."

"No, not at all, she's fine."

"I take it you met the American chap, Kaplan. Quite a decent bloke isn't he? And his wife is absolutely charming. Salt of the earth. They're taking care of you, introducing you around and so forth?"

"They've been wonderful, Peter," he waits for it and it comes.

"So do you think you might have some pages to send me soon?"

"Soon, Peter. I'm actually thinking of staying here a while longer. There are a few things I'd like to look into. I'm thinking I may introduce a bit of a political angle on this one." Give him something, throw him off the scent. He cannot suggest he stay longer to avoid coming back to his life, to the real world where expectations await him.

"Political? Why I think that's a splendid idea. Could be just the infusion you need. How much longer were you thinking?" Peter sounds a touch worried.

"Three weeks, maybe four."

"Three weeks," Peter is surprised. "Well I suppose that's not a problem. I'll have Lorraine make the arrangements. The accommodations are satisfactory?"

"They're fine."

"Oh, by the way, George Clarkson was asking after you. When I told him where you were he said something about how much he loves the tropics. I think he may intend on visiting you."

"Old king George, ha. Thanks for the heads up, Peter."

"Well, I just wanted to see how you were getting along. I'm looking forward to getting those pages, so keep working."

"I will. Thanks again, Peter."

He rests the receiver back in the cradle and sits back on the bed.

—

Porter strolls through the scattered crowd when he sees her. He takes his time approaching her. She is examining some battered books in a wooden stand, a makeshift bargain-bin outside of one store. She is dressed in a pale red summer dress with quarter-sleeves and a rounded neckline. Her hair is tied back and he likes the way her bared neck looks, even with its visible scar.

She looks up at him when he is almost beside her and she smiles, "Hello. I'm so glad you could come."

"Well, I'm glad you invited me."

He leans in and kisses her cheek lightly and she smiles again.

"Picking up the local customs I see."

"Only the pleasant ones. Shall we eat?"

"Sure. Come with me." She takes his arm and leads him slowly along the walkway and they talk casually. "I asked Jack to join us but he couldn't get away from work."

"Well, I would say that I asked Nadia to join us as well, but that simply wouldn't be true." Ana looks a little surprised but he has the sense that she already knows that Nadia has left him. Her surprise is more likely at his easy admission. "The truth is that Nadia and I have been having problems for some time. She left me," he offers a tight smile. Ana does not offer condolence. She peers at him as though expecting more. "It's for the best really."

"Forgive me for saying, but you don't seem too upset."

He hesitates a moment but decides that they have crossed a line, that the truth is what she would want to hear, yet it still has the tug of confession. He stops walking and she faces him and he has a sudden doubt that she even cares one way or the other. "Look, I'm not a fool. Though, God knows, I've done my share of foolish things. I know what my relationship with Nadia is, what it's always been. I knew it would run its course and come to an end. I was always prepared for it. In fact, at this point, it's somewhat of a relief."

She watches him for what seems like a long time, her face impassive then it suddenly seems to soften. "Sorry, I didn't mean to sound like I was accusing you. I mean, it's really not my place."

"No," he touches her shoulders, "no, I just wanted you to understand." He tries to smile and she smiles and suddenly all of the apologies and explanations seem childishly clumsy and unnecessary.

"I hope you don't have any allergies to seafood," she says brightly.

He releases her and they continue walking, their mood light now. "Not that I'm aware of."

"Well, I suppose we'll find out."

———

It is raining outside in the night and he sits on the bed in the blind blink of the television and stares at the phone. He wants to call Ana — or 'Anais' as he is coming to think of her in his musings. He remembers her standing in the water, her skirt hem in her hands, the glimpse of honey thighs, smooth shoulders and pale scar. He pictures the curve of her neck, turn of her jaw, her eyes looking back at him with some message of sorrow or salvation he still cannot read.

For the first time it is cold in the apartment and it is the relief of standing before an open fridge door. He lights a cigarette and smokes ritually. He tries to think of a pretext to call her but can think of none. He sees the book she gave him on the desktop, the inside flap still blank, his words still unfound. He picks up the receiver, listens to the dial tone and imagines Anais on the other end.

He hangs up without dialling and smokes another cigarette. Eventually he rouses himself, dresses and goes out, to the same bar where he meets the same people. He speaks with Monique, their eyes linger, they speak but make only the connection of unspoken and unresolved attraction. He sits and listens and feels apart. His mind lingers on Ana, back again and again to their connection in loss. But he wonders what it is exactly that she has lost.

—

Nadia is walking among the stalls as vendors try to get her attention, most with goods, others more interested in her than pedalling wares. She drifts absently and he watches from a distance, a voyeur in this sea of people. As he watches her he feels his first pangs of loss, his first longing for the youthful limbs at his side. Even as his mind holds no regret, his gut seems to scold him, churn and almost weep. She does not see him.

He had never fooled himself that he and Nadia would last, had never believed that she could understand him, be that soul mate of consolation he assumed he must be seeking. He knew that it would end sooner or later and that most likely the rift would be violent — that is, violent in the scope of emotions. He had known and yet still now, as he stands in the arcade looking across at her in the sunlight there is this sense of loss that pulls at some gut-string.

It is about possession, he thinks. It is the male instinct, to dominate and claim. But did he ever really have dominion over Nadia? He watches her now and imagines those thin limbs curled beside him, but he cannot formulate them into a posture of rest at his side. Not with him. As he remembers she is either asleep, oblivious of him, in spite of him, or on the attack. The irony of his foolish libido; that he was not the keeper but the kept, the spoilt flower.

The thought does not comfort.

Nothing comforts him but the thought of Ana. Nothing specific, simply her: Ana, Anais, walking beside him, her eyes on him. This is the ghostly blossom of his relief, the remembrance of her eyes on him, her voluntary attention as they engaged each other across the lunch table. She laughed a few times, but it was her eyes, on him, attentive, as his were to her, drinking her in.

He needs to see her again.

Ten

Kadeem was a member of the Minister's so-called Watch Guard. Like some political pope these men were his Swiss Guard — 'Elite' or 'Gestapo' depending on who you asked — his inner-circle and personal soldiers, until Kadeem branched off, found religion and formed his own temple. The Minister could not abide the appearance of religious bias and so Kadeem left. He took most of his men with him and they maintained militant ties, forming others as well (so the rumours went) with the Middle-East.

That they continued to work for the Minister, in league with his political party was widely speculated but never investigated. This failure to investigate a politician with possible once-removed ties to Middle-Eastern fundamentalism struck Porter as very strange. He resolved to make some calls. Even if local media had no interest in laying out the story he was certain that foreign interests would have been. Luckily he still had some contacts.

Porter closes the laptop and lights another cigarette. The feeling of instability in the tropical air has increased from his reading. He looks out over the streets in the amber afternoon light, dust motes and patchwork cars, a vagrant kicking a can along the street, jabbering, making noise just to give himself relevance.

It feels strange sitting here in his suit (sans jacket), all dressed up for a charity function — one of those affairs that encourages luxurious indulgence as a means to raise awareness for its antithesis — just as awareness is dawning of the struggle going on at the ground level, the grit behind the scenes. Behind the everyday some still felt the need to effect things, to make an imprint for better or worse. People struggled to make their voice heard, so much to convince others of their choices, of their relevance, ideas people would kill for.

Porter does not know much about the charity being served tonight. All he knows is that Ana has invited him, and so he picks up his jacket and puts it on. He does not feel he has any such ideas, none worth dying for, not worth killing for. But perhaps he simply has not found it yet. Perhaps in all of his books he has just been an empty beggar kicking a tin can for attention.

—

Men and women dressed sleek as seals — seals and penguins they fill the room. Jewels and champagne tilt and glitter in the light and bubble in the conversational hum. Porter looks for Ana and finds her, an exquisite face in the crowd, sleek as well in a fitted black dress that rises in a collar covering her scar and leaves her shoulders bare. She does not shine here, she would not want to. She smiles at the man in the couple she is speaking to, but she does not shine for him, Porter notes. She is uncomfortable here pretending to care for another's cause that will change in a month, but no one but Porter seems to notice the fear of discovery in her eyes that flashes and disappears when she laughs, eyes narrowing and glancing away and back before anyone else should see.

"Are you going to write about us?" a woman at his shoulder asks in a plastic gloss smile.

It would probably be a waste of ink, he thinks. But he just smiles, "One never knows," he says as mischievously as he can muster. The woman stands uncomfortably next to him for a moment and he ignores her and she fades off into the crowd.

He moves down the stairs and makes his way between humming bodies. He moves into view of Ana and detains a waiter with a tray of glasses until she excuses herself from her couple captors. Then she approaches him and smiles and their smiles echo each other in their exhaustion. Her hair is pinned up with two tendrils free, framing her jaw-line. She is relieved to find him among the sea of faces but her relief is faint and he wishes he could raise that thing in her that would force her into bloom.

"Thank God you're here," she says and her smile, though tired, is genuine.

"Where's Jack?" he asks without thinking, as though his first order of business were self-sabotage.

She is immediately disturbed. "I'm sorry," she says. "I really do have to apologize. I was most upset with him, but . . . well, apparently he ran into Nadia. He said he blurted out about the function before he thought. So I'm afraid he invited her."

Porter thinks of Nadia drifting in the arcade, her fingers trailing across the edge of a stand and then the hand appearing at her waist, her free hand captured, the bodies coming together briefly, pressing as Kaplan squeezed her to his side and their mouths met quickly and they kept walking. They did not see Porter. He remembers as he looks at Ana now, her eyes on him, reading his thoughts it seems before they break away to circulate the crowd.

"She's here then," Porter says.

"Yes," Ana says, somewhat stiffly, "Jack was talking to her a moment ago. But I'm not sure where they've gone to."

We are such foolish children, he thinks. He considers telling her about Kaplan and Nadia. He thinks to but looks at her and sees the pain of her loneliness. She suspects or even knows, but is not ready or, for whatever reason chooses to deny the truth for now. He cannot be that light that would burn her eyes. Let her arrive at it in her own time, he thinks. He is content to stand here beside her.

They talk for a while, saving each other from being absorbed into the other cosmos that drifts eerily about them; conversations like so many black holes, swallowing any sense of individuality. They anchor each other, form their own micro-cosmos (or perhaps he is but her orbiting moon).

"How is the book coming?" she asks.

He looks away and she smiles wider her eyes showing a playful pity. "Oh, you must be so tired of that question."

"Just a little bit," he laughs.

"Still," she says, "I do admire your ability to do it. I always wished I could be more creative."

"Well, it's a pretty effective means of hiding from the world. I mean, there is something juvenile about it when you really consider it; a grown man sitting by himself, making-up stories."

It is her turn to laugh. "Well, when you put it that way. No, not at all." She looks around at the crowd. "People make up stories every day. People pretend. People lie. It takes skill to make them whole, to create something for people to lose themselves in, to find expression through."

"Well I just failed as a dancer so I had to fall back on something," he says jokingly.

She smiles, "You're not such a bad dancer as I recall."

"Well, thank you."

"Definitely a better writer though." She grins and he laughs and they revert to watching the crowd from the safety of their bond.

Still he looks at her and is happy to just do so and she shows no discomfort under his gaze only smiles, shifts slightly, and sips from her glass. For over an hour there is no sign of Kaplan or Nadia and it is the unspoken stone between them. They are caught in small whirlpools of conversation, the kind that dimple the surface of the water and capture small items in their orbit for a moment but are unable to hold anything substantial.

A few drinks in and released from one of these dimples in the fabric of the evening, they go outside for some fresh air. They discover that it has been raining, the streets already blackened, sidewalks glistening and drops on car windows glinting like sequins. They stand at the top of the wide stairway and she shivers. He drapes his jacket over her shoulder like an old French movie actor and she accepts it with a smile of thanks.

There is something almost peaceful about this moment. Then he sees Nadia and Kaplan and a second later Ana does too.

They stand on the sidewalk just a little down the road, just outside of the light of a streetlamp. Nadia wears a dark glittering dress of crystal wine that is short and opens in a V at her flawless back. Her hair is pinned. She has turned away from Kaplan in his black suit, as though she is upset with him, and he talks urgently, pleading. It is their body language which says it all and then, to dispel any doubt, Kaplan steps in close behind her, still cooing, still trying to appease and he places his hand at her waist, plants a slow kiss on the back of her bare neck. The corner of Nadia's mouth betrays the hint of a smile.

Porter feels Ana stiffen beside him, turn hard. She looks away, avoids looking at him even as she gently returns his jacket, then she walks towards her husband and his lover. He follows a short distance behind her, tries to remain outside of her circle but he wants to be there should she need him, does not want her to be outnumbered, and for some reason wants Nadia to know that he knows.

Nadia becomes aware of Ana first and begins to shrink from Kaplan's hand. Kaplan remains unaware until Ana's voice reaches him.

"Jack?"

Kaplan looks up but he does not seem startled only disappointed and frustrated.

"Hello, Ana," Nadia tries to smile, to pull the veil of normality.

Ana ignores her, but Porter sees her jaw tighten. "Jack, I'm ready to go."

Nadia sees Porter in the shadow behind and glares at him as though he is the tattler and so he is robbed of any play of injured pride or triumph.

"Jack!" Ana says again when he does not respond. He is looking away, wipes his face, rocks on his feet. She speaks more sternly now, though her voice betrays a tremor. "Jack!" Porter sees tears well in her eyes aflame, her jaw set challenging.

"Not now," Kaplan mutters then wills his eyes to meet hers. "Not now," he repeats more firmly.

"I'm ready to go," Ana insists.

Nadia turns and begins to walk away along the sidewalk, dark heels clicking. Kaplan swings towards her, then towards Ana, seems to see Porter for the first time then turns back in Nadia's direction. Porter realizes Kaplan is somewhat drunk.

"Jack, I want to go."

"Not now, Ana," he snaps.

Porter has taken a few steps back with Nadia's retreat. He feels an intruder, but he cannot bring himself to leave. He stands there in the shadow. Only Ana remains half lit.

Kaplan's eyes flicker past Porter before he speaks absently, "Porter, be a good chap, see Ana home will you."

Kaplan looks his wife straight in the face and holds her eyes with a challenge of his own. He waits a beat, a dare. Ana is silent. Then he turns and walks away following the fading clicking of heels.

—

They don't talk as they drive. This time Porter is at the wheel, Ana keeps her face turned staring unseeing out the window at the dead streets unrolling. "I don't want to go home," she says suddenly, her voice ghostly. "Can we go somewhere else?"

His mind wanders momentarily. He wants to hold her, comfort her. "Of course," he says quietly. But he is uncertain of what she has in mind.

He takes her to the guest house and the bar there. There are a handful of people, more than he expects, but it is not noisy. Someone tinkles away at the piano playing at tunes composed for wind-chimes and they find a quiet seat at a wooden booth in a dim corner. He does not wait for the waiter. He needs to regroup, perhaps give her a second to do the same, so he goes to the bar, orders two drinks and returns.

She looks drained but smiles as he places the drink in front of her. He sits back in the booth. She stares into rum drowned ice cubes and he watches as a frail old couple takes the dance floor. They are more agile than he would have imagined and he sees them stare into each other's eyes with an intensity reserved for the very young or the very poor. He takes a deep drink and watches Ana.

"Did you know?" she asks without looking up. There is no accusation in her voice, it is almost casual.

"I suspected," he lies.

She sips her drink and looks at him. "I did too," she says. "It's not the same as knowing though, is it?"

He doesn't respond just studies the curve of her cheek.

"Is that why you two . . . ?"

"No. I don't know. She left me." He realizes it must sound strange, but then he supposes not to her. He lights a cigarette. "There were other issues though. She would have left sometime."

She studies his face, his face etched with resignation.

"It's not Jack's first affair," she takes another long draw of her drink. "You must think I'm an idiot," she grins.

He downs his drink. "I think you're perfect," he says.

She looks at him sharply. By her look he could have just slapped her, and now she seems to question if he is mocking her. He studies her lips, looks away, ashes his cigarette.

Her face softens. "May I?"

Her fingers brush his as she takes the cigarette from his hand. The piano tinkles sounds of swept glass and she looks out at the couples on the dance floor, inhales with a furrow of her brow and exhales. It is not designed to be seductive but purely to relieve stress, but Porter watches the furrow of the skin between her eyebrows, the slight squint of her eyes and he wants to raise his hand and touch her. He keeps his fingers tight on the cold sweat of his glass.

"You are smart to have never gotten married," she says, still staring out.

He hails the waiter for two more drinks. "I was actually."

She is surprised now, curious. She looks back at him, rests her elbow on the table and leans forward tilting her head. "You were? Really?"

He nods slowly.

"I thought you were the confirmed bachelor," she smiles. He is relieved when the drinks come, a moment of distraction for him to steel himself. "So what happened?"

He sips deeply. "She died," he tells her. He looks at her, gives the brief smile designed to try to prevent the barrage of pity that usually follows.

Ana grows sober again. "I'm sorry."

"It's okay. It was long enough ago." He thinks of adding that she had left him too, that perhaps he had no rights to the role of the grieving widower, but there is a twist in his stomach that persuades him to simply let it rest.

Ana stares at him a long moment. Her look is not one of pity, but something else. It is, Porter thinks, the recognition of what he had seen on their first encounter, their shared communion with loss. She raises her hand and rests it gently against his cheek. Her hand is cool in the smoky bar, her fingers shift, stroke his cheek only barely before her hand lowers again rests on the table beside his. He closes his hand over hers and she sits there a while just looking at it, their hands clasped on the tabletop.

He can hear nothing, see only her lowered face, all sensation concentrated in his hand and the trace against his cheek.

"Let's dance," she says softly.

In the time he takes to rise and meet her on the dance floor he is desperate for contact with her again. She puts her hands on his shoulders and his own touch her hips, circle her waist and he feels drunk and heady. She moves herself to rest against him. He can make out almost the length of her by feel. She looks at him briefly, then away. Her head is just above his chin but she tilts it, rests it against his shoulder and he inclines his cheek against the soft warmth of her hair. They drift in a slow circle and now he cannot see, only feel her against him. He tightens his grip just a little and after a moment her body responds, holds him just a little tighter, a bit closer. His blood pounds even as he feels an almost overwhelming peace. He can smell her, beneath her perfume, the scent of her skin.

The song ends and they are tight in each other's arms. It takes them a moment as they slowly release each other and it is like waking up in a new place. They stand holding hands studying each other and he finally finds courage to do what he has so longed to do. He brushes back a lock of her hair, tucks it behind her ear and touches her face. His thumb traces her narrow eyebrow, the corner of her eye, fingers travel along her cheekbone, the edge of her jaw. He studies this miracle of creation, a being so unique. He wants to kiss her, those wide lips slightly parted now, but she touches his hand where it rests on her cheek and squeezes it lightly, then lowers it gently to her side.

"We should go," she says softly. "I should go home."

—

He offers to drive her but she insists that she will be alright. That is the extent of their conversation as they walk to the car. He feels her shoulder brush against his at one point and feels a rush, but she avoids letting it happen again and he does not try to orchestrate contact himself. He does not want to pressure her, does not want anything from her that she may regret later. He is convinced that it is better to let her go forever than to cause her any further suffering. It does not occur to him that letting her go may cause her to suffer and she shows no sign of it. For now her suffering is non-specific and all-pervasive. She faces him and for a moment he struggles with the desire to kiss her and then she is applying soft pressure to his arm in what may be gratitude or reassurance, smiling sadly and getting into the car.

"Good night," she musters through the car window.

"Good night," he says. And then he is standing watching the taillights disappear in the distance.

He slowly leaves the sidewalk, hoping to hear the car return. He climbs the stairs to his room, hoping to hear the front door open. And he lies in his bed in the darkness quietly praying for the phone to ring or a knock on the door. He falls asleep in the silence, the taste of her brow lingering on his lips.

Eleven

They have reached the point where they can enjoy comfortable silences. Porter stares at his paper pretending to read the articles, his mind secretly consumed by Ana. Coraline looks through her pocket diary, her lips silently citing random passages, the small apostrophe appearing between her eyebrows as she scratches with pen and marks her notes.

Porter glances at Coraline. There is still a sense of mystery about the girl, that element of wildlife still persists. A sudden movement on his part or a whim on hers and she might bolt, he knows, and he would never see her again. The thought stirs the edges of the implosion Ana has left in him.

"How is the book coming along?" he asks her.

She looks and pouts a moment. "I get frustrated sometimes. It's like I can see the whole thing clearly in my mind but I can't seem to string together the right balance of words to, you know, get that specific image. Does that ever happen to you?"

He just smiles. It seems like forever since he has had those kinds of firm images in his mind, but her words remind him that there was a time when he did. He wonders if it is that he has lost some confidence of vision, or is it something more organic, more permanent to do with artistry, the flagging or failure of his talent.

"It's not progressing nearly as quickly as I would like," she concludes and continues to doodle in the margins of her diary.

"Perseverance is a necessary quality for any artist. And sometimes when you're seeking to define something in your writing you come across something unexpected in the process. Sometimes you find it's even better than what you were initially trying to get at." He tries to sound reassuring but he is constantly plagued by doubt himself. "Hang in there. I'm sure you're doing fine."

He lights a cigarette and thinks of Ana, the tracing of her body against him on the smoky dance floor, the brush of her skin, taste of her sweat. He thinks of her hand on his arm and then Ana in the car. Ana who has to go home — whose home lies with a husband, a husband by a vow now broken.

He looks up and Coraline is watching him with dark studious eyes. "I suppose we never get it all figured out, do we?" she says.

—

As I age I should learn more. There seems to be a singularity in all of life's experiences, but what if I am alone in feeling what I feel?

The lover loves and is left behind in his pain. It wasn't love, some may say. But the love of an illusion is still real to the person experiencing it. Would you have died for that love? Yes, they say, I would have. The object of affection no longer being what they perceived, they mourn not for the individual, but for the loss of an idea.

Every day, millions of mourners, millions of would-be lovers, shed tears for the death of a dream, for the loss of an idea. This we hold in common: that we have all unwittingly worshipped false idols.

—

He feels alone as he wonders into the guesthouse with the sun setting at his back.

"Good evening, Mr. Porter." The girl behind the desk smiles at him and hands him a slip of paper. "A message for you. And your friend is waiting for you at the bar." He takes the slip with what he knows is false hope

He flips the paper and sees: 'Call Peter,' scrawled in black ink.

He wonders into the bar where the lights have not yet been lit. The fading sun smiles along the window shutters, Cheshire cat beams, barely reaching the white-suited back of the old colonial figure seated plumply, elbows on the bar and shaggy gray hair overlapping his greasy collar. Porter recognizes George Clarkson, 'Old King George', without having to see his face. When Clarkson does turn there is little new to add to the ruddy-red cheeks, black brows (despite grey and white hair), watery blue eyes and thin pink lips. He is as wide and bullish as ever, though his cheeks have perhaps softened slightly and the bags beneath his eyes are crossed with some additional lines which had not accompanied him on previous trips.

"Tobey!" he wavers delightedly, a few drinks in. He totters on his barstool without getting up but shakes

Porter's hand firmly with the weight of his body. "Looking bloody well, chap. How goes it?"

"George," Porter smiles as he slides onto the stool beside him. "What brings you to paradise?"

"Paradise? Hardly. A powder-keg is a powder-keg no matter what dress you put on it." He grins with sudden inspiration, "This little island may as well be my ex-wife." He nudges Porter with an elbow and signals to the bartender.

"Marlene was never so tolerant of your drinking, far less for encouraging it."

George laughs a wheezing bellow that causes the bartender to reconsider before placing the two new glasses before them.

They drink and reminisce, or at least Clarkson does, while Porter drinks and pretends to listen to these anecdotes he has heard repeated a million times. Occasionally he chances to look in the direction of the table that he has now claimed in his memory as belonging to Anais, as much so as if it had a flag planted in it.

"This new shit they put out is just, well . . . well, just that: it's shit!" Clarkson practically spits in a doddering slur as he lowers himself over his next drink. The night has spun on and Porter's bones feel saturated. Clarkson smells of paint thinner, an acid tinge high up in the nostrils. "Goddamn write-by-numbers. Like everything else. Like the music . . . stagger and posture without any real artistic merit . . ."

"Oh come on, George, sounds to me like you would have burned Joyce."

"Bullshit, it's totally different."

"It's no different. To dismiss the new is the beginning of the end for an artist. You stop growing you start dying," Porter adds looking into his own glass, "it's as simple as that."

"Over simplification," Clarkson counters. He starts up shakily turning on his barstool to face his companion. His body turns, but his eyelids remain at half-mast and he directs his argument to Porter's belt buckle. "I'm talking about the churned-out spoon-feed-the-ignorant-masses and give-me-my-Hollywood-movie-deal-already pulp that is dropped into these, these . . . spit-shine super-market book store." He slaps his hand on the counter, his dark, shaggy eyebrows seeming to bristle even more. "Backed up to their sanitized, pander-to-the-commonest-denominator, plexi-glass doors . . . in dump trucks . . . . Ever notice these mega-bookstores, the whole fucking place looks like a sanitized grocery store. As though their research has shown that the commonest denominator is most comfortable being treated like a three year old. This catering to the commonest denominator — that's what I'm talking about! Spoon-feeding the public shit, by authors who couldn't create a beautiful sentence if Nabokov wrote them a crib sheet."

Porter lets the rant hang in the air a moment. He sips his drink and pulls on a cigarette. As he watches the smoke billow and curl and hang around him, it does not escape him that each successive book of his has done poorer and poorer sales. It also does not escape him that Clarkson, a writer himself, has not written a word in almost fifteen years, having found the profession of barstool philosopher to be more suited to his affinity for alcohol. (Q: 'How do you take your whiskey, George?' A: 'Why, in excess, thank you very much.')

Sweat runs down Porter's neck. "It's always been this way, King," he smiles. "There have always been more shit writers than good ones . . . more hacks with tracing paper than artists who understand and explore their craft. That's always been the way, it's nothing new."

"Pffft!" Clarkson sighs, red-faced drunk. "I don't see it."

Is it age, Porter wonders. *Will my mind cloud with this milk-skinned cataract, so that I can no longer see? Has it begun already?* He suddenly has a clear image of Ana standing with him on the dance floor. He wonders what she sees when she looks at him.

—

He has put it off for days but he knows he cannot avoid Peter forever. He flips through his notebooks and tries to formulate a more solid idea, to string the beads of his thoughts as it were into something he can show his agent. Beads for an island, Porter thinks. How history repeats itself.

He chooses to call the office on a Friday afternoon in secret hopes that Peter will be out, but the line connects on the second ring and Peter's voice is alert and business-like. "Hello."

There is a brief moment of panic where Porter considers hanging-up. "Hello, Peter, it's me."

"Tobey, how are you? I was beginning to worry. I must have left you about five messages."

"I'm fine, fine."

"So when are you coming back? How's the manuscript coming along? I still haven't received those pages. Did you send them?"

A pause as he considers. "No, Peter, I don't think they're ready as yet. I need a little more time. I'm supposed to meet with some reporters next week and I think that should be very informative." He can almost feel Peter slump in his chair, hear the sudden exhaustion transmitted through the line. Porter plays his card in desperation, "Peter, Nadia has left me."

"What? Shit, Tobey, I'm sorry. What happened?"

"I don't know. I think she met someone else. But, look we all knew it was going to happen sooner or later, it's just that it has thrown me off a bit. I know it's come at an inopportune time but . . ."

"Of course, of course . . . take some time," Peter says betraying some reluctance.

"Thank you, Peter."

"Look, Tobey, maybe it would be better if you were back here. I mean, for you personally."

"No, it's alright. I'll be okay. I'm making progress. I'll send those pages soon, I promise," Porter says, with no idea of whether he can fulfil his word, "after I meet with the reporters."

"So, next weekend then?" Peter interjects hopefully.

Porter does not have the heart to push his luck any further. "Yes," he says resigned, "by next weekend I'll have something for you."

"Thank you, Chris."

"No problem, Peter. I'm going to ring off, I've got King George waiting for me downstairs."

"Oh hell," Peter sighs. "King George is probably the last thing you need right now."

"He's an entertaining distraction," Porter tries to sound light.

"Very well, I'll let you go." Peter hesitates before adding awkwardly, "Oh, and you know, if there's anything you should need, well you can always give us a call. Me or Jeannine, I mean."

"Thanks Peter, I appreciate that."

They say goodbye and he hangs up the receiver, falls back on the bed and watches the ceiling fan rock and revolve. Clarkson is not in fact waiting for him downstairs. No one is waiting for him.

Twelve

He finds himself in a small office building housing the Sentinal Newspaper, an independent, local publication. There is the sense of important things happening, news, selling and the past-era scent of newspaper print. He is lead down a narrow flight of stairs to some offices in the basement to meet his latest contact. There are walls of free-floating shelves stacked with books and papers.

The first thing one notices about Laura Narinesingh is her wealth of thick wavy black hair. There are copious amounts of it even tied back as it is. She is tall, attractive and elemental with dark intelligent eyes. She speaks to him of the coup as she fiddles and adjusts a camera. Occasionally she snaps a picture as though for a test. She sketches out more of the political landscape, speaks of the local minister thought to be corrupt, the Americans' involvement and their threat to invade, using the coup, she suggests, as a possible excuse to occupy territory for the offshore drilling rights. She speaks intelligently and he makes notes, but he cannot help feeling distracted, outside of himself.

She is casual, off-hand in her responses. She does not belittle the questions, but they are part of her everyday and Porter can feel that he has not delved any deeper than she has already gone.

"There is a broader picture," she says, "a place where this island fits into the grander scheme of things — its place in the world. People are slowly waking up to that. It's not in the interest of foreign powers to let this place fall into just anyone's hands. You know, in the past messages would take months, sometimes years to pass from here to the outside world. Most of us in today's world can't imagine what that means."

There is a snap and a whir (a sound the digital camera makes just for show) and he realises she has taken his picture. He does not ask to see it and she does not offer to show him. She rests the camera down, finally finding full engagement in workings of another kind.

"Can you imagine waiting a year for a response to a question?" she muses. "You wait as a ship crosses oceans one way, bearing the question, a question which may very well have lost all relevance by the time it is posed. And then you have to wait while the ship makes the return voyage. Perhaps the ship is attacked or falls victim to a typhoon, and the response is lost and the question must be asked again, the response waited for."

She studies Porter as though answers were written in the lines of his face. "I don't think most of us today can even imagine that sort of thing. Miscommunication was rampant. And wars were fought over those types of things." She affects a shrug. "That is the culture of this island, one of miscommunication, that's the history we come from. That and a sense developed as a result that the affairs of outside governments and ruling powers-that-be are not our concern. That they don't affect us."

She picks back up the camera and resumes tinkering. "Things are changing, but very slowly. It's the only way things will ever change around here; slowly. It's like waiting on one of those ships. But what can you do? Big news doesn't come every day. And one has to live in the interim, till the ship comes in, so to speak."

—

In the night he sits before the dead glow of his computer screen and the blink of the television and stares into the heartbeat-throbbing-shadow in the corner of the room. He catches an occasional glimpse or apparition of the spider's web. *These moments where you wonder who you are, alone in the dark, mind focusing on black holes receding into black holes*. He can remember writing years before, remember dreaming, but it is like he is watching it in a movie. He seems to have a memory of dreaming stories, of a crystal image in his head, complex characterizations and potent prose. There were days early on where he would sit in the little apartment, the one above the furniture store, and the lines would pour out. He would write through anything; cold, tiredness, hunger, because the words owned him then. They were a stream from somewhere in his soul, his inner-self communicated most purely with the world. He would read back what he put down and his dry eyes would sting and emotion would well up in him, choking him because the beauty was undeniable. There was the insecurity afterwards of course, the fear that it was precious only to him, that others would not understand it, not comprehend its honesty, its purity. It did not matter.

What he misses most now, he realises, is not the praise of others but just that feeling within himself, that sense of accomplishment that comes with fulfilling one's purpose. And it was his purpose, he knows. He knows it because he felt it back then. And once you feel it, it is unmistakable and undeniable.

But how long do these things last?

The phone ring cracks his thoughts.

"Hello."

"Hello . . . Chris?" A silence reigns. She sounds small and far away.

"Ana?"

"Yes."

"Anais."

He can hear her soft smile. "Yes."

—

The buildings on the Rue Sanctuary are squares of solid primary colours as though constructed with children's building blocks. The sidewalks are fairly quiet but only because of the overcast sky, since he has been told they are normally bustling with activity. Porter stands waiting briefly before he sees her approaching. Ana smiles catching the little bit of sunlight available and he watches her approach in a beige sleeveless dress, cinched with a broad belt, and heels. Her hair is tied back and she looks happy and he wonders what has transpired in the time he has not seen her, and if she has mended her marital bliss.

She smiles as she takes his hands in greeting, presses her cheek to his. There is a warmth to her that acknowledges something passed between them, but it does not admit intimacy — nor does it exclude it. As she takes his arm and steers him along the sidewalk, he feels as though they are old college sweethearts meeting again after years of being out of touch. The initial suggestion is that their intimacy has passed and he cannot help but feel disappointed.

"Thank you so much for coming," she says.

"Of course," he says. "Of course I would come."

Her hand tightens briefly on his arm then releases. "How is the writing going?"

"Well. Quite well. It's coming along."

"Oh dear," she says, smirking up at him, "sounds like it's not coming along at all."

He smiles despite himself, for he is beginning to feel irritated by her casual attitude.

There are seabirds drifting in the distance and he can see the seaside not far off and the shadowed outline of an oil ship in the distance. She looks out and he suddenly catches the three-quarter view of her face in the sun, the glow on her cheeks also deepening the serious line of her mouth. He is suddenly aware of her performance; like that first night, only this time he was too caught up in his own affairs to have noticed the mask. She looks back at him with a smile, but something seems different now in her eyes. They stop walking and they look at each other for a long moment, the lingering of the eyes like the intertwining of fingers, the lace of flesh and bone. She looks away, the smile gone.

"Let's get something to eat," he suggests, throwing out a lifeline.

She looks up, smiles, takes it, "Yes," she says, "let's."

They find a small restaurant, its striped awning creating the appearance of a tent so that when they enter, they are surprised by the depth of the place, though not the darkness. They find a table in a corner and are quiet until the menus arrive. They make conversation over the food choices for a while, place their orders and wait. He cannot help but look at her and she seems to waver back and forth between pleased and uncomfortable.

"I wanted to apologize for the other night," she says eventually, looking into the folded menu.

"What on earth for?"

She looks away embarrassed.

"Really, what are you apologizing for?" he says more gently leaning forward.

Her brow furrows, "I'm not sure. I mean, well you know what I mean. Our last meeting just wasn't quite . . . appropriate."

"And are you apologizing on behalf of your husband too?" he sits back. He has spoken flatly, without conscious intent of malice, but now he wonders if there is not some subconscious attack in the question.

"I suppose I am."

The answer stings him and he falls silent. He straightens the napkin in his lap. "You have no need to apologize," he says eventually. Then looking at her he repeats, "There's no need," and this time he means it.

She searches his face seriously for signs of insincerity before squeezing his hand on the tabletop. "Thank you, Chris."

They fall silent until the food comes before they resume casual conversation. He tells her about Coraline and her uncle, Stellan, about the reporters and Old

King George. At his prompting she speaks about her childhood. He is surprised to learn that she is Canadian, from Burlington. She moved to the U.S. when she was seventeen with a boyfriend. They lived in New Jersey. It did not work out with him, but she stayed and a few years later she met Kaplan. She digresses at this point, circles back to her childhood, cold winters and pinecones, a happy house with three siblings, two sisters and a brother. Her parents, she thought they were happy, and in her memory they stay so. She tries not to let the divorce years later overshadow the younger days, the happier times.

"People make a lot of excuses to say their childhood was difficult," she says between bites. "The truth is that, as I remember it, my childhood was straight out of a Norman Rockwell painting. Well, until I was about twelve."

"What happened at twelve?"

"Boys," she responds, and she wrinkles her nose at him and they laugh. "I thank God for my brother and sisters though. I almost feel bad that I was so oblivious to how unhappy my parents were before the divorce. Though maybe it was for the best. I doubt I could have done anything about it."

He feels that she is speaking half-truths, telling him what she would offer any stranger, but he will not challenge her. "Children shouldn't have to worry about those things," he says.

"They shouldn't, but life doesn't work that way." She folds the knife and fork in her plate before her and touches the napkin to her lips. "So what about your parents, did they live happily ever after?"

"My parents? They never separated or divorced. They remained thoroughly miserable together until their deaths," he says.

"Is that what good parents are supposed to do?" she studies him.

He folds his napkin long, holding the end pinched in one hand and pulling it down with the other. "No," he says after some consideration. "No, I don't think so. My house was a morbid place to grow up. You could feel the discontent in the air. When I think about my childhood home all of my memories seem to be filled with slate, as though there were some eternal rainstorm hovering outside the window."

He tries to smile but she does not return it, only studies him, her eyes again on his, seeming to take his hand. The waiter arrives and breaks the spell and they are left with only the reckoning.

———

Out on the street she moves close to him a moment. "There is something I wanted to ask you," she says. "We're hosting a gathering for Kinbote, the artist I introduced you to. I'd like you to come." She looks at him, but he senses a complication, a ghost lurking and so he waits. The shoe drops quickly. "The thing is I know that Jack has invited Nadia."

Porter stops in his tracks. He stares at her incredulously, not knowing what to think. "Wait, you mean to say he's still seeing her?"

Ana sets her jaw, holds his gaze defiantly without saying anything.

"Ana. He's still seeing her? And you know. And he's bringing her to your house."

Suddenly she seems to crack, she takes his arm, "I know, I know, it seems downright . . . sordid. I just . . . I can't bring myself to fight him, Chris. I just can't seem to bring myself to care enough to fight him. But, I was hoping . . . I mean, I can understand if you don't feel comfortable, but I was hoping you would come, just so I could have someone there who . . . I guess, knows how shitty everything is. I guess it's so you can rescue me should I need it." He can see that she is only now working it out for herself. "It is too selfish of me, isn't it?"

He touches her head, smoothes her hair with his palm and he almost swears she shivers slightly. She is not crying but he feels she is on the verge. It does not matter, he knows he will go. He tells her so. He says simply, "Okay, I'll come."

"Thank you," she breathes and she rests her head against his shoulder and he puts his arms around her for a moment, standing there, on the sidewalk in the sun. It is a brief embrace before they part and he stands and watches her go.

—

Lavelle Rampaul is dark with unremarkable looks. He has none of the glamour and suggests none of the sophistication of Narinesingh. Porter comes away remembering the man only by what seem to be fitted accessories; his matte-white hair, thinning on top, black plastic-framed glasses in a fifties style that is being revived, but not the way Rampaul wears them.

He wears short-sleeved dress-shirts, the kind worn outside the pants, chocolate-brown slacks and cracked black-leather shoes.

The man speaks in a heavy local accent, goes on and on cheerfully about his life and accomplishments, which are spoken about circularly, few told as many. They fall into a comfortable rhythm. Rampaul talks about himself and Porter listens, being required only to nod lightly and emit the occasional one word response that suggests he is absorbed, while his mind is free to wander. He does follow the thread of Rampaul's life, a constant attempt to make his impression on the world; as union leader, as politician, town councilman, failed again and again.

A whole world is out there, Porter thinks, with people like Laura Narinesingh and Lavelle Rampaul, people prepared to make their mark on it, who get involved in politics, attempt to make change or reveal truth, effect the world or fail to, but at least try. There are issues so large and yet he has no interest in any of them. Should Armageddon come tomorrow and everything be blown to dust, he would only want to hold her once more as he did that night in the guesthouse bar. He can no longer contemplate any other justice. He cannot find in himself a belief in any other definitive truth.

—

The colonial-house-cum-bar a block from the hotel is crowded, but he has managed to secure a tall table in the corner where he sits across from Monique and nurses a drink with a pleasant glow about him. Monique is sedate and cat-like and her male companion several feet away seems taut, sweating and agitated as he shoots looks at Porter, and Monique's unseeing but bare back.

Her dress laces behind her neck and her shoulders are also bare and she seems to use them to full effect, exaggerated movements of mirth and pleasure telegraphed the distance to her jealous lover.

"Why are you torturing him?" Porter asks, although even the cold bloodshot looks cannot dim the sunshine in his centre. Perhaps his gentle smirk is not helping matters, but he is convinced it is not his concern. He leans back on his chair, arm propped on the back, corner of his jaw propped against his fist.

Monique smiles, rolls her shoulders. "It's good for him," she says, "reminds him that he wants me."

"A dangerous game. What if he decides to say to hell with you, and find some other girl?"

She laughs, leaning low over the table flashing brilliant teeth. "You think it's that easy?" She pats his knee condescendingly and ripples stir across the room. "Besides, men want the challenge. He will want me more because other men want me. Then he can feel as though he has won me from all of you, all of you 'other' men."

He glances at her hand still resting on his knee, then across the room at the muscled back of the man now facing the bar. "Well maybe you should consider my safety then," he says with no real sense of urgency.

She slowly takes back her hand, toys with the straw in her drink and looks up at him. "If he felt he had me, he would lose interest. Isn't that true of all men? It's like a game. And you must win the prize, to prove that you are a big man. And the best prize is the one hard won."

He cannot help but laugh at her depiction of men as little boys. "Maybe," he says. "Maybe it's only in time that honesty becomes important, and maybe trust."

"That? That only becomes important much much later. That is love without passion. That is convenience, which comes later in life," she grins wickedly, "when you no longer think you can hunt your prey."

He laughs again. "I think the idea of passion does maybe change the older you get. But love based on a false idea or impression, is that love at all? And lust isn't always passion."

"Oh," she looks at him sidelong teasing, "you don't have to defend it. I don't think you're so old you can't still hunt your prey."

He laughs out loud, the lover tenses, and Monique raises her glass in salute.

Thirteen

The house is set far from the road, windows peeking over its high walls with long, vacant glass eyes. Joseph drops him at the entrance where a beautiful suit holding a dishevelled security guard opens the gate for him without asking any questions and Porter begins the long walk up the path to the front door, a cheap bottle of wine in his hands. He hears the voices and music, that social chorus of the successful gathering, even before he walks through the arch of the door into the front hall. A few people linger there in cocktail attire, halting their conversation long enough for a synchronized effort in sizing him up, before they resume. No one greets him.

He makes his way down the hall and the house opens into a large step-down living room with vaulted ceilings and a wrap-around second level. The room is populated like a subway car at rush hour. When he locates Ana she is on the far side of the second level listening to an olive skinned, wavy haired Latino who speaks animatedly and leans towards her from the waist. Porter can tell even from this distance that she is bored and when she sees him she makes her excuses and begins to make her way down.

Porter is suddenly aware of this thing in his hands. He raises the bottle for her to see but she only raises her eyebrows in turn and laughs. He makes his way through the crowd to meet her part way and shoves the bottle grinning at an unsuspecting guest. The man takes it with a confused smile and Porter pats him on the shoulder and quickly moves past.

The atmosphere is festive and he almost feels as though it is Christmas as she leans in to kiss his cheek, saying, "Cristobal, I'm so glad you're here."

"Really?" escapes before he thinks about it, and her eyes narrow and her smile blooms. She tugs lightly on his sleeve and he follows her lead back up to the second landing.

"It's a disaster," she snickers.

He looks across the almost packed room of bodies below. "It looks to be quite the success."

"It wasn't supposed to be nearly so many people. Kinbote and Lana seem to have invited everyone they've ever known and told them to bring everyone and their families as well. It's ridiculous. We've already had to send out for more food and drinks." She runs her hand through her hair and breathes a heavy sigh.

"Well I promise to eat very little," he says.

She laughs, looks him over. "So how are things with you? Is the book coming along?"

"Very well. It's coming along, very well."

"How well?" she smiles and looks at him sideways, narrowing her eyes in mock suspicion.

"Well, I believe I'm damn near ready to maybe actually start writing it," he confesses boldly.

She laughs out loud and her eyes shine.

A woman appears suddenly beside Ana and leans in, speaking desperately. Ana leans in to Porter, "I'm sorry, more catering emergencies. Just try to mingle.

I'll see if I can't send someone over to keep you company." She starts to move off, "I'll be back."

He watches her move away and winding her way through the crowd being greeted and greeting in turn as she goes. People beckon her to join them and she declines always smiling. He tries to decipher if it is the same smile that she gives to him. He wants to believe that there is something more personal between them, something more open which she offers him, more full and of herself, but he could be wrong.

He makes his way to the upper landing and looks around at the jubilant strangers, everything bathed in champagne light and he can feel the bubbles.

"Hello Chris."

He is surprised by the voice and more surprised by the cold turn in his stomach. He turns around and Nadia shimmers with everything else. Dark and sleek as always, she has cut her hair in a twenties-style bob that splays a wisp across one cheekbone. She looks waif-like but glamorous.

"Hello Nadia. How are you?"

"I'm good. Have you been writing?"

Her eyes measure him, scan over him again and again, sticky fingers prying at a lid and he feels a blush to his skin, a remembrance in his gut that warms down there. Is it the smell of her that he can somehow distinguish? He knows now that his mind feels little for her, but his body still remembers.

"I have," he says. "And how are you? What've you been doing with yourself?" he asks with a hint of the barb, as he sips his drink.

She seems oblivious, just stares at him in complete control. "You know you never even tried to find me," she says. Her eyes are piercing behind their mask and she presses her back against the wall and he is aware of her body drawn out.

He takes a deep pull at his drink looking out across the crowd to see if he can find Ana, but she is not to be seen. Funny, you think about it, prepare for it, but it is never what you think. It always catches you off guard. "So where have you been?"

"I'm staying at the Marriott," she says. She looks down and stirs her drink with her finger, licks the tip.

He feels tired now, notices the heat for the first time, oppressive humidity from the press of bodies. "Well, that is the sort of 'better' place you wanted," he says casually.

"It is not good for a girl's self-esteem that you don't even look for her," she says, eyes still sizing him up. "I'm not saying it for me," she adds deciding something and releasing him from her scrutiny. She leans back on the wall again looking out. "I'm just letting you know, for future reference. Everyone wants to feel wanted, needed." She is not looking at him now as she moistens her lips, he holds no more interest.

Kaplan arrives beside Nadia. "Hello Chris," he says pleasantly as he comes up beside Nadia.

"Jack," Porter tilts his drink in acknowledgement.

They seem to have nothing to say after this. It is apparent that Kaplan is looking for Nadia and his discomfort seems to translate into an embarrassment for Porter as the interloper.

Porter quickly drains his drink and excuses himself, shaking the empty glass, and begins to wonder aimlessly through the crowd. Somewhere down the stairs he finds a waiter and another drink. He holds up in a corner for a while then hangs on at the elbow of some aimless conversation passing more moments. He tries not to drink too much. He scans the landing for Kaplan and Nadia and finds them after a moment not far from where he left them but further in the shadows of a doorway recess. Kaplan is leaning in close beside Nadia's neck, perhaps kissing her, he cannot tell. Nadia arches her neck outwards and laughs, ruby lips and razor teeth.

Porter needs a cigarette. He works his way and squeezes from the crowd, spilling outdoors as though being expelled from a womb. He keeps walking, across the patio, onto the lawn under the black sky, the night air cool against his perspiring skin. He lights up, pulls deeply. The din has faded to a blur behind him. He looks up, lets his eye run across Orion's belt. To see stars at a time like this, as though it is the universe that is telling him how small he is. His mind runs randomly on thoughts of purpose, of greater meaning. A strange sensation creeps through him, pins and needles through his shoulders. He wants to cry. He wants to destroy something. He wants to lie down and sleep and waking up ever would be optional.

He glances back at the house, the false light, like civilization beckoning to him. Beckoning, but not welcoming. The moth's false moon, the electric light. I should go, he thinks. What good could possibly come from this? He thinks of Ana . . . Anais. He wants to be beside her again. He wants to be close to her. But what good can come of that?

He finishes off his second cigarette, drops it on the lawn and drives it into the dirt with his shoe. It has begun to feel chilly and it reminds him that he has left

143

his jacket inside. I can get another, he thinks. He wipes his shoe on the grass. He will get his jacket, he decides more reasonably. He will get his jacket, find Ana and tell her he is going and then he will leave. He glances back at the line of trees that border the property, the unknown lurking in the darkness between them. He heads back inside.

There are mirrors here, panelled along the wall before one reaches the kitchen and people reflect in them back and forth endlessly. He has always had an aversion to mirrors. As a child their reflective depths suggested another dimension, a world beyond where everything was back-to-front, and somehow more artificial. Perhaps the artifice arose from the idea that the Cristobal Porter standing in the mirror was only a replica. He would turn quickly, or force his eyes to peek achingly from their corner in attempts to catch that world in a moment of lapse — that Peter Pan's shadow moment where it would slip and reveal itself as a separate entity, where its synchronization with the 'this-side' world would falter. The falsity of that world on the other side morphed in time into a falsity of narcissistic tones, and he would hate to see someone standing there, trying to meticulously prune the image of the 'other-side' world (the other-side figure always resistant, forcing that one strand free).

He does not find her in the kitchen and works his way back outwards. He cannot see Nadia, nor is Kaplan in sight. He works his way back to his original perch in hopes of a better view — also following his childhood instruction to remain in one spot if lost, so that she may find him. He smirks at this thought, its Freudian reek. There is nothing of his mother about Ana, of that he is certain. Perhaps there are similarities in those attributes they lack, he considers, then wonders if he has in fact drank too much. Suddenly he sees her standing in the mouth of a doorway, her back to him. He recognizes her shoulder, her hair, the three-quarter view; tip of a nose, corner of a mouth, line of jaw and chin . . . give the man a cigar.

He arrives beside her shakily and forgets his reason for seeking her out when she smiles at him. She smiles warmly but there is something mournful in her eyes. He should offer condolences. "There you are!" and her hand is on his arm. She excuses herself from the woman she is speaking with and leads him away, through the doorway. "I just remembered, I wanted to show you something."

He follows her obediently, aware of her arm entwined in his, breast against his elbow, fingers on his hand, her hair brushes against his shoulder. She does not rush but walks steadily and it is only when she releases his arm to open the door and lead him into the study that he remembers he came to say goodbye. Alone in the study it is too late.

She walks to the bookshelf and covers her mouth with her hand, keeping her back to him and, after some hesitation he closes the door behind him. "Ana?" his throat is dry. She turns her head further away, he cannot tell, thinks she may be crying. He approaches slowly, whispers, "Ana."

He is behind her and she sniffs.

"What is wrong with me?" she gasps. His hands close gently on her shoulders and she does not react, allows it. "I'm a fool."

"No," he whispers holding her more firmly. He feels her body drift back slightly so that now she is against him. Suddenly she turns and he embraces her and she buries herself against him.

"I thought I could do it," she says as much to herself as to him. "I thought I could pretend that nothing was wrong, in front of all those people . . . I thought it didn't matter . . . It doesn't." She lifts her head to look at him as though imploring his belief. "It shouldn't," her eyes well with tears and they run silently over. He touches her face, wipes them gently. "The irony is we haven't been together for over a year now. I've been pretending for over a year now, lying to everyone, to myself. I don't understand, this emptiness, this numbness. It's like a limb gone numb, that discomfort, that fear you feel that . . . that the sensation won't return."

She is beginning to sound tired now but her eyes have not stopped searching his face. He leans forward and kisses her cheek where it is tender and salted from tears. She closes her eyes, breathes deeply and he kisses her again, softy on her face. "Anais," he whispers. He feels her close, warm skin against his, her cheek slide against his. He kisses the side of her neck, tip of the tongue brush her pulse and feels her respond, her lips' kiss against his temple. And he kisses closer now, their arms holding each other as he finds her mouth blindly and feels her lips against his in their fullness, feels them part moist, tongues brush, past the edge of teeth, and taste. He pushes firmly against her and she responds with equal pressure. Something quivers in him with the feel, the taste, the smell of her — his head swims, a knot of emotion rising in his throat.

They are locked like this for a long moment, holding each other, kissing and Porter does not want to pull away as he knows he will have to, does not want this moment with her to end. Their mouths move exploring in so many ways, a million different sensations, drawing reactions in degrees; the light bite, small steady kiss, then lips barely brushing, teasing before sinking down.

In the back of his head the party sounds that have been almost completely stifled suddenly shift. He pulls away abruptly and she steps back. They look at each other for a moment and then the sound seems to explode tumbling into the room as the door swings open. All of this in an instant.

"There you are," Kaplan says. He strides into the room. "I was looking for you. Some of our guests are asking for you."

Porter's concern is for Ana. For a moment she looks confused then her look is of defiance. Porter wonders if she is daring her husband to comment, to speculate or confront, or if this is merely her natural poise towards him now. Porter wonders if he would suspect them. It is Porter's experience that the guilty see perpetrators in others. There is a brief moment where their eyes meet, where Kaplan seems to gauge and then reaffirm to himself that Porter is not a threat, even should he want to be. He acknowledges Porter with a nod of the head and tip of the ever-present drink. "C'mon," he says to Ana, "it's Carrie-Ann and Lorna."

Ana moves towards the door. Kaplan moves over to Porter, touches his shoulder, "Porter and I are heading out," he says. Ana stops and turns with a look of concern. Kaplan takes it as disapproval. "The party's running itself and it's all of your artsy types. We're heading over to Faverau's with Mike Benjamin."

Ana's eyes pass to Porter a moment. "It's alright," Porter says to Kaplan, "I can stay here, in case Ana needs a hand with the guests."

"Don't be silly," Kaplan says. "Like I said, the party's running itself. Besides your friend, what's his name, Clarkson, he'll be there and I told him, pretty much promised him I'd bring you along. So come on, grab your jacket, let's leave the ladies and the fags to this mumbo jumbo and go grab a real drink."

Ana looks at Porter but neither seems to know how to protest, nor if there is any purpose in doing so. "They're in the kitchen," Kaplan says to his wife by way of dismissal. She stands defiantly a moment then turns and goes. Porter watches her as she walks away, wanting to go after her, trying hard to hold the taste of her in his mouth.

—

Faverau's is a fake hole-in-the-wall, a lot of money having been spent to make it look cheap. It is a bar designed for a higher-income clientele who want to get drunk and be rowdy. When Porter arrives with Kaplan the other bar patrons are already drunk. Kaplan introduces Porter to a couple other men in shirt-and-ties already loosened and then abandons him to Clarkson, much to Porter's relief. The drive down was uncomfortable. Kaplan spoke very little, Porter even less. He feels grim, tired and his mind still swims in the kiss.

The bar front is open to the street, a few benches and picnic tables in the front area and a low wrought-iron fence, thigh-high, around it. Clarkson grapples at Porter's elbow, leading him down to one of the tables. Drunker than usual, Old King is sweating and blustering, jabbering incessantly, like a monstrous fly that will not be shooed. Porter looks out at the street, car lights passing, night air cool and he can sense moisture in the air, rain somewhere to come.

". . . Absolutely, wonderfully naïve, these people," Clarkson is saying, wavering back and forth so that Porter feels his weight pull at him and then ease. "It's so quaint, but they have no idea of order. Groceries, restaurants, bars, even the hotels . . . no one queues for anything, you just jostle, stick your hand up and hope for the best," he laughs.

Porter feels disgusted by him. You have no self-restraint, he wants to say, you drink to excess every day, drown yourself, and you would be one to judge? He extricates his arm forcibly from Clarkson's grip when he hears the voice from the street.

"Cristobal?" he turns and is surprised to see Coraline. "Cristobal, it's you."

She smiles brightly, her face painted with eyeliner, shadow and lipstick, making her look older, her eyes more coquettish, lips blushed. "Coraline," he steps towards her to block Clarkson and the others from them. He feels the cold gate against his legs. "How are you?"

"Good. I'm good." Her two friends stand a distance away on the sidewalk and exchange words. He cannot guess their exchange, has no idea what Coraline may have told them about him, if anything at all. "Uncle Stellan would like to see you again. He enjoyed your visit. He asked if you have the time, maybe you could come talk with him again."

"Of course, I'd like that. How has he been?"

"He has his good days and his bad days, but he's been much better lately," she says. "I think some intelligent conversation would do him good."

Porter is suddenly aware of a shadow at his shoulder, the looming spectre of death, something haunting. He feels somehow threatened. He catches the quick movement of Coraline's eyes. Perhaps she reads his expression. For his part he does not want to turn, does not want to admit Kaplan into the conversation. "Well, I best not delay you. Call me and we'll make arrangements."

"Of course," she says and she seems aware that they are speaking not only for them. "I'll let Uncle know." She begins to walk away then turns, "It's nice to see you."

"You too," he says.

She joins her friends and the three girls walk away under false yellow light. Porter hears ice shift in a glass, the sound as Kaplan swallows. "Not bad at all."

Porter feels a surge inside. An image of Coraline in Kaplan's embrace flashes in his mind before he douses it, preventing it from going any further. The twist in his gut is protective for sure but also something else, he knows — possessive. "She is young," he says trying to sound dismissive.

"But not too young, I'll bet," Kaplan still watches over his glass.

Porter forces a smirk, clapping Kaplan lightly on the shoulder in a show of camaraderie he cannot begin to feel. "Too young for the likes of us," he says and strolls back inside, willing Kaplan to follow, to break the line between Kaplan and Coraline's retreating form. Kaplan smiles, not fully convinced, but his glass is empty and he slowly follows Porter back inside.

The night is interminable. There is nothing for Porter to do but drink. The conversation does not move him and he avoids it by raising the glass to his mouth, taking in liquor instead of offering responses. He expels only smoke where he can help it. He tries to remain on the peripheral of conversations and eventually finds the edge of a table to hover at where he can seem a participant while remaining apart. He tries to hold on to Anais, as she was in the study, in his arms. He tries to recall every detail, every subtlety, every line of her, the scent and taste. But it is already fading and the recollection seems to fall short, to lose form and consistency, to hold the shape of the smoke exhaled.

He sees Jack Kaplan almost similarly positioned on the peripheral of another group. Kaplan stands near the edge of the upper steps. He wears his suit, the shirt unbuttoned at the top, a bit wrinkled as is his jacket but still well fitted. He is a bit dishevelled, moist with sweat from the night and the alcohol. But there is something suave about him still, the way he swills his drink gently in one hand, holds the cigarette poised in the other, raises it to his lips, squinting slightly as he inhales, like the frontiersman gazing at the setting sun on the horizon. Kaplan's mind seems somewhere else, and Porter wanders whether he is perhaps trying to capture the scents and textures of Nadia. Or is it perhaps Ana that his mind runs on, that he is trying to call into substance just as Porter himself is. Trying to find her in his memory, to reconstruct the pieces into that solid whole, so that he can get a firm grasp, so that he can hold her close, hold her down.

Is there competition between the two? Porter wonders. There is something in Ana that he has felt a connection to from the beginning, a sorrow that echoes his own, that he has the need to comfort, as though to do so will somehow allow him to mend himself, to be able to fill the hole in him. But is there any sense of confrontation, his physical desire for Ana goaded by some deep-seated want for revenge on Kaplan for Nadia?

He pulls deeply on his cigarette and glances at Kaplan. His only jealousy of Kaplan comes from his familiarity of Ana, his possession of her and his memories so much more solidified by years of experience. This Porter knows. If there is any desire for revenge it is buried so deeply as to not matter to anyone. But what about Ana?

He flicks the cigarette butt out into the street with a firm gesture of decisiveness. He is leaving, and if any questions are asked he will tell them outright to fuck off, that he has no desire to be here, that he has wasted enough time with them and that he should have stayed with her. He will tell them, any of them — Kaplan himself — if he should ask. If any of them should ask.

As he walks briskly out onto the sidewalk and down the street, walking in the direction of the guesthouse, he does not look for a taxi. He is almost daring them to stop him, to give him any excuse to proclaim his feelings; his love, his loathing, himself. Let them ask. But they do not, and he walks leaving the sound of life and laughter echoing out of the mouth of a bottle and fading behind him, on into the night.

Fourteen

He sits in the café, sober in the cool morning light, still replaying his moment with her, in the study. There is the longing to be there again, to savour things he may have missed. He wants to write about it, about her, a sonnet or a symphony, but it is all too overwhelming, too much at once and he cannot squeeze out a word beyond the etching of her name, *Anais*, which now holds some power on the page, on the tongue, the taste of her there that has captured him. He finishes his coffee, folds his paper unread beneath his arm, and walks back.

—

Joseph takes him again to the small house on stilts with the mongrels in the yard. It feels warm and inviting now. Coraline is as natural and luminous as ever though she is perturbed. She smiles and ushers him in, explaining that her uncle is having one of his bad days.

Inside one can feel the shroud of illness before even laying eyes on Stellan. The room is dim and Stellan is sitting at a desk in an under-vest and shorts, glasses perched on his nose as he goes through some papers. As they reach the doorway Stellan begins to cough and it is a phlegmatic hacking that gurgles from deep inside his ribcage. He covers his mouth with his hand at first before pulling a handkerchief from his pocket and using that. They wait patiently and then after a moment, when he has collected himself and resumed his examination, Coraline knocks.

"Uncle," she says in a sing-song voice, "Cristobal's here."

Stellan looks up, tilting his head back to peer down his nose through his spectacles at them. The leather cord that slopes from the hinges of his glasses, the dark circles under his eyes with their wrinkled bags and the folds of his drooping cheeks all conspire to give him the look of a bridled pack animal. His eyes are watery and uncomprehending for a moment, then he smiles. "Hello, hello, Porter! Come in. I apologize for not standing but the sudden shifts play havoc with my stomach. Pain, when I tell you."

Porter greets him, amazed that a man of his complexion (like rich dark clay usually) could change colour to his present sickly gray. A flicker in the eyes betrays his sharp intelligence, but his body is worn and tired. Coraline pulls a chair for Porter and seats herself on the bed further back. Her youthful glow gives added contrast to her Uncle's pallor.

Porter listens as Stellan talks, interjects occasionally. His mind wanders even as it is provoked by the themes Stellan raises. Somehow they are talking about human nature and revolt. "You know, I always wanted to believe in the innate goodness of people," Stellan says. "That people are basically good deep down inside. But the longer I have lived, the less I find I can tell myself that. I have come to respect nature more and more. I don't think morality is a given. What do you think? I mean, a man steals. We say it is wrong. Society says it is wrong. But a man steals bread to feed his family, we see this differently. It is not wrong, per say, but necessity. Now suppose the man stolen from also had only this one loaf to feed his own family . . . We would again reset the scales. Morality can be divided, hairs split, based on intentions, circumstances."

Porter considers adultery in this light. The mistreated wife, does she deserve to seek comfort elsewhere? But perhaps this argument could then be applied to Kaplan. If, unfulfilled in his marriage, does this give him some sort of absolution to seek fulfilment outside? Is the happiness of the adulterous couple, the happiness of the adulterer in her lover's bed, a factor when weighing the guilt of the act? Or are they all condemned?

"So then morality is purely a fashioned concept," he says by way of encouragement. He is happy to let his mind wander, at the same time to feel that he is giving this ill man some pleasure in allowing him to voice his ideas.

"I think so," Stellan says, as though just arrived at the concept. "I think so. But interestingly enough, a concept fashioned to guard against what is probably the most driving force of man's nature. I think man's nature is to change," he leans in, raising his eyebrows high, "any and everything." He looks at Porter with great relish. "If it is broken, we must fix it. If it is fixed, we must break it. Man is in constant revolt against any and everything."

Is it true, perhaps? Porter thinks. A man loves a woman, then decides he wants another woman. A woman is a lover but becomes a mother and then she is something else, no longer the same as before, because nothing must stay fixed.

"So man must change his environment," Porter says. "And morality is a sort-of basic thread run through to prevent a too drastic upheaval."

"Exactly!" Stellan is almost ecstatic. "You are a pleasure to talk to, Porter," he says. Coraline grins from her seat as spectator. "Look at the world and it is revolution after revolution. Cycles go on and on, one system generates another, rises and then breaks down. Son rebels against father, takes what he knows, shifts it slightly, fashions something new he can call his own. Until his son now comes along, and rebels against this new thing, must change it, must fashion his own. On and on it goes, until eventually one son, the latest rebel, unbeknownst to any, fashions the very thing his great-great ancestor once held as his."

"As with religion," Porter suggests. "God creates Man. Man destroys God, but must immediately fill the void. He seeks to erect something in its place, a system, an idea. In time too, the system is revolted against, and eventually fundamentalism returns. Man returns to God."

"Yes. And in this way Man is slave to God," Stellan says.

"But Man returns to God, only so that he can once again revolt against him."

"And in this way, God is slave to Man," Stellan nods slowly.

"Hegel said, 'God without man is no more than man without God,'" Porter says. Would he destroy this? Porter wonders. Will his feelings for her change?

"Tell me, what are your views on God?" Stellan asks and leans forward, arm propped on his knee.

Porter is taken aback, reminded of his college days and conversations on the green, or in the pubs. He wonders at the naiveté of these conversations, these musings. Perhaps it is life afterwards that became less important. Perhaps when he stopped wondering, questioning, formulating ideas and philosophies on how he would choose to live, perhaps it was then, when 'everyday life' overtook him that he lost his way. Perhaps, he muses, without that conscious idea of how to live life, life instead lives me.

He is smiling lightly when he responds. "I always envied those who could have true faith. I'm not talking about the zealots, the ones who follow blindly without questions, but the ones who ask questions, search and still believe. Personally, I've always felt it was a sin of pride to state with too much certainty. I struggle to map, in my writing, the complexity of the human conscience. Human motivation is intricate and varied. It's difficult enough to hazard guesses as to human intentions, I could never submit that I'm intelligent enough to understand the workings or intentions of God."

Stellan nods slowly, dramatically, like a sombre game-show host. Coraline looks at the Englishman curiously, as though seeing him differently, as though his face had changed and she is undecided whether she prefers this new one, but accepts that it is necessary and can respect it as such.

"So one simply does one's best," Stellan says in a tone of summation.

"I suppose so."

"I agree with you," Stellan says, leaning back with a sigh. "And yet I will have a Catholic burial."

"Uncle!" Coraline chides.

"Do not think too badly of me," Stellan continues to Porter and he laughs.

Porter smiles but his mind is drawn to his wife's funeral — standing in cold aisles, feeling like a stranger, an imposter there. People throwing shadows in the shape of salt shakers, bowling pins on a conveyor drifting past and over him. They forgave his unseeing eyes because of the loss they knew he must feel. So certain were they. But his eyes did not rise to meet theirs for pain, but rather for the fear that someone would look back at him knowingly, seeing his falsity and expose his feelings as he stood there, not mournful but numb, not heart-broken but guilty.

—

There is the knock on the door and he opens it to see her, Anais, standing there.

SHE: Hello.
HE: Hello
SHE: May I come in?
HE (*embarrassed*): Of course.

> SHE *enters and* HE *closes the door behind her and they stand there.* HE *wants to take her in his arms immediately, to kiss her immediately, but he hesitates and in that moment of uncertainty the naturalness of that gesture is lost, so that if he were to gather her to him now*

*it would seem too calculated.
So they stand there awkwardly a
moment,* HE *staring at* SHE.

SHE (*looking at his desk*): You've
been writing?

HE: Yes, yes, finally making some
progress. Thank God.

SHE: That's fantastic.

HE: Would you like something to
drink? Some wine?

SHE: No. I can't stay.

SHE shifts *uncomfortably while* HE
stands.

SHE: I needed to apologize . . .

HE: No. No you don't need to do
that.

SHE: Really, I was drinking. I was
upset. It was unfair of me to
put you in that position.

HE (*smiling*): Unfair? Do you think
you overpowered me? Is that it?
You think you took advantage of
me?

HE *has come closer.* SHE *lowers
her head looks towards the
doors, towards the light.* HE *has
come up on her now and rests
his hands on her shoulders.* SHE
cannot meet his eyes.

HE: Do you see me as that defenceless?
That powerless against your
charms?

> SHE *looks up and* HE *is still smiling.*

HE: I am.

> SHE *smiles too. And they study each other like this a moment.*

SHE: I'm just . . .

HE: Please don't apologize. Don't say you're sorry.

SHE: Perhaps I should have that glass of wine.

HE: Would you like to?

SHE: Yes. Thank you.

> HE *pours two glasses of wine, the unsanctified blood of their Saviour, and hands one to her.*

—

"I can't stay long," she says again, and he feels the oppression of time ticking down, running out. Watching her everything moves slowly except for the sand flowing through the hourglass. If time is of the essence then he wants her now, to lie naked with her.

Let us whisper our endearments as we taste each other, let our words spill from one tongue to the other's mouth, let our promises be locked in the twist of muscles, a pact sealed in the press of flesh. I can bare my soul to you; cleave it open as you cleave to me.

He stands and watches her sip her wine and sips his own. He studies her. She seems more distant, someone else and at the same time so fragile, open and vulnerable to him.

"I wanted to call you," he eventually says.

"Did you?" she smiles almost teasing. She is studying him now, like that first night, turning the light, taking the upper-hand so that he is the one feeling uneasy and for her amusement. Only there is something softer behind her look, comforting him even as he becomes this bundle of nerves uncertain how to proceed.

"Yes. I just, well, I wasn't sure . . ."

"I understand."

He wants to ask her if she has been thinking of him, needs the reassurance. But he does not want to say it first. He cannot give her everything, cannot surrender himself into her hands, not when he feels he has so little by way of collateral.

She smiles. She does seem to understand but she drifts away anyway. Both hands on her wine glass, she strolls towards the desk, the light behind her. She seems to have retreated into her shell, curled smaller inside the gilded cage of her body. He wants to coax her back out but he does not know how. She stands in the balcony doorway, her posture thoughtful, then drifts back towards him. She gives him a wistful smile, touches the small stack of books on his desk and examines them as a point of interest. He feels he wants to speak but does not trust himself and simply admires her.

She picks up one of his books, "Any good?"

"They're some of my favourites."

She goes through the small stack he always carries with him when travelling; a Nabokov novel (usually *Lolita*, this time *Ada, or Ardour*), *Art and Lies*, Ovid's *Metamorphoses* and a collection of Shakespearean tragedies.

She turns over Ovid. "I used to love mythology," she says. "Like such grown-up fairy-tales, fantastic and magical and no guarantee of a happy or even a just ending." She rests down her glass and raises the book in both hands, examining the cover, as though absorbing the tales through touch. "Magical, but at the same time so much more like life."

They are there for a moment with myth between them, frozen in time, he still wanting her, awash in history and words, she who stands locked in some dream fantasy echo of her life. She could begin her transformation, he thinks again, and become the weeping willow like one of Ovid's nymphs. He would approach her, fall to his knees and kiss her skirt hems, and he would feel her fingertips brush his forehead and look up to see that it is the tracing of leaves, that she has been transformed by tragedy and he is collapsed there at her roots to turn to stone.

The moment passes, she rests down the book and comes back to stand near him. "You know I wanted to be a painter. Did I tell you that?"

"No, you didn't," he takes a step towards her. He is always aware of their proximity, but she seems to take no notice. "I didn't even know that you paint."

"Well I don't anymore. I used to. Oil paints, when I was in college. I used to do these large paintings, abstracts mostly. I could never stand realism. I always found it so," she considers, a furrow in her brow, "it's so locked in. There's no art in faithful reproduction, no imagination in that kind of mimicry." He is momentarily caught in a play on her words; 'faithful reproduction,' as opposed to 'unfaithful reproduction'. Were they to reinvent truth?

"An artist should attempt to re-invent truth, don't you think?" she asks.

"Yes, I agree," he says, but it is spoken without conviction. He feels a disappointment at himself for this statement, eager to please, before assessing the truth of his own opinion. She looks at him as though guessing that he has fed her a line, has not sought for the answer but simply returned the gift of her thought. Love is not the path of least resistance. "Actually, I don't know that it's the same for painters and writers, but I tend to feel it's more about re-presenting the truth, so that it's perceived differently, so it might be understood more fully."

"Like shining a light on an unseen facet," she says.

"Yes. I mean, I guess first and foremost you'd need to figure out what 'truth' is. Is it intrinsic, or just a matter of perception?" His words feel thick of lecture, but she smiles.

"Then again," she says, "the truth is the truth, isn't it? To reinvent it or reinterpret it is just to create a lie, however white a shade." She looks at him a moment with a gleam in her eye, as though enjoying the sparring. It dims briefly and then she laughs. "I never really thought of any of that when I did my work anyway. I just tried to be passionate about it and hope that something worthwhile would spill out. It's probably why I wasn't very good at it."

"I'm sure you're being modest."

She smiles mischievously but also with appreciation. He suddenly feels there is something sexual come into her.

"Maybe I am," she says. "Anyway, it's in the past."

"I would love to see you work."

"See my work?"

"That too," he says, touching her cheek. She turns her face away and his hand lowers. He presses on to distract himself, "But I would love to see you at work, actually in the process of painting, surrounded by brushes and canvas, swatches of paint and all that passion pouring out."

She smiles, apologetic for her shying away. "You are sweet," she says with no sense of patronizing.

She steps closer and she is in his sphere now. She raises her chin and he does not miss the opportunity. He kisses her gently then harder and longer. She pulls back, plants another small kiss. "I really can't stay," she says. "I have to go." She comes back, head down, hugs him, buries herself against him. "I have to go now." She steps away, straightening herself, then moves towards the door. She stops there, looks at him and he crowds close to her, fills himself with her scent. He tries to imprint everything about her on his senses.

"When will I get to see you?" he asks.

She seems hesitant, studies her hand on the door jamb, the cracking white paint.

"Jack's going away," she says eventually. "In two weeks. He'll be gone for a month."

It is the first time he has heard conspiracy from her lips. It is not the thrill the romances say it is. There is however a grip at his gut, like the warm sensation of liquor, an excitement at the thought of having her to himself for a month. In fact it overwhelms and, coupled with his current arousal from her kisses, the two week wait seems impossible. He catches her before she turns and tells her so, "I can't wait two weeks. Can't I see you sooner?"

He is pleading, at the same time his hands on her demand. She searches his face, her breath quick and he kisses her hard on the mouth, a display of his desire, to illustrate of the necessity of his request.

"I'll call you," she says. It is his turn to search her face. "I promise." She seals it with a kiss and her fingers trail across his cheek. He watches her go and waits for her full shadow to descend the stairway before closing the door.

Fifteen

In the following days, Porter forces himself to work to get his mind off of things. He makes phone calls, writes notes, drinks coffee and smokes cigarettes. He sits before his laptop, puts on his glasses and labours over the keys. His mind wanders, thinking of her. He forces himself back to his notes. He feels the frustration of a story taking shape but trapped behind a gauze curtain, its shape blurred. The hints are there, suggestions of an outline, silhouetted figure moving behind a sail. He presses at the fabric wall, prods and probes with the dullness of his pen's intellect, but the membrane will not rupture. He tries to relax, let it form naturally, as though to coax it shy from behind its hiding shroud. He visualizes it this way now, the shadow image behind the shroud and it becomes Anais.

He sits back with a sigh, pushes his glasses up and rubs his eyes. "You fool," he says quietly to himself, "you're behaving like a boy, a damn adolescent schoolboy." He stretches, stands, walks to the French-doors and looks out pulling his cigarettes from his pocket and lighting one. He exhales smoke out over this island city, more familiar now but still exotic, still with mysteries. Some of these mysteries tug at his curiosity, a flirtation desiring to be unravelled. Others he has no interest in exploring, fat logs half-submerged that inspire no want of knowledge as to what has taken root and festered beneath.

He looks out at this now semi-familiar cityscape as he smokes. He takes in the pitted walls with their visible cement patch jobs, paint splashed single-coated strokes visible, cracks run ant-scaled chasms. Everything is of the heat and of the sea, earth and fire and salted wind. So is Anais, he thinks, despite her sometimes caged and reserved attitude, there is still something elemental about her, something quietly natural, of the heart, flesh, bone and blood. Though she is a foreigner she belongs to the island.

It begins to emerge: a mother and son, a revolution. The veil is suddenly splitting . . . No, not so much splitting, it is suddenly worn through in places, the fabric showing holes, light filtering through and glimpses of that beautiful idea on the other side are starting to show . . . A mother and a son . . . A fallen and unknown father . . . A beautiful, mysterious woman. The mystery woman is Earth, whom the mother cares for, whom the son simultaneously loves and attempts to destroy . . . Porter is beginning to see it . . . The story . . . The Story!

He turns with a notion to grab his notebook and pen when the phone rings, louder than ever. He staggers a moment between two worlds. The phone screams, demanding. The notebook is meek.

He grabs the receiver because it may be her, and the boat of his imagination capsizes . . .

"Hello," the dogged voice, "Tobey? It's Peter . . ."

. . . And the entire story is swallowed in the sea, figures in a great shipwreck slipping through foggy water — Mother, Son, Earth — skirts billowing, seaweed hair, wrapped in the canvas sails, like so much bed-sheets, lost in the murky depths.

"Tobey? Tobey, can you hear me?"

"Yes, Peter, I can hear you," he closes his eyes, pinches his nose-bridge, then pulls another cigarette. He listens to Peter's demands, his predicaments, his perfectly justifiable veiled threats. Porter promises soon, as he has done every time before, but this time, for the first time since coming here, he has hope — hope that he may be telling the truth. His subconscious can be dredged, the shipwrecked retrieved. Some will be lost on the seabed, some changed by the press and crush of the tide, but now he finally has reason to believe that there is something worth seeking in the silt.

—

Night time and he sits restlessly, the adolescent churning has turned to childish want. The questions abound. He wonders if she could be thinking of him as he is thinking of her. It seems unlikely. He finds his own thoughts excessive. He is sure she must be preoccupied with other things; her daily life, her husband. He doubts she has time, as he would wish her to, to lie and think of him, to remember the feel of his hands on her or try desperately to close her eyes and conjure his scent.

And then there is the imbalance, the unfairness of his surroundings. How she moved around this apartment, made this contained environment hers, so that items evoke her still, Ovid's pages retaining her touch, and then abandoned him here while she returns to the real world, to exist in spaces he has not touched, he has not seen, that she would have no reason to imagine him in.

He picks up the phone. He wants to call her, but then he hesitates because he does not know if he can risk Kaplan answering the phone. He can find no pretext, as hard as he tries. Left to him he would tell Kaplan directly, "I am not calling for you. I want to speak to Anais." He would provide no explanation, nor any denial should it come to that. But then, once again there is the realisation that this is not his decision to make. This hornets' nest stirred would be Ana's to deal with, no matter how much he may try or wish otherwise to take the burden on himself, to shield her. It would be impossible.

He realises that he is not fully sure of Ana's position either; whether she retains hope for her marriage, whether her feelings for her husband are still tied by love. Or is it only appearance or tradition that holds her, the impropriety of divorce, the fear of accusing or disapproving eyes. Perhaps she would fear the change. The story of life after marriage may seem set to her, so that she may fear the question of what her life would become if not guided by that principle; who is she if not the wife of Jack Kaplan?

Then again, perhaps she has finally become disdainful of her husband. Perhaps even now she awaits only the confirmation that she has somewhere else to go, someone else's support, and with one call he can liberate her. Perhaps she waits by the phone for his call which does not come. His thoughts run over it in circles and the fact that he does not know in which direction her mind lies stings him all the deeper.

He eventually falls asleep in the still dark of early morning hours. His feelings are mixed. There is the sense of accomplishment, as he has started to order his notes, has begun to sketch an outline and to write. He has finally begun to write. Then there is the restless hope, thinking of the potential of a new book, a new love, the memory that fuels him, his mind charged with memories, some real and others speculations on future encounters.

These thoughts keep him up almost as much as the fears which accompany them, filling him sometime with doubt, a fall of the stomach given way to the medicine-ball weight of that fear which comes from wanting something and now having something to lose. But his sleep is dark with only shimmers of dreams that reflect like moonlight off of some moving car's windshield, to glide in its uniform shape across the ceiling of his room.

—

The malls here are even more depressing he finds than the ones at home. The building desires grandeur but does not begin to scale it. The shop windows are dull and uninspired and one has the impression that it has all been dug-up from some sort of time capsule, a haze of dust having muted everything, the appearance like sound through cotton-plugged ears.

Porter walks through the small arcade, mounts the escalator which rises at a steady rate even though the hand rail slips and jerks beneath his palm, slowly overtaking his feet. At the top he steps around a woman who stands dazed (one of his personal pet peeves: those people who arrive at the top of an escalator like newborns blinking in the blinding light of a new world, uncertain of where they are or what direction to take, untrusting of their legs to carry them any further than where the escalator has deposited them, so that they stand there stupefied while people like Porter try desperately not to be shuttled barrelling into their backs). He walks briskly through the mall looking left and right for a suitable store. He has never learned to enjoy shopping. In outdoor markets he can perhaps drift, taking in more of the multitude of faces alongside the multitude of odd and intricate items. In a mall full of the same clothes, shoes, jewellery, he can summon no enthusiasm. The bookstore here is uninspiring, filled with text books of every nature and a few cheap productions of popular books, written for easy conversion to movie-rights, books which, if Porter were fully honest with himself, evoke his envy in some small part for their success, even though he knows he would never wish to have written them.

The only positive thing about this bookstore is its selection of books on local history. For the most part the tomes are weakly researched, non-delving looks into the island's recent past. Yet strangely enough the ones that are well done seem extremely well done, their writing heady and detailed. He picks up a couple of these and carries them to the checkout.

As he exits the bookstore, with his straining plastic bag like a pained ghost-white scrotum, the corner of his eye catches on an attractive girl seated in the nearby food court and his head turns instinctively. It takes him a second to recognize Nadia, with her dark new haircut, short at the back showing the sculpted nape its translucent bone-gloss beneath the freshly mowed follicles. She wears those large shades, like a new-age Audrey Hepburn, the look that always puts him in mind of a human personification of a blind bee — give her a white cane and tin cup. The look seems designed for the reveal, the conversion of Holly Golightly from this cartoon-esque caricature, hiding behind her Minnie Mouse ears, to be revealed as the feminine royal butterfly and commander of the male sceptre.

Nadia does the reveal, but not for him. He sees Kaplan come towards her table, in a white shirt, sleeves rolled up, light khaki pants. He looks relaxed and vibrant, like a magazine advertisement. He should be standing with Nadia beside him on the deck of a yacht, in bright sunlight. Porter can picture it now; Kaplan staring beyond the camera, wearing Nadia like an additional piece of jewellery, draped like a scarf, and he smiles out to the camera into the sea and sun, commander of the new frontier.

Porter feels his stomach turn and he walks quickly away. It takes him a moment to understand the quickening of his pulse, a nervous excitement that coils in his centre and pushes past a quick wave of something crossed of butterflies or nausea. At first it flits across his mind and he is surprised to think that he could have been made jealous by the sight of the two lovers. However his deeper-self quickly reveals its own dealings, as he unthinkingly gets in the car and has Joseph drive him home, straight home.

The sidewalks cannot go by fast enough. He is nervous, but excited.

Kaplan is there with Nadia.

He imagines the phone receiver in his hand, what he will say, but he cannot fix on the right words.

Kaplan is there, in the mall, with Nadia. He is not at home. He is not at home with Ana.

And this is what some deeper part of him has understood, seeing passed all the rest, the part that seems to have crouched in wait for some such chance. Porter can call Ana, his Anais. Kaplan will not answer. His only hope is that she is not also out, but he does not allow himself to entertain the notion long. He is thinking of the cold receiver in his hand, the heavy ring, her voice on the other end.

"Hello?"

"Hello, Ana?"

"Yes."

"Anais?"

"Yes . . . Yes."

Sixteen

He enters the lobby and Ana is there as arranged. He seems to shift in his shell with complete uncertainty. She looks at him and approaches in a red dress, almost plain but for the fact that it is a vessel for her and she cannot be plain, not to him, not now. She smiles casually and he realises that he was holding his breath in anticipation, uncertain of the mood the moment would call for.

"Chris," she presses her cheek to his and he is enveloped by her scent.

"Ana."

"I hope you don't mind my coming." Her words are formal, but she smiles and looks at him with a directness that speaks otherwise. Then he realizes her words are for the girl at the counter behind her.

"Of course not. Please, come up," they smile politely and he moves ahead towards the stairs. "I have your book for you."

Bars of shadowed light fall through the stair railing. He does not want to turn away from her, does not want to take his eyes from her. Still there is a delicious excitement that tickles his spine, his entire back prickling in awareness of her presence.

"So have you finally decided on an inscription?" she asks and he can imagine the tweak of her smile.

They reach the door and he fumbles at the lock. His mind flashes to Nadia, how she pressed him at the door of his apartment in that other world of London. Would Ana do the same? And he immediately suppresses the memory, becomes angry with himself for comparing the moments. For surely what he feels for Ana is something different. Although the physical desire for her is there, there is something further, a desire to connect with her, to gain intimacy. He would lie still and listen to her secrets whispered in his ears. He would watch her sleep. He would curl up in her rib-cage and give up himself.

He is thankful when the door opens and Ana passes through without event. She stands in the middle of the room, looks around. He wonders for a moment if he should take her in his arms now, kiss her. Would she allow it? She is here after all.

"Would you like a drink? Coffee, or a glass of wine?"

"Well it's early," she begins, then shrugs, "but one glass of wine won't kill."

He goes to the kitchen and she strolls to the open French-doors. It has begun to drizzle, but the light outside is still clear white and bright.

When he comes back with two glasses of wine she has seated herself at the foot of the bed, her legs crossed. He hands her the glass and they sip silently a moment. For the first time her composure falters. The silence appears to go a little long, as though she had planned everything up to here. She opens her mouth to speak hesitantly a casual remark, then stops.

"I wanted to see you," he blurts, his voice sounding too abrupt in the silence. It sounds like a faltered step in a dance, feels clumsy.

Then she smiles. "I wanted to see you too," she admits quietly to her glass.

They look at each other then, the moment changed. He takes her in, enjoys the anticipation. She rests her glass on the ground. He touches her chin, turns her face up to him. Her hand grazes his hip. He bends and kisses her, then lowers himself kneeling before her. She touches his hair. His hand holds her ankle and slides up her calf and they kiss again. It sends an ache through him. He can hear the rain falling heavier outside now and he kisses her neck just behind her ear. They look at each other, so close he can feel her breath.

His mouth sinks on her shoulder, tongue tasting her skin and she breathes in sharply. She is subtle. They take their time. He can sense that they both know the first time will be awkward, that the anticipation may overwhelm, that they must learn each other, but there is something pure and brave about their exploration here in the midday light and the falling rain outside. And in this knowledge there is too the sweet promise of more.

—

He can feel himself changing, an old life dissolves. Perhaps this state of change really is man's true nature. God is here in her, in the fullness of realisation of self, for he is only what exists in her eyes. Her realisation makes him — and for as long as his faith resides in this, she is his true religion.

—

They lie in tangled sheets and tangled limbs. He studies the bareness of her back, her smooth bronzed shoulder blade, the sweep of her hair away from the nape of her neck, and marvels at the beauty. Even the thin candle-wax scar that runs along her spine to fade before her hairline speaks its own word of beauty, embodies a nature at odds with the Greek sculpting of her form that imbues it with something richer, of the world itself. He wonders if he will ever fail to see her as such, if this could become mundane. He hates to think it and for now is happy to believe it could never be so.

She sighs, snuggles back against him. The smell of her now is more natural, skin and sex and sweat, thick in his nostrils, on his tongue and it makes him want her again, even before he is able. He raises himself up on one arm to glimpse her expression. She is smiling, looking out at the white day now fading and the falling rain. The rain cools the breeze and drifts against them, reminds Porter that he is slick with sweat. He kisses her shoulder. The rain falls heavy and he looks out at it. It increases the feeling of the world washed away, the two of them the last in the ark of this room.

"What's going through your mind?" she asks. She stretches like a cat and again eases back against him, pulling his arm around her like a well-worn sweater. She laughs at the juvenility of the question.

"My mind is blissfully empty. I am completely in the now. Completely here with you," he says, punctuating his sentences with small kisses along her neck.

She smiles, closes her eyes. Then softly, "Does my scar bother you?"

"No," he says honestly. "I like it."

She turns in his embrace and again he finds himself studied, those eyes intense, as though being mocked, to find the clue on his face. He studies her in return but his look is different; he is drawing, etching in his mind the lines and curve of her face, only it changes, with the slightest shift of the light it alters and he will have to study her face forever to get it right, to recreate it. He wonders how God does it.

She smiles as though reading his thoughts. She touches his lips. "You don't have to feed me empty words."

"I haven't. I wouldn't."

"Writer," she smiles.

"They aren't empty," he says. "Your scar, it adds history, makes you fuller." He smiles and touches her face. His eyes focus on her earlobe, mind wonders momentarily dipping into the ocean of the past, something vague and foggy, an image of his wife perhaps, only out of focus so that it is impossible to tell. It is momentary, brief, but it brings a hint of sadness with it, the sense that all things must end. "We all have our scars, don't we?"

She puts her hand on his cheek and studies his eyes before finally bestowing a kiss upon his mouth. "That last line was a bit cliché," she says, "but I liked the rest." She grins wickedly and he laughs.

"Why you . . ." he grabs at her waist suddenly, tickling her and she laughs as he rolls over her and grabs her wrists, pinning them beside her. He takes nips at her neck and she laughs and struggles now turned sensitive, everywhere ticklish.

They are both laughing and they kiss, playfully, hard, then deeper. He grows hard against her and her hands pull at his shoulders and they are no longer playing, as far as this is from life.

———

The rain halts as the skies go dark, then it begins again. Seasons, clouds, sun and moon move beyond them, but none of it matters. Theirs is a complete sustenance.

———

He kisses a line down her centre, laps the fleshy thimble of her navel and below. His hands cup her hips, a bone bowl he drinks from, the heat of her thigh against his cheek as her fingers lace into his hair tightening, the press of her heel between his shoulder blades. She moves against him. He slides one hand blindly upwards, feeling, his fingers filling the space between ribs, fingers entwined — sensations of flesh, bone and sinew, and the pulp of plum against his tongue. After she will kiss his mouth, the mingling tastes, his and hers no longer. The scent, the taste, the feel is of them. There is only Them.

———

He lies on his back, her head resting on his chest, rising and falling with his breath. It is frustrating at times because he wants to kiss her and can only reach the top of her head, but at the same time his arm holds her comfortably and strokes a fitted curve along her back and flank. He can feel her breath, warm against his skin, grown even. He realises that she has fallen asleep. He would keep her here but looking out at the dark night he begins to wonder about Kaplan. Will her husband be expecting her home? Maybe he should rouse her and mention it, but he does not want to break the spell. If he reminds her she may have to go, and he wants just one moment longer — always one moment longer.

She shifts and raises her head to look sleepily up at him. "You alright?" she asks.

"Perfectly," he smiles.

She looks out at the night. "I should probably be going."

"I think you should stay," he says.

She considers this. "Jack wouldn't care," she says. "He would assume I went off coast, or to the apartment. He wouldn't even ask me."

In his mind he bristles at her mention of her husband. Can he be jealous of her thoughts being on him, even these passing mundane notions? He does not want Kaplan here with them in any form. But he tries to focus on the reality. "Then there's no reason for you to go," he says.

"No," she says quietly, then smiles at him blushing, "I suppose I wanted to make sure that you didn't want me to."

He laughs out loud, embraces her, rolls over her kissing her.

—

He is seeking his way back to life, bit by bit, picking his way over the stones.

—

"My dad died when I was young," she says. "My real dad. I don't like to admit it, even to myself, but the truth is I barely remember him. And the memories I do have I don't trust to be real. I'm not sure what are actual memories, and what's stuff that I made up from old photographs or stories my mom told us."

He is in the kitchen pouring two glasses of wine which he carries across to her now. She takes hers with both hands, sitting cross-legged wearing his shirt, and drinks a few long swallows. To Porter the effect is a bit childish and completely charming.

"I feel guilty for not knowing. I'd look at pictures and I'd try to conjure his smell or his voice. I so wanted to remember his voice." She is silent for a little while.

He has sat back against the headboard and she moves closer. He kisses her temple.

"I can't really miss him. It's more the feeling of having missed out on knowing someone very special," she continues. "There's that feeling from all the stories I've been told. Of course the stories you're told are all warm glowing ones. I'll never know if he had a temper, or if he drank. And then too there's the feeling of resentment, because I should've got to know him. It was my right to have known my father."

She rests her head on his shoulder. "It's like not being invited to a party that you had every right to be able to attend, and then to have to listen to other people afterwards talk about how fantastic it was, and what a great time they had. They tell all these little anecdotes and you smile and nod, but part of you wants to tell them to go to hell, to shut them up, because you should have seen these things yourself, should have been allowed to experience them first hand, and the stories, well the stories just aren't adequate."

—

She comes out of the bathroom and strolls over to his desk, brushing her hand across his notebook. He likes to see her here, touching things, claiming them. It will make it more difficult when she goes, he knows, seeing her in every corner of this room. But for now he wants the yearning, will look forward to any form of her.

"You were telling me about your mother. Oh my, don't I just sound the psychologist," she grins at him, then continues her inspection.

"A quiet woman. You see my father did things the old fashioned way; married first, then fell in love — unfortunately not with the same woman." He lights a cigarette. "My mother meanwhile was in perpetual search of 'the Norm'. She was obsessed with the idea that other families were supposedly normal and we weren't. As I got older I tried to convince her that the normality she saw in others was mostly a façade. But she wasn't convinced. And I think in time she actually convinced us, against our own better judgement." He pinches a piece of tobacco off his tongue.

"We eventually all felt abnormal. Which I guess is why we all tried our own different ways to escape. My father was there physically, but he had no interest in any part of our domestic life. He was like a boarder. My sister Belle, Isabelle, ran away. Now that was more of a surprise. Took off with a sailor, moved to Denmark, married him, divorced him and is now happily settled in Copenhagen with a real estate agent and two children, a boy and a girl."

He takes another pull, staring into the long ash. She stands holding a book, finger on the spine, watching him. "My brother was even more theatrical; tried to kill himself. Luckily he did it by trying to wrap his car around a lamppost — a German automobile no less. Needless to say, he was unsuccessful and we all refer to the unhappy accident as 'that terrible near-tragedy'. The tragedy for Lucius of course being that he survived."

He looks up and smiles, opening his arms, "And I became a writer."

She rests down the book and comes towards him. "So you became a writer to escape?" She climbs over him. "Running away from yourself?"

"But wherever I go . . ."

"There you are." She grins and kisses him on the mouth, planting her knees on either side of his hips, straddling him.

"I blame my mother for my entire life of failed relationships," he says playfully.

"How very Freudian of you," she whispers into his ear and bites the lobe.

"She made me believe that there was such a thing as normal; that one could believe in the fairytale of two people understanding each other completely. It's only in time that I realised there's no real complete understanding. There's always compromise, and without ever being fully understood."

"But there are connections," she says, looking at him as though he has said something dangerous.

"Yes, there are connections. But we can never find that complete understanding we search for. There's too much we hide, too much we're ashamed of. And then there are the things we don't even realise about ourselves." She looks at him, her hand still cradling his head. "It's not a bad thing," he says, in response to her sobered look. "People can love each other despite this. It's to see the beauty in the mystery, in the ever unknown. It's to marvel at creation."

"You really believe that?" she touches his cheek softly with her hand. "Is that why your eyes are so sad?"

"My eyes are sad?"

"Yes," she kisses him gently. "Since I met you, I could see you had sad eyes."

She kisses him again and he smiles. He puts his arms around her and holds her, kisses again and again. "Not tonight," he whispers.

—

He tunes the radio quietly to a station playing music by The Beatles. It is something they can both agree on. She lies on her stomach, chin propped on her hands, bare legs kicking so slightly, like palm trees in a breeze, until the music finds her and they begin to wiggle. He sits beside her and she rolls onto her back and he kisses her. How could he not be tired of kissing her by now? He wonders this as he feels the spring inside at the taste of her. He must have kissed her a million times tonight, and yet each time has been different, each variation a new exhilaration. How many chords are there, he wonders, and then how many songs?

He remembers the night in the bar and he asks her to dance. As they stand and sway to the music he holds her body, aware of her physicality, of the odd mystery of the body and mind, that tenuous connection — the body in his arms, real and there and the mind reeling with thoughts like a galaxy reeling with stars, beyond his sight.

"You know," she says, holding onto him, and he cannot see her face, "I know how your brother felt."

"What do you mean?"

"I mean," she hesitates. He can feel her grow small within herself. He caresses her back, kisses the top of her head. "I mean, I tried once . . . to kill myself as well."

They are quiet but for the sound of *'Michelle'*.

"The car accident, you mean?" he asks.

"Yes," she whispers.

"The one where you got your scars?"

"Yes."

He waits, but they drift in their quiet dance without her saying anything, and he holds her, encases her, intent on keeping her safe.

—

She sits up in bed smoking. He likes the way she sits, one leg curled towards her, the other knee up, a pillow in her lap. She leans on her knee and exhales. "I'm supposed to have quit," she says.

"I think you can make an exception. Here of all places." He shifts on his side, rolls over, looking up at her.

She looks at him quizzically, tilts her head, "What do you mean, 'here of all places'?"

He pulls himself up so that he is seated with his back against the headboard. He reaches for the pack of cigarettes on the sideboard, but she hands him hers. "I just mean that here you aren't bound by the normal rules. It should be a retreat from the world. Because here, well, it's different." He feels he has not explained his thought, cannot find the right words. "Here is . . ." he pulls on the cigarette and hands it to her.

"Here isn't real," she smiles.

—

Flesh slides against flesh, slick with sweat. His hand tightens in her hair, her back arches. Her breath, a sudden intake, rouses him further, pelvis grinding against pelvis, sore from lovemaking but still intent — a passionate bout that fills their heads drunk and sets the room spinning, swimming. They are part, everything disjointed, a mosaic; limbs and torsos, biting teeth and glazing tongues, fingers and limbs entwined, sweat slicked bronze and pale. He closes his eyes, filled with her scent, feels her push, feels himself release, feels her hold tense shudder as she breathes heavy in his ear — an exchange of souls.

—

The moment he has tried to push away comes. They lie in bed. She is sleeping and he has just come awake. Morning light is a white patch through the doorway to the small balcony. It is still cool but starting to warm and he tries not to move, not wanting to wake her but eventually unable to resist planting small kisses against the side of her neck.

Kisses planted, a crop sowed. Sew a stitch in time . . .

She groans, smiles, stretches and finally, so slowly, she opens her eyes, lashes fluttering, turning into him, burrowing against him. He holds her, kisses her. They keep shifting slightly. Each shift is greeted by a string of small kisses as they drag out the ritual of waking, stretching it to last as long as it will dear hold.

They are quiet when they rise. Both know the night is over, the crest passed and now the downward slide to an inevitable conclusion. A conclusion that is no conclusion, because beyond it awaits the unknowable.

He makes coffee and they drink, hardly talking but taking each other in with their eyes. When she says, "Perhaps I can shower," he is happy for her presence, and when she enters the shower leaving the door ajar, her glance from beyond it a subtle invitation, his heart lurches. He makes love to her beneath the cool flowing water; awkwardly at first, but they laugh and she pushes against him, as he tries to hold her against the slippery tiles, until eventually they twist, slippery limbs and he enters her from behind, and as simply as this he holds her and kisses her until he would disappear in her and he feels her grip tighten, feels them tense in unison, feels the starburst in his head and warmth that is followed by a sort of sadness, that guilt-lesson of Catholic school.

In fact he feels it is that burst of moment where we discover we are one with another, that our happiness is dependant and can be granted by another, that lasts so briefly, is so fleeting and the sorrow afterwards, that it cannot be held onto, that it cannot last. He holds her for a long time in the shower afterwards not wanting to let go and she lets him until he feels her shiver with cold and he releases her, wraps a towel around her and holds her tightly again and then they part.

After that their rituals become separate once again. They dress, dawn their old skins. He observes her, the way she steps into her heels, the tilt of the head and flick of her hair as she pins her earrings in place. When she is done she stands there as though about to board a ship. He wants to kiss her, one more time, but she has already applied her lipstick. The fear grips him that he will not see her again or, more honestly, that he will not have her again.

They walk to the door. He wants her again immediately, imagines pulling her back, tearing at her clothes, throwing her back on the bed. Instead he opens the door. She kisses him lightly so as not to smudge. He leans in, smells her perfume and kisses her neck, slowly, with parted lips, the hint of her on the tip of his tongue, tasting her, savouring her.

"I have to go," she says sadly. She puts her hand to his cheek, he kisses her palm. "Goodbye."

"Goodbye," he says.

She smiles, then turns and walks away. He watches her go, watches as she descends the stairway and then he returns to his room, now larger and vacant. Every object seems foreign, every item different for her having touched it. He picks up her coffee cup, two inches remaining and he sips it, trying to find her taste. He lays in the bed and inhales her scent from the sheets. He stares at the ceiling, at the fan spinning, an indifferent witness. When the phone rings he barely hears it, then, when he does, he wants it to be her, but it is not.

"Hello, Cristobal," comes the smiling voice.

"Hello, Coraline."

Seventeen

Dry leaves and grass crackle beneath their feet as they walk along the clay bank. The procession is already gathering and Porter cannot help but notice the lack of congruity. There is a motley bunch of mostly men, about forty people in all, the spectators mixed in with the actors. Individuals who are part of the faux-ritual that Coraline and Stellan have invited him to see are distinguished by dry-grass skirts and greasepaint on their cheeks. But just like the spectators a number of them wear rubber flip-flops or sandals and some even wear faded tee-shirts. It breaks the mood immediately for Porter, is the image of a tribe already colonized.

They mull around some sort of central point and it takes a moment for Porter to make out, what first appears to be a monolithic nest, what is actually a chair on a litter made of wicker and rough saplings.

As they round the litter Porter's eyes alight on the chair's occupant, an old weathered Indian with grey and white hair which touches his shoulders, and skin the stuff tobacco pouches were made of. He sits bare to the waist, a crown of weaved twigs on his head. People mull around him as they prepare to start, the mundane co-ordinations of county fairs.

But the Indian in the wicker chair remains stolid. He appears to be in a trance, imbues a sense of the ancient, of the mystical. Porter is reminded of his first encounter with Coraline, that sense of something close to the earth. Only this Indian shaman embodies something so otherworldly and foreign as to create a hint of the sinister. His marble eyes appear unseeing even as he takes in his surroundings dispassionately with a turtle's pace and care.

The light is dying and the moon can already be seen seeping into the pale blue afternoon sky. Porter is aware now of Coraline beside him, her simple dress which could be mistaken for buckskin. She draws a magnetic pole in comparison to the old shaman and caught between these two poles the first tingling of mystery and sense of the ancient creep over him.

The actors lift the litter with an excess of exhalations and scuffles, as the everyday conversations die away and they take up a chorus which is a plaintive cry underscored by a steady hum. They walk for some time, heading towards the river and the hum becomes the drone of flies in Porter's ears, the high pitched whine like the drawn complaints of a dog. The light incense below him seems to fan in the shaman's direction.

When they reach the riverside they settle the old Indian at a good vantage point where his unseeing stare can feel its numb fingers over an expanse of the muddy water. The actors move forward, bringing out thin bows and arrows with balls attached to the ends like fibrous marshmallows. They light the balls and raise their bows towards the new moon pale in the clear evening. The chanting stops. Someone calls out a snapping series of yelps which Porter translates to himself as an ancient native variant on "ready, aim, fire," and the archers unleash their volley as a squad of drunken recruits.

The arrows for the most part shoot upwards, though some vault sideways. They leap feebly up momentarily and then drift awkwardly back downwards to flop into the water. Porter watches the flames sputter on the lake surface, the dying corpses of slain stars.

Coraline beside him again seems to read his thoughts. "One can only imagine the excitement of what it used to be," she says, "a pack of wild hunters with their shaman to protect them from evil spirits, stalking out to hunt down the moon herself."

The participants already seem to have lost interest and are slowly sauntering around in good cheer. Iceboxes are opened, bottled and canned drinks with pre-market-tested logos shouting from their labels are passed around. The shaman alone maintains the charade. He watches out at the dying flames, his face impassive, studying their pattern like tea leaves.

"He's quite interesting," Porter observes.

"The shaman," Coraline says. "The shaman was a holy man who was revered as a conduit to the spirits. He was the only one in the tribe who didn't have to hunt or forage. They would bring him gifts and worship and fear him. They would make him offerings. Bring him women too."

"The divine translator?"

"He was practically a god himself, since he was the only one who could talk to them."

"Might be interesting to be a living god," he says lightly, but Coraline does not smile.

"To be revered in that way means to be isolated," she says. "I would imagine he would be the loneliest person in the world."

They make their way back as so many have dispersed. The old Indian still sits in his chair although he has grown tired of looking out at the water. He turns his head slowly to survey everything around him as though none of it really existed. Porter sees no further interest taken by the remnants of the ritual party in the man or his litter and fears briefly that the old shaman has been abandoned here. It is a flash of thought before they are out of sight and he begins to wonder if Stellan has at all recovered.

—

We are all members of tribes.

He writes it down, tries to order his thoughts, his opposition to being defined by the shift of masses, and yet he finds himself trapped in his own personal history. *These people*, he writes, he finds himself thinking, and cringes internally, for he has no desire to see them as a single horde, as though they were all — Asian, African, European — a tribe apart on this island. *Families. Nations. There are always exceptions*, he writes, *and yet there are overwhelming cultural influences of thought.*

He remembers back in London, a writer friend of his speaking of his wife's family from Hong Kong: "They are Japanese," his writer friend explained. "Studied at Oxford, but she was the only one born here. Yet they go back to Hong Kong and they are more English than she is. They are more English than the English."

"That's because, unlike the English, they don't feel the need to apologize for it," Porter had responded.

It had come across at the time as clever cocktail banter, had elicited the requisite chuckles, but now his mind turns it over. This heavy rock he had spat out takes on different dimensions and he wonders if it is in his cultural genes this feeling, this need of his to feel apologetic for his being. It dawns on him that part of his steady discomfort here is his constant treatment as an outsider, always a guest, toasted and introduced with warmth and welcome, to be taken special care of, to be handled differently, but always as a foreigner. And it harps upon, or perhaps grates against is the better term, his own instinct: to feel a need to apologize for his intrusion, for bringing this reminder of history with him into their perfect world-of-the-present. He now a leper, infected with the past.

And he who would see only individuals, would wish to relate to them as such is excluded by reason of his tribe.

Eighteen

The boat glides steadily.

He waited and she called. Whispers across the phone line fully into the conspiracy. "Jack wants to throw a party," she told him. He still felt something when she would speak his name, no longer the pierce but the slight pressure of jealousy's blade at Kaplan's legitimate claim on a piece of her, while his moments were all stolen. "A going away party." She hesitated. "I want you to come. My God, that must sound so selfish."

He was uncertain, "I don't know. Why do you want me there? Do you think he knows?"

"No. No, I don't think so. He thinks I'm using you as a flirtation though, to try to get back at him, for Nadia."

"Are you?"

He took her momentary silence as honest thought. He wondered if it even mattered to him. He could not imagine he would refuse to see her even if it was just a ploy on her part to inflame Kaplan.

"No. Maybe . . . I do want to see you . . . but my feelings, they're, they're a bit confused. I feel I haven't had anything for a long time. Anything for myself, that I really wanted. I feel like that with you. But I don't know if a part of me wants him to know. I don't know."

Words, he thinks, remembering the conversation as he rides over the waves, wind lashing him, *they are binding me to you. And it is never the words you think. Not the sweet nothings but the lost and confused words that are the truth. Love is the feeling of drowning, of sinking in the embryonic waters, sunlight filtered through, not knowing which way is up. Like a shipwrecked carnival.*

"I'll come," he had said.

"Nadia will be there," she said, laying all cards on the table.

"I'll come. I'll come to see you." I will be whatever you need, he added to himself.

The boat drives now through the waves, the rough wood feeling unequal to the power of the motor behind it. Joseph sits at the tiller of the single outboard motor, his chin up to see past the raised bow. They had been talking about life on the island, the discontent running heavily among the populace and the rumours of gathering shadows. Porter pried for sociological factors, his story moved away from the small family tragedy to something else, to an exploration of something new to him, a different culture, a different way of being. Joseph gives the usual answers to his questions, ones he has heard many times before from the interviewees, rehashes of television anchors. They both fall silent for a while after the boat becomes airborne over a crest and lands heavily back down onto water. Then Joseph speaks again, going off-script.

"We, all of us, suffering from the same malady; the Modern Problem," Joseph says casually, a distant smile on his face as he stares out at the pale sky, face in the wind. "All people want the same thing."

Porter smiles, trying to assume the same casual attitude as his guide, "And what's that?"

Joseph looks at him, expression unchanged, but his eyes behind the face are more penetrating. "Well, what do you want, Mr. Porter?"

He is taken aback, chuckles, "To be happy, I guess." It comes out like a question but he is amused at his guide's simplicity.

"Yes." Joseph looks back out to sea, "And what would make you happy, Mr. Porter?"

He tries to smile, but there is something stoic now about Joseph, something timeless about the way he sits, chin jutted out to sea, wind whipping his shirt in the fading evening. He thinks of the apartment with Anais in it. But how long would that last? Could that be enough for an eternity? Could they grow old in that bed together?

The breeze carries fine sprays of water and Porter finds himself growing chilled. "I don't know," he says absently.

He does not think that Joseph has heard him above the motor, but then the guide leans slightly towards him without turning, smile broadening. "That is the malady," he says casually. "The Modern Problem," and he resumes his vigil on the horizon, marking things in the seascape that Porter cannot decipher.

Again Porter tries to smile, tries to enjoy himself and assume Joseph's ease in the wind, in the smell and taste of saltwater. But he cannot. His hand keeps tightening on the gunnel. He makes a conscious effort to loosen it, only to find it has involuntarily tightened there again. He feels a sinking in him, feels alone and by the time they reach the house with its extended jetty and string of lit bulbs along the veranda, the sun has already begun to set. Porter climbs up onto the wooden deck feeling cold and hollow.

—

Two days later he sits in his usual spot, umbrella-shaded from the morning sun, so crisp here. The steam rises off of the dark coffee with its sharp rich scent and Porter shakes the paper open, holding it slackly as his mind wonders unseeing. Images float up, sensations, and he is once again submerged in that intoxicating pool of her memory, time slowed and disjointed.

He had entered the party cold and sober, feeling the pauper at the ball. He doubts in retrospect that anyone even noticed him come in. He found her and she greeted him, a polite smile, "How lovely that you could make it," casual meet-and-greet until he kisses her cheek, breathes in deeply and hears her whisper in his ear, "Cristobal.".

He nursed an unnecessary drink in a corner of the veranda, happy and replaying her voice in his head. He avoided the guests as much as possible, smiles and nods at the edge of others, and tried to find her, tried not to stare, wanted to. His name whispered like a secret, some spirit-animal that is only hers to know. And in his mind the name that calls his spirit; Anais.

In the cafe he turns a page despite having read nothing, looks off down the sidewalk a moment. He wants to see Coraline. He would like to talk to her this morning, hear her ideas, to look upon that face of youth and beauty that speaks of ideas and life eternal, filled with hope. He wants to bask in her potential with his newfound spirit, to say, "I have hope too. A kernel of yours, but I can once again nod and understand that the world is full, that life can be feasted on. It is a banquet and not a dried nut in an iron shell."

At the party he did feel the intruder, a stalking stranger. Everywhere it seemed to him people knew or suspected. He saw Kaplan but said nothing to him, his mind was preoccupied. Uneasiness pervaded his body, the confusion of restrained desire, guilt — he the cowed old wolf stalking a golden deer, pelt of burnt honey. His memory of the experience would have been miserable if it were not for their moment. One moment.

Nervous anticipation filled his stomach. He knew what it was to be a spy now, to engage in espionage, harbouring a secret purpose, a desire to undermine all of this festive normality. Each time her eyes engaged him was a stolen secret, a dossier of wonders to carry back to his room and pore over. He tried not to stare, not to give away his game. Eventually he had wandered away, sick of the shallow conversations, words like shiny plastic beads with their predictable ridges of mass manufacture. He found his way downstairs in a small room converted to an office. He thought of it as a study only because of the small bookcase with its preserved paperbacks which sat behind the desk — the only books in the house. Needless to say this was Ana's retreat. A place she could come and do what, he wondered.

The books, a notebook, in a corner on a small sewing chair — the kind whose seat could open and stored colourful spools and pins and needles, a limb of her life gone numb — on it a sketch pad, dusty with stained and slightly curling edges. She had pulled it out he realised. She had retrieved it from some treasure trove of the past. Was it after talking with him — after speaking of her desire to be a painter in her past? Had he revived something in her, perhaps inspired her to try again, to reclaim herself, starting with her body, following with a dream? It would have made a good story.

He was tempted to pick it up, to scan the pages, but something in him feared to. There was too much undiscovered that could be discovered there and some things now he would rather not know. It would hurt him now if he found out that she was without imagination or possessed no real talent. He could not imagine it being so, but still. It was a similar sensation as to when she had said that she had read his book. He feared her finding it empty, boring or uninteresting. He would not have wanted her to see him that way, no matter how much he felt it himself.

The sound of the party swelled and faded as the door opened and he could see her figure slip in against the hall light. He had not turned the light in the study on and so when she closed the door it took a moment before she emerged from the shadows, a smoky silhouette solidifying slowly. The words play in his mind now — "smoky silhouette solidifying slowly" — their slithering repetition, something suitably fluid, an elusive idea.

She approached him, eyes watching. She came close to him. He could see that she had had a few drinks. She watched him in that same curious way, studying, gauging. "I saw your sketch book out," he stuttered quietly, suddenly nervous with her this close.

She did not say anything. Her eyes shifted to his mouth without a change of expression. Then she was against him, the front of her body pressing his. He leaned closer, her head tilted back and he kissed her. It was like sinking. He felt a fearful excitement and the room tipped a moment, her mouth full and open to him. His hands moved over her. She pulled his hips against her as he eased her partially onto the desk. Someone laughed, but far enough away that his heart only jumped at first. He kissed her neck as her hand found him hard beneath his trousers, held and stroked. His own hand found the hem of her dress already bunched partially in his hand, slid beneath to the burning warmth of her inner thigh.

Her breath was warm and moist in heavy gasps against his neck as he moved his hand in her with increasing intensity and her own hand griped him hard. For his excitement he may as well have entered her, aching for her, he had felt her press against his palm, fingers buried. And if he had entered her there as he had wanted so desperately to, he knows he would have been quickly lost, the moment gone before she had begun. So this way was better, his arousal growing with hers, the crescendo of her staggered breath, the strong grip of her fingers and her face pressed into his shoulder, teeth biting down. She shuddered to stillness, then inhaled deeply, once, twice, her body shaking with each breath. He found her mouth, tender and full now, as though swollen, moist as she was.

The blinding light on the sidewalk cafe flickers as a group of schoolgirls walk past, and he is suddenly drawn back to the present, head swimming groggily, the shamed awareness of his aroused state buried unnoticeably beneath slacks, paper, table, still pulling blood from his mind. He leans forward with a nervous laugh, to nobody, the sidewalk bare now, passersby gone.

She had slipped away from him as she had come. Backing out in semidarkness, a smile glinting a moment in the lying wink of the door's light, the brief, vertical horizon that swallowed her like another dimension. When he found his way back to the party, it was an assault on his senses — too loud, the crash and smash of conversations and banging laughter. The partygoers reminded him of children, with alcohol-sugar-rushed minds they made noise for the sake of noise. Words, all those empty words, he heard them saying as though decibel added weight, volume provided import. They may as well have been shouting vowels, blasting into hollow drums. None of it could reach the place inside of him that replayed the sound that called up all of nature: her sigh and a shudder — the almost-silence that could split the atom, that would unravel the universe.

Nineteen

This was revolution, how it started, whispers and conversations, the first spew of the rebellious mind. Before the act comes the fermentation of the idea. 'Loose talk'; it circulated, had always been circulating, since he arrived. Displeasure and discontent, in the bars they complained but the majority shrugged their shoulders. What could you do? Others began to demand action, and the saddest thing to Porter was that the most fervent rebels seemed to be the ones with no plan. Their rebellion was not an overthrow to replace. There was no intellectual idea or ideology with which to replace the one they wished to destroy, there was simply the desire to destroy. As though shackled they wanted only to be released, to be free to roam where they may. They had no intended destination, but this was beside the point. They were being 'oppressed' (their word — they spoke from a colonial heritage, with a linguistics that echoed the memory of a slave culture). It passed with other catchphrases in conversation, but he had heard it more often recently, had seen it etched in faces grown less exasperated and more outraged.

And now here a protest, people marching, raising signs and fists, chanting in what could barely be called unison. It takes him a while to figure out what they are saying. They drift forward as he watches from his cafe. They are calling for change. A small dark man in the front in a short-sleeved work shirt raises a megaphone. The feedback burns through the crowd, further confusing the scattered chants. The majority of the protesters are women. The man calls through the screech of the megaphone, so that when it rights itself to its static-blare he is already in mid-sentence. ". . . in Parliament! This Government want to bury the worker, when it's the worker puts bread on his table! What we want to know, Mr. Prime Minister, when you dining at your big table . . ." The man seems rather uninspired, rather uninspiring and the crowd herds like cattle, lazy in the heat, passed Porter along the opposite sidewalk.

The lady from the cafe has come to stand in the doorway, wringing her hands in her apron. "It start," she mutters quietly. Porter looks up, but she is not talking to him. She shakes her head sadly and turns back inside.

—

Coraline meets him and they are driven to Uncle Stellan's house.

The visits have taken on a routine; they talk with the family, eat a quiet lunch and then sit in the dry yard and speak. Stellan is in better condition this time, but still seems unwell. A shadow hangs about him, his illness palpable and occasionally Porter's eyes meet Coraline's and he can see her awareness of it. He is gaunt despite his extended belly and he sits heavily.

They talk of many things before coming to the attempted coup, to the man who led it, some would say successfully.

"Do you know who he was? Kadeem?" Stellan asks.

Porter shakes his head. He has read of the man, but wants Stellan's version unadulterated.

"He was a Holy Man," Stellan says. "He was once a great spiritual teacher, teaching of beauty, the beauty of the Koran. He was a Muslim, a very pious Muslim." Stellan looks away to the worn dirt patch of the yard. "Well, he was once." He looks back at Porter and smiles sadly.

"You knew him personally?" Porter ventures.

Stellan nods, looking away again and out at the trees. Then he seems to sigh, waves it off with the brush of a hand. He is about to speak when he is cut off by a fit of coughing that overtakes him suddenly. He coughs heavily for some time, a phlegmatic wheezing, until Porter is tempted to slap him on the back but instead sits at a loss looking towards the house for help just as it subsides. Stellan spits heavily into the dry earth at his feet.

"Sorry," he says, clearing his throat. "Most people do not understand the Muslim religion. It is a harsh religion, made for a harsh time. In many ways the Prophet Mohammed speaks to those who require a faith truer to their circumstances. Christians became, early on, comfortable with their own hypocrisy. I mean no offense; you come from a Christian country."

"No offense taken."

"Christians preached of Jesus as God. Jesus' words were words of love and peace. Therefore these were the words of God himself, by Catholicism's own reasoning. And yet in the name of this God they wage wars, the Crusades, launch the Inquisition," he counts off on his fingers, scowling. "Is this not hypocrisy?"

Porter says nothing, leaning forward elbows on knees. It is his turn to study the dirt-patch yard, the trees. Again he is aware of a sense of expectation, a role laid out for him by history — the white European, Cristobal the Catholic, Columbus' heir, invader of the indigenous. He tries to remember when last he has been in a church and can come up with nothing since his wife's funeral.

Stellan's voice brakes his musing. "I say this only so that you will not judge too harshly. Understand Kadeem is not the bad man, the cold murderer, many would have you believe. Nor is he the selfless prophet, others would claim. He is somewhere between, something between." Stellan pulls the old slipper from the puppy's mouth and tosses it out. The puppy gives chase. "And something else entirely."

"It's normally the case, isn't it," Porter says.

Stellan chuckles, "Yes, I suppose." The puppy returns and Stellan wrestles with the end of the slipper gently for a while before winning it. "He is political." He throws the slipper out again. The puppy gives chase, the cycle continued. "I suppose we all are, in one sense or another."

Porter hesitates a moment, waits for Stellan to rise at least partially from the past, out of that current of regret before asking, "Can you arrange for me to meet him?"

———

He is invited to a performance at the Government's new Opera House, a monstrosity of glass and steel like

207

some industrial bubble belched up from the ground on the verge of popping. He walks with his hosts, friends of Peter's; a pleasant art gallery owner and her husband, whose line of business will forever elude Porter. He smiles and nods, is aware of speaking while his mind contemplates each moment of his time with Anais. He replays it searching for clues, inflections in her voice, the tilt of her head, shift of her shoulders, piecing together a million versions of the same scenario, combinations of meaning which will reaffirm or deny the crashing down of the house of cards.

The Opera House is so supported by webs of steel beams that what would have been a vast open hall has shrunk down to very little floor space, the grandeur only stretching above where one can see reflected in the distant ceiling well-dressed ghost images adrift in a sea of black night.

They are afforded good seats, high up, just before the section railing of the reserved box. Porter sits feeling warm between his jacket and skin and hollow beneath. Slowly the auditorium lights go out and the shifting restlessness of bodies in the dark subsides. A spotlight rises. Sharp notes resonate. Sharp struck single keys that jar, coughed forward at random from the piano and the single figure crouched over it, the only things illuminated on the wooden stage. Slowly the pianist seems to gather the notes, find a footing, and formulate some sense out of chaos before the notes escape again in a cascade now from his pulsing fingers. It is the tune of an epileptic, but slowly subsides into a low background cacophony of hollow drum beats.

A woman in a floral dress takes the stage. Her shoes clop like a horses hooves, the sound of blocks of wood striking each other. She bursts forth a long wavering note, a tribal call that wakes the ancestors, wakes all of their ancestors, lights something primal. There is something stirring in her plaintive cry, the broken coarseness of her song, but it is out of place here. It is a spectacle, overly produced and robbed of its naturalism by the surroundings of the Opera House and its attempt to fulfil some European idea of grandeur. The audience in their ties and slacks are a new age imperial court reducing what may have once been a meaningful ritual to trifling entertainment. It puts in mind those animals brought in cages from the New World to be displayed in king's courts.

Porter suddenly wants to be sitting with gypsies around a fourteenth century fire, to see dusky-skinned girls with their dark hair dancing, twirling through smoke and stomping their bare feet in the clay soil. He pictures Coraline, tambourine to hip, as the gypsy Esmeralda. He sees lines of trees in fog on a wet English countryside and he longs for it, to walk up into the hills, to disappear into the fog of his own land, devoid of history, at least his history, where he can start anew. He pictures Anais lying in his bed, turning towards him, folds of sheets like snow covered mountains.

He barely notices when the performance eventually ends until a barrage of applause assails him. He sets a waxen smile in place for the sake of his hosts. A man comes onto the stage and gestures broadly with one arm up to the reserved box, behind to the right of Porter.

"Our gracious Prime Minister, the Honourable Baxter Clairmont," the man on the stage announces.

Bodies turn and a stocky black man, like an African Churchill waves magnanimously as though he were the composer and orchestrator of the evening's program. And perhaps, Porter thinks, he is.

Porter is relieved when they eventually file out. He would be anywhere but here in this Opera House with its reek of school auditorium. He bids his hosts goodbye, thanking them for the evening's entertainment. He is grateful for their consideration, but his words still stick in his throat the bone of a lie. He finds Joseph smoking in the parking lot and gets into the car, sighing relief.

—

Dr. Baswani is a small fragile-looking Indian with a Ceasar's laurel of white hair. His eyes are clear and everything about him speaks to the intellectual. Baswani is pleasant and well spoken, his movements precise. Porter cannot help wonder if this man has ever loved a woman passionately.

They sit in Baswani's living room and speak for some time of general politics, of the old government, the new, of colonial stigma, a lack of real cultural identity.

"We are at a bad time in history to be a new country," Baswani says. "In order to become a strong nation one must develop one's own cultural identity. In order to do this one must want it, you understand? You cannot force an identity on anyone, because even if they play along, it is still only that; a play. Deep down inside the identity does not take root, it is resented. And, as with people, a cultural identity is not who you pretend to be, but rather who you are."

"You think history discourages it?"

"Well yes, that too, but my reason for saying we are in a bad time in history for it is because many of the binding traits of cultural personalities have diminished. Firstly, we are bombarded by the media of other countries. This is a constant reminder of what the outside world has and tends to diminish the idea of what we have. It's like a man looking at a farm that has been operating successfully for several years, with a beautiful estate house and lush fields, and then you give him a plot of overgrown jungle and tell him, 'Here, make something of this.' Most men do not have the vision to see that the grand estate came from this same type of plot. They want what the estate owner has, but they don't want to build it. Because it already exists they think there must be an easier way to attain it."

"You think they desire what other countries have then. Do you think foreign cultures contribute to the problem?"

"Foreign governments are looking out for their countries' interests, and rightly so. That is their job. But our government is more interested in people liking them enough to get them re-elected. They are like parents spoiling a child, agreeing with everything the child says, no matter how ridiculous or unobtainable, simply because they want the child to like them. We can only blame ourselves, but it is a difficult time for such a project regardless.

"Religion is another factor that can bond a country and foster this cultural identity — this is the case with most of the first world countries. But in today's global society religion itself is fractured and marginalised. Don't get me wrong, I'm not a very religious man, my point is simply that if you were to take a poll of the island you would find that you have almost equal portions of Hindu, Muslim and Catholics — the Catholics probably being the majority by a fine margin, but you can't unite a nation based on a fine margin — not to mention the smaller movements; the Shouter Baptist, the Bobo Shanti, and so on."

"Do you think there's any way it can be done?"

Baswani sighs and removes his glasses, polishing them on his shirt-tail before replacing them. "I'll be honest with you, Mr. Porter. I try not to be a pessimist. People are not patient animals. And here, well we have been let into the race late. We make progress a little bit at a time, but we always see ourselves as behind. Many are happy to tear down, they do not think enough is being done and they revolt, they rebel. Look, there was a coup, and there is violence and the people who see themselves as patriots for their country effect change — but at what cost? The coup instilled a government which built monuments to its own authority, hollow symbols of a supposed progress. And many were happy to accept this because it gave the outward appearance of progress, of development. But others will be dissatisfied by this and then this government too will be replaced, it is happening now. It goes on and on. Modernity is forcing certain advancements. These are mostly being done by the private sector and basic economics, because this is the one area where the majority will state their voice, or at least the economic majority. As consumers we are developing a personality.

"Unfortunately, this seems to be where we're heading. While we will fail to develop a cultural personality — the very thing a government would need to be elected on in order to plan a way ahead for this country — we are becoming instead a country defined by its consumer personality. I find this sad, but then I see this trend worldwide. We are becoming a society of wants, like bodies to be clothed, but bodies containing no soul."

———

. . . Bodies containing no soul.

Porter walks the sidewalks and feels that he would be one. He recognizes a feeling now as others move past him, that he would be envious of them all for the lives he assumes they live, the personal histories they walk with concealed behind their skins, that he has so carefully avoided all his life.

Only now he has a secret: Ana, his Anais, the secret that fills that space in him empty for so long. He feels no need for history as long as there is the suggestion of her in his future. She is the sun that warms his edges, defines its outline and reminds him of his own presence.

Yes, Cristobal Porter does have a soul after all.

Twenty

They talk quietly across the wire, whispers like revolution. There is no one in his apartment, no one in her house. They whisper so as not to wake the silence, not to shatter the air which moulds its intimacy around them. Voices in quiet make love to each other, broken only by occasional whispers of static.

After that it happens in starts and fits of unreality. Kaplan leaves and she arrives as arranged, meeting him in the darkened guesthouse lounge. She arrives at his table, a darker more sophisticated version of her, phoenix raised from the fires of that night, that night of the party. That night where she daringly seduced him, found satisfaction and left him happily wanting while her friends and husband drank upstairs. He stands to greet her silently. He kisses her cheek. She looks steadily at him with that challenging stare, but with something else behind it, something of control, a comfort in control. He feels nervous, as though he no longer knows her — yet it excites him; that he thinks he knows something of her only to have her raise his uncertainty, make him question what he thought was. A dark cloud drifting, she guides his hand and shifts and he is holding her on the dance floor.

They are dancing.

—

At the door to his room he senses a moment of pause. Some line burns across the threshold and when she crosses it she quietly exudes a sense of exaltation, even as it is touched by a sense of loss for the skin that remains on the other side. He comes to stand behind her, wraps his arms around her and she enfolds his arms in hers. He feels her sink back into him, a release of herself, surrender. She turns to face him and he kisses her mouth gently, her face and neck, slow exploration of her skin, her curves, hands and lips seeking slowly for the hidden catches that will open her desire. The spring of his own desire is coiled so tightly in him he fears he may snap, come too soon, or break into tears.

Oh, you fool. The words escape in his thoughts, but everything else is muddled, carried on a warm clear fog of drunkenness, everything moving slowly like honey. *Golden bronze, like burnt honey.*

He feels alone, a sense of stage fright. It is washed away by the sensation of her hands tracing labyrinths over him, then fingers entwined in his hair. He feels like the first time that she was here with him as his. Slowly he removes her dress, runs his thumb along the curvature of her shoulder muscles, down the length of her back, following the riverbank of her scar, and she bows her head, hair falling to the side. He can see the tip of her nose, her lips parted, hears the whisper of her breath as he kisses the nape of her neck.

Time. We have time now.

He explores with his fingers, with his mouth and he would drag this moment on forever, would learn and memorize every inch of her. He kneels fascinated by the soles of her feet, enthralled by the press of bone against flesh at her hip, even more so by her movements, the intake of air as he presses his tongue there, the pleasant rise and twist as he applies light pressure with his teeth and kisses. He would spend forever chartering this land, but her quickening breath, her coaxing hands, her writhing body all conspire, move them both to an ever increasing rhythm, African drums pounding in their chests, rising to a frantic pitch.

For the night they are locked in each other's arms. They sleep soundly. He wakes once, kisses her shoulder and the side of her neck until she stirs. She does not open her eyes, just smiles and pushes back against him, and he lets her fall back to sleep and drifts off himself, her hair against his cheek, the beginnings of rain outside.

The first day they barely rise. He prepares them food which they eat in bed, sitting cross-legged, smiling naked at each other. Draped in sheets, they sit like gurus on their mattress raft and eat with their hands. The sounds from outside drift past like the rushing river of life going by them, happily forgotten.

They make love, they drink, they fall asleep against each other. In the early afternoon he lays back, his head against her breast. Her fingers play through his hair, sliding soothingly through damp locks. They are quiet for a long while, bodies pleasantly exhausted. He watches the light sliding through the French doors, creeping along the blistered paint on the far wall. When she speaks it is sudden but slides naturally as the light, seeping from their thoughts.

"Why do we grow afraid? Our minds grow old first, don't they? Old and afraid and the body just follows. We collect our lives around us like a security blanket. Memories, friends, routines . . . like so much dust."

He cannot see her face but reaches back to gently stroke her hair. "I feel that you have broken the rust off of me," he says.

She does not move. He cannot see her expression. He kisses her arm. She touches his jaw and he turns and she kisses his cheek, then his mouth, solemnly.

"You've woken me, Christobal. You have woken me." She says it without a smile, a statement of fact, neither of gratitude nor of blame.

He kisses her, kisses her because he can think of nothing else to do. He kisses her because he wants to. He can be safe in it. There can be no negative interpretation of a kiss. It is the one thing, he thinks, that should always be honest. He kisses her and tries to let the scent of her, the taste of her, her physical being fill his mind; a cleansing fire to clear the doubt, the uncertainty. Here, in this kiss he knows her. He is certain of it. Certain of it only here.

—

People say passion is either fed or it dies. But sometimes, when locked away inside it can feed on itself, it can squeeze down to such a concentrated mass. And then, like the atoms compressed at the dawn of the universe, it must eventually explode. Creating galaxies . . . or obliterating all in its wake.

But of that concentrated teaspoon of mass that was the universe, nothing remains.

—

He cannot stop touching her. His hand traces patterns across her skin. While she sleeps in the heat of early afternoon, his hands glide lightly over every inch of her body, a blind man mapping an image for his senses to recall later, acknowledging that there will be a time when she is no longer here. Occasionally she shifts, sighs sleepily with content.

He forces himself from her when the images have formed into words in his head, when they begin to torrent in a waterfall through his mind and they become too much for him to be sure of recalling later. He rises carefully and sits at the desk, begins writing, stopping regularly to look across at her sleeping soundly. He writes words of ridiculous poetry, shakes his head and laughs internally at himself. He lets the pen move and the torrent continues and the pages fill faster and faster. He will sort it later, figure out what is of use and what not. Everything now seems related to her, to that warm body at rest in his bed. Every relationship is a preparation for this, every event in the distant world is but an analogy for this event.

His head is down scribing furiously when he slowly becomes aware of being watched. He looks across and she is looking at him through freshly woken eyes, watching him curiously. He smiles and her lips tweak in a response, but it is a distant response as though her mind is crossing other fields. What does he represent to her? She does not look away, but watches, a silent observer, or one who feels they cannot be seen.

He rises and comes back across to her, climbs carefully onto the bed and she smiles more fully at him now, but there is still something civil in it, something distracted but acknowledging the correctness of the gesture. He kisses her and she returns the kiss and here he is finally reassured. This she puts herself into, does fully and pours into him. They make love slowly, affectionately. There is something beautiful and communal about it, but at the same time a solitary act.

—

I try to paint these portraits of simple moments and mundane phrases, these subtle movements of body-language, dolphin cries of infinite combinations that try to speak of something buried deep beneath the sea, fathoms upon fathoms below the surface. Why are there so many books — tomes upon tomes of words, tombs for words? What language can describe a soul?

—

He wakes and extracts himself carefully from beside her. He showers and dresses but stops at the bed to sit beside her before he leaves. He strokes her hair and kisses her face until she wakes. She smiles up at him, looks down at his clothes. "You're leaving me?" she smiles and stretches. "You do remember this is your room?"

"I'm just going to pick us up some breakfast, and maybe a paper."

She stretches again, wipes her eyes. "I should probably get changed too. One can't shut out the world I suppose."

"Why not?" He kisses her, "At least for the time being."

"Just pretend the world doesn't exist?" she looks to the French-doors. "Can we live in a bubble? Make up our own world?" She smiles softly at the prospect, strokes his hair as he leans close over her.

"My dear," he says, "I'm a writer. I make a living of it."

He kisses her and forces himself to the door. "You had better be here when I get back."

"Is that a threat?"

"Most certainly, if you want breakfast."

—

The world is changed outside. The air seems clearer, crisper and there is energy in his steps, a heightened sense of awareness to the sounds, the smells and tastes of the world. Sex does this, he thinks, it awakens us, peels away the dead layers of skin that husk over our senses and exposes the newer bud beneath still tender. But it is an assault as well. His body seems to flex in the openness, while his insides urge a return to his cave where time may rob him of his happiness in increments.

He comes to his cafe and orders some pastries and two coffees, receives them quickly and pays. As he steps back onto the sidewalk the sun blazes but not unpleasantly. He blinks to accustom himself and begins walking when a voice calls his name, "Cristobal."

Coraline smiles at him as she steps out of the blinding rays. He smiles at her and she seems fully young and innocent. "How are you, Coraline?"

"My Uncle wanted to see you," she falls in-step beside him.

"How is he feeling?"

"Better for the moment, thank you, but he's been in steady decline," she furrows her brow. "I think the doctors know more than they tell us."

"They usually do."

Pasiphae appears from nowhere and begins trotting alongside them. They walk and talk until they are outside his gate. He faces her and Pasiphae sits cheerfully, whipping her tail.

"What an odd little family we make," Porter jokes.

Coraline seems to blush. "I'm sorry to be following you."

"No, come on. I meant nothing by it. We're friends enough to not need apologies at this stage. I only hope I haven't taken you out of your way." He shrugs the two cups of coffee. "I'm a little preoccupied."

Coraline glances between the coffee cups and does the math, she smiles, blushes more deeply. "Sorry." She steps back, recovers, "But I will give you a call? You will come and see Uncle?"

"I will. I'd like to talk to him, well, to you both quite actually."

She smiles waves and walks away. Pasiphae seems torn between them. "I would give you a bit of a bite, but afraid my hands are full, old girl." She follows him along the path, up the stairs. "Don't suppose you could get the door?"

Beady eyes look back at him dumbly, tongue lolling from happy jaws.

"Didn't think so." He manages to turn the knob and pushes the door back. He makes his way up the stairs, having to rest a cup on the landing to unlock the door. The hollow sound of the lock clicking transmits a sudden thought through him that he will find the apartment empty. He opens the door, retrieves the cup and enters.

She is seated on the edge of the bed, clothed in one of his shirts. Her hair spills tangled down her back, but the highlights show up dramatically. She turns sleepily towards him and he offers a cup of coffee which she takes.

"I'm sorry, I should have opened for you," she says.

"You couldn't have known."

"Oh, but I did. I saw you from the balcony, you and your young friend. I'm sorry, I wasn't thinking." She sips, looks contemplatively at her cup.

"Well I managed to make it."

She eases herself against his shoulder and he kisses her temple. This comfortable familiarity, existing in each other's space, he wonders if it could last. It is what he would want from a life with someone. It does not have to be marriage. It never had to be.

He tries to remember if he ever had this with his wife. They would sit after making love. He would hold her. He brought her coffee or wine, dependant on the time of day. He would read the paper and she would lie against him while she read a book. He has spent so little time remembering those early days. They are pleasant to recollect. How did things go cold between them? So gradually a routine develops. So gradually life slips out of your hands, you drift off, become distracted and lose the reins. He inhales the scent of Anais' hair. He wants to hold on tight to this way of being. But is that even possible? How can one contemplate the future with another man's wife? He is forced to live in the now. That is what is good, he thinks. That is what is important.

So he tells himself.

—

I am like a child. Writer's make up stories. They never grow up.

—

He has been unaware that he has been this lonely. As he lies in bed with her he feels himself changed. The ghost made flesh through her acknowledgement, her approval. He wants to say those words, watching her resting quietly, everything so perfect. He kisses her neck and studies the subtle flare of her nostril as she breathes in deep, the delicate lobe so carefully moulded they are the best argument for the existence of a divine hand. But one must not say the words unless they are sustainable. As much as he loves her, does truly love her here and now at this moment, their tomorrow is so uncertain as to not exist. So he takes her in, memorizes and categorizes with all senses, tries to retain all that he can of her scent, her feel, so that he may relive it when she is gone. So that he might hold onto the spectre of her until she is with him again. He dreads her departure. Dreads the prospect of this shadowy interval lived only for a hope of a future moment of happiness. And how brief is that to be?

—

He rolls onto his side and watches her as she dresses. A woman dressing, how does it take on such art? She climbs into her dress and he finally rises, holds her from behind kissing her neck.

Moments later they sit silently across the table from each other, drinking coffee. He cannot take his eyes from her. She seems more casual, yet aware of his eyes. She will look at him and smile. It is a conversation of smiles. His is fixed; a man in a daze and he would have it so. Hers shifts playfully, then self-consciously, then, he can tell, simply allowing herself to be happy.

She slips away at the door, the last taste the tip of her tongue, her cheek, her face turned, her hair tracing across his hand. She descends the stairway and he hopes for her to look up, back at him. She doesn't. She disappears from their world, returns to the other.

Twenty-one

CESTRUM NOCTURNUM (or "Night-blooming Jasmine"): a stunning evergreen shrub that grows in warm, tropical climates, Night-blooming jasmine is especially favored for the greenish-yellow, tube-shaped blooms and its exquisite scent. Although it will bloom during the day, it is after the sun goes down that the sweet fragrance becomes especially intense. Night-blooming jasmine, is also known as 'Lady of the Night'.

—

Absence. Everywhere in his room there is the lack of her. He feels it most strongly in his bed at night, where he can lay and summon her scent. He can close his eyes and imagine her body, the press of flesh, the warmth of her living breath on his neck. Outside in the night she haunts him pleasantly. It is the desire of memory, but it is touched too with the lover's burden, the price of joy which is the fear of losing it. Loss will creep in, with the fading of her scent from the pillow. But for now, in her fresh departure there is a pleasant longing and the notion held most dearly that he will see her again, have her here again.

—

MELASTOMA DECEMFIDUM: A medium-sized shrub that grows to about eight feet. Its blooms are a rich pinky-lilac in colour and almost two inches across. After flowering, the calyx of the flower forms seeds that are covered with a pulp that attracts the Semp (a bird often kept caged for its whistling ability — hence its dwindling numbers in the wild).

—

He tries to write but can only think of her. He writes a few lines more fit for some senior school binder, scratches them. This reoccurrence of childish ways — love returns us to a state of innocence where pure feelings are possible. It is a fantasy world for the adult, which is why words written about it can so often seem overly simplistic, the snips and snails and puppy-dog tails of nursery rhymes. But is it love? Some other word should be available, something in between that over-used complete commitment, the offhand forever, something of fondness, of sentiment and of need.

He thinks hard; can he form a character of her? Can he see her objectively, capture her in words? He begins to try. Her body a shell, a vessel that has endured travel and travail, he describes it as an artefact unearthed, its history to be deciphered. Its contents are more elusive. He feels innately that he knows her, understands her desires, her hurt, the hesitance to reveal anything of herself and her longing to do so. He understands it as he understands it in himself. But so much remains mysterious, unfathomable. He sees her clearly and yet cannot pin it down, like a sail flapping loose, blinding in the sun but roiling, shifting, constantly changing shape, still dazzling. Who she is cannot be bottled or caged on the page.

—

BOUGAINVILLEA GLABRA: Named for Canadian explorer Admiral Louis de Bougainvillea. The actual flower of the plant is small and generally white, but each cluster of three flowers is surrounded by three or six bracts with the bright colors associated with the plant, including pink, magenta, purple, red, orange, white, or yellow. Bougainvillea Glabra is sometimes referred to as "paper flower" because the bracts are thin and papery. Bougainvillea plants are very hardy and can survive some degree of neglect, but care is required for them to truly flourish. Sunlight is essential to the healthy growth and flowering of bougainvilleas, ideally six to eight hours of sunlight per day. Less than five hours will prevent bougainvilleas from blooming. Under the right conditions, bougainvilleas can bloom 11 months out of the year.

—

Porter finds himself suddenly defined by her. It is exciting and in moments worrisome. Their bond is tentative, a difficult thing to be defined by. He sees the fragility the more time they spend apart. The more he thinks of her in activity with what he begins to perceive as the real world, the more he imagines his presence in her mind fading. This is the fertile soil of jealousy.

He imagines her again and again in his room, drawing from memory, reliving moments shared, looking for every nuance of meaning in her words and actions. Building on this he creates future moments, time they have not yet shared, words they would exchange. He writes and re-writes scenes in his mind, adjusting her responses to allow for variance in her feelings, moments of abandon or moments of uncertainty.

In his own moments of uncertainty thoughts creep in, the tendrils of insecurity. He has visions of her in her husband's arms and it burns him. The other's fingerprints stain her skin. Can a lover ever receive enough reassurance? Porter fears his faults, his failures magnify his lacks. How easy he would be to dispose of. It rises like a swell of water, a wave which turns his stomach, twists his insides, then breaks with an image of her face, her eyes fully on his, subsides as the warmth of her hand caresses his cheek. There is no lie in her eyes, in her touch. She could have been anywhere, but she was here with him.

Porter smiles to himself again. He touches his lip lightly where the memory of her lips resides.

—

ANAIS (or "Anais-Kaplan" formerly "Anais-Heighton"): Named for Anais Nin, a French-Cuban author (whom her parents supposedly never read). Anais' stands five foot six inches tall with skin the colour of burnt honey — two shades lighter across her breasts and pubic area — and brown hair with sun-streaks of gold. Anais, notable for her prickly glare and too-wide smile, gives off an intoxicating fragrance of vanilla, amber and sea breeze.

—

Porter walks in the small avenue with its shops and strange Arabian Jazz, echoing its exotic call like an enchantment. He studies the plants and flowers of the florist, their design for survival in this harsh terrain. Fearsome thorns bare tooth at him even as they offer the treasure of their brilliant blossoms. These sharp devices that would tear at the creature approaching them wrongly, blend with the unassuming stalks and lurk beneath heart shaped leaves with their juicy pulp. He studies these elaborate nature's designs and wonders at the feelings of plants, the analogies that present themselves so glaringly obvious to the human laying of roots, reaching for sun or glory, and fear for protecting their beauty.

What thorns lurk beneath your blooms?

He considers buying flowers for Anais, but he would not know how to present them to her nor where she would keep them, and so he exits the shop empty handed, only tracing a finger over the cool surface of some leaves.

He enters the strange shop with the dusty dolls and crude wooden carvings instead. He finally settles on a pendant of a snail's shell, white laced with gold and a slight blue-metallic stain. It hangs on a chain of small cobalt blue stones. The girl behind the counter accepts his money distractedly without a word. She does not tell him, does not seem to know what he knows; that it is a Fibonacci shell, its spiral containing the proportions of the golden ratio, the divine scale of nature's building blocks.

Twenty-two

He sits in the back of a large black vehicle. Joseph has been left behind. The windows are down but the air inside still seems stale and still, a slight odour of musk and the men who are sweating backs of swarthy necks. He stares over the shoulder of one, through the windshield, but the image quickly blurs as he focuses on the man's strangely curled earlobe. They have not blindfolded him, no hood, no dramatics. Everyone knows where to find Kadeem, he is not an outlaw nor a fugitive. This is not the hero's quest of the noble correspondent, even though these are men of violence. Porter feels a tense sense of anticipation, trepidation but not fear. Perhaps it is the other men's natures; stern, barely speaking, they look him up and down with open suspicion. They are would-be heavies, wishful assassins.

He thinks of the dead stone of the telephone in his apartment. He had wanted to call her, had wanted her to call him. And as quickly as those thoughts occurred, the reasons against poured in again, driving questions: Did she want to leave her husband? And if she did, would it be for a failing writer? He could swing the hammer and she would have to stand in the hail of splinters. And who would pick up the pieces?

The car turns and twists and Porter may as well have been blindfolded for he could never find his way here again, nor back should they abandon him at the side of this dusty road bordered by dry brush and trees obscuring all and nothing. They eventually pull into a compound, white walls, something mosque-like about the structure although it appears to be a home. The yard is dry almost-sand and seems to soak the sun's attention. Porter is already sweating profusely as the men lead him across the threshold into the musty shadow of the indoors.

The air here is stagnant but spiced with sweet incense. The rooms are blocks of various sizes, simple rectangular windows with light golden drapes and high ceilings. An ornate fan of wicker set into maple-stained blades turns slowly overhead, but the house is sparsely furnished. Kadeem stands in the centre of a modest living-room suite wearing all white, a long loose shirt and pants and sandals on his feet. He looks at Porter with the same harsh suspicion as his subordinates have. Porter tries smiling slightly but Kadeem's expression does not change. He gestures to a chair and Porter sits.

Kadeem's face is narrow, ears and nose protruding, like roughly moulded clay pressed in place. Porter waits for the pleasantries, the offer of a glass of water or a cup of tea but it does not come. Kadeem sits leaning forward, elbows on knees, less in anticipation and more a man about to berate a child. Porter feels appropriately subordinate.

"So," Kadeem finally says, "you wanted to see me?"

"Yes, thank you for taking the time."

"This is for what, an interview? You are with a magazine?"

"No," Porter shifts, "I'm not a reporter. I'm a novelist. I write fiction."

Kadeem seems taken aback. His wiry eyebrows clench as he deciphers this bit of information. "You write fiction."

"Yes. Novels. Dramatic novels."

Kadeem leans back slowly, then his face relaxes. He smiles showing big teeth. "You cannot find enough to write about in real life? There is so much goes on in the world, you still feel the need to make things up?"

Porter feels silly once again. "I suppose things in real life don't line up so neatly. Morality, development, they're all there, just not necessarily in one story, not as neatly as some people would like it. I guess I trim off the fat for those who like a lean steak."

"So you would make life 'neat'? I can understand that. I know people would rather not get their hands dirty. 'Make me feel, but not too much.' A nice, neat resolution. These are the same people who lose themselves in fantasies and become passive in the face of government abuses. It's like an opiate these fantasies."

Porter is not sure how to react. He sits still, tries to hold Kadeem's gaze, but the man is casual in his insult.

"I cannot blame people for doing this," Kadeem continues as though discoursing with himself. "They have done it for centuries. It is easier to do nothing, to close your eyes and imagine or pretend things are better than they are, than to risk yourself for something."

The two men look at each other in what is for Porter an intensely awkward silence. Kadeem gives a smirk which acknowledges his own upper hand. "But you know Stellan," he shifts forward again.

"Yes," Porter says, happy to move on.

"He is a good man. More a man of ideas than action. History admires men of action, not necessarily ideas. Men who are of both action and ideas are rare. History remembers them most of all."

"And would you say that you are such a man?" Porter crosses his legs, watches Kadeem blankly.

Kadeem smiles slyly. He has been interviewed before and is wary of the pitfalls. But his smile says it all. He leans back comfortably to spread his wide arm span across the back of the couch. "History will decide that. But I know that I am but a servant," he says in a rehearsed voice, a flourish of his hands.

From here the conversation takes on the tone of an interview; Porter asking questions and Kadeem answering them with practiced calm, precise passion and conviction — always conviction. As Porter listens to him, as he asks more questions he likes Kadeem even less. The leader's lack of education is evident to Porter. Kadeem references revolutionary leaders, political manifestoes but it is all with the rehearsed reverence of someone who has overheard talk. He mentions names like Marx and Gueverra casually, as though everyone knows their histories and what they stood for, but the context is lacking and Porter recognizes the ploy meant to imply an intellect while deflecting a deeper probe. He wonders if any reporter has ever pushed that defence, if any journalist has ever taken this man to task. Porter himself does not. It is not what he is here for, he tells himself.

He wonders how men like Kadeem garner followers. But then Porter would venture that these followers are more likely than not less educated than Kadeem. His followers would be men stirred by passion. Like most men. However their intellect will not hinder them in action. Their reason will not override with its poignant or stale (dependant on your aims) protests of "What next? What will fill the void?"

Anger is the most active emotion. It is easier to hate because it requires no secondary emotion, thought only in the present. It is easier to destroy than to create. Creation requires thought — what to create, how to go about it, a place for it, a caring — the act of destruction requires only a focused power, a force strong enough to oppose and obliterate the object of displeasure. These men are not here to rebuild. They will strike the blow, destroy the object of their hate and stand proud upon its ruins. But that fire does not easily die and it will fester in their bellies until they find something else, another object to focus their displeasure upon.

Porter asks Kadeem about this at one point, about what he would have in this government's stead, but the man has no real response. "They will be forced to make something better," he says and continues in this vein. Porter does not bother to ask him who 'They' will be. These men are not up to the task of creation. They would defer and hide behind false modesty. They do not have the will of restraint, the strength of that kind of sacrifice, the fortitude to love an ideal. They are a lynch mob.

It is their anger that Kadeem has tapped into. Porter sees it staring into the man's eyes, dark and focused like a mesmerist's, forcing their conviction, that righteous fervour, convinced as all men are that they have been wronged by the powers that be, cheated of their victory. The land of milk and honey promised them has been sucked dry by others. Kadeem would work his magic on all, his fist clenches as he tells of the injustices wrought upon the working man by the slippery fat politicians. But Porter, a man removed from history and lost in fate, feels none of it. For one brief moment a sulphur flare ignites and he sees the telephone, that silent stone seated and he does feel cheated, but in the next instant he sees Anais standing in the water, looking back at him and it snuffs out, the ember fades.

We have cheated ourselves, lost our own way. Our parents robbed us of innocence and opportunity, as theirs did them and so on for generations before, back to Adam and Eve. Ours is an inheritance of guilt, sticky and curdled; the used up world which the meek shall inherit.

One of the men brings tea at some point, in a patterned kettle on a tray. He rests the tray on the low coffee table and Kadeem helps himself. Porter can smell it warm and fragrant but Kadeem says nothing, makes no gesture of offer. It is unclear whether it is assumed that he should help himself or if he has made himself unwelcomed. The interview goes on, Porter asking questions and Kadeem answering them like a fielder in a cricket match. Kadeem performs sufficiently but without any great flair. His answers are essays, they do not open the doors to discussion. They are designed as closed rooms.

Porter eventually runs out of questions and they sit awkwardly again in a moment of silence, no mutual points of interest hit upon to further conversation outside of the professional curiosity.

"Well, I do very much appreciate you taking the time," Porter says.

He is relieved when Kadeem stands, gives a slight bow of dismissal and Porter follows the underlings back to the car.

———

On the drive back Porter observes the billboards and advertisements patch-worked everywhere. He begins to see the identity crisis of this island, the adulation of empty symbols.

Perhaps it is that: Greatness is based on the past and the future — what you have achieved in the past, your prospects for the future. In the now all men are equal. So wash away the past and future and you wash away the divisions of inferiority or superiority.

There are of course still divides, cracks in the system, but these are only where the past and future seep their way into daily life. The rich man has more prospects for the future as a result of the successes of his past. This allows him more freedom in the form of options in the now. And so the society objectifies him, sometimes even vilifies him, treated as though this wealth simply sprung into being or was possibly achieved through corrupt means (In many cases it is), because there is no room for a slow trudging progress in this society of the Now. Only men of instant action are afforded the role of hero here; sports stars whose vibrant successes can be attested to thanks to the instant-replay. These men of physical action can be deified, allowed to flaunt the wealth and sex their physical prowess has achieved them. For the physical is the now — just as the cerebral is always past and future.

Twenty-three

He has not heard from Anais and the absence has begun to grow solid. Porter's world turns back inwards, his separation from the everyday manifesting itself in a numbness that the thought of her intensifies. Like cold, one can measure the absence. When the phone rings he tries not to anticipate, not to hope for it to be her. He forces himself to take another pull of his cigarette, to out it before answering.

"Hello."

There is silence for a beat before the feminine voice comes in almost a whisper, "Cristobal."

"Coraline?"

"Yes. I'm sorry to bother you . . . I mean, I wanted to let you know, thought you'd want to . . ."

"Are you okay?"

"Uncle Stellan," a catch in her voice and he knows already, "he's gone. He passed last night."

"I'm so sorry, Coraline."

He is uncomfortable with these moments. He remembers his wife's funeral, the desire for everyone to just leave him be, their words making no dent in the haze surrounding him. He would force out the words expected, 'Thank you,' when in fact he despised them all for being there, as though they magnified his loss and his shame with their presence turning mourning into a spectator sport.

"Thank you," she says. There is an awkward silence and he can hear her breathing on the line. "I have to go."

"Of course. Coraline, if you need anything at all . . ."

"Thank you."

She hangs up and he rests the phone in its cradle, standing alone in his room with that resonance of mortality that takes all of the fuss of life and wipes the meat clean from the bone.

—

They sit in their dim circus restaurant.

He has just told her about Stellan. Ana's hand finds his fleetingly, two fingers that trace the back reflexively before she is aware and withdraws. She is still careful. She cannot be open as her husband is, walking in daylight with his lover. And so they remain in shadow, eyes devouring while their bodies carry out the marionette restraint of formality. The touch is electric to him. If they were friends she would hold his hand in reassurance, but her wariness causes her to overcompensate and so the lover is denied a simple pleasure he would have appreciated all the more, as though his status were a demotion. The Fibonacci Shell is tucked into his shirt pocket, wrapped in tissue paper, awaiting its time.

"I'm so sorry to hear," she says.

Her face is sorrowful and his first instinct is that she is overacting, overcompensating from a lack of practice in being insincere. It is an uncharitable thought and he quickly realizes it is incorrect. She is in fact close to tears. Whether her emotions are stirred for this man she has never met, a young girl's loss, or the overwhelming dilemmas wrought from life in general, he cannot tell. That she is so high-strung makes him uncomfortable at first, as though a leak has sprung from the dam, and he sees her fragility. But then he is moved by her sensitivity and moved by a desire to protect her.

He places his hand on hers leaving it only a moment longer. "It's alright. How are you holding up."

She takes a piece of garlic bread from the centre basket. She gauges him. "Jack has been acting erratic . . . strangely, with these . . . outbursts. He picks arguments, gets aggressive. Just randomly it seems."

Porter simply looks at her.

"It's not to do with me, I'm sure," she says. She begins breaking pieces from the bread, slowly pinching them and discarding them in her plate in jerky movements. "I think he and Nadia are having problems. I don't know what kind of problems, but he's on edge, preoccupied all the time and very agitated."

"And he takes it out on you."

"It's what I know from home. I don't know, he may be the same way at the office." She looks down at her plate as though surprised at what she has done. Her shoulders slump visibly and she seems again on the verge of tears. She squeezes her eyes tight, one fighting a migraine. "I'm just so tired of it. We act like strangers, fight like strangers, as though we were just random people forced to live in one life together and resenting each other for having to share the space. Like there weren't enough space." She looks up at him with the tweak of a smile beneath red-rimmed eyes, "Sounds like a bad Sartre play."

They are quiet for a moment. She stares at the table cloth. He stares at her hand on the table beside his, inches away, a distance so difficult to travel.

"Leave him," he says flatly.

He is aware of her eyes on him, hears the exhalation. She smiles, something patronizing which squeezes his insides uncomfortably. "And would you marry me, Chris?" she asks.

'Yes,' is the first thing that springs to his mind but he stays silent, forces his eyes to meet hers. There is so much about her he does not know. Can he trust what he feels now, or is it just discovery that intoxicates him, that burst of hope one gets from seeing yourself through approving eyes? Right now her eyes are not approving. She is not Anais, but Ana, as she has made clear by reverting him to Chris. Who can speak for forever?

"I don't want to grow old alone," she says.

"Is life with a man who's become a stranger that much better? Doesn't that make you alone now?"

Her eyes flare for a moment. "You don't know all of it. This isn't all that's between Jack and me. I didn't marry a stranger and you don't know someone for years and then just stop loving them. It's not what I was saying. Jack and I were in love. We got married because we loved each other. That doesn't die overnight."

The words lash. He feels his footing slip, the crack of eggshells. She has defected back to the Other's camp and Porter is the intruder. He wants to grow angry, to rail against her betrayal, to explain that it is what is now that matters. Love doesn't die overnight, it dies by increments, getting old and weak, cut by each wrong, bled a little by each transgression. It is weak and must be constantly guarded. He says nothing because he is uncertain of her mind, what she feels for him. He has no guarantees to offer her. She knows her life with Kaplan. With Porter there will be only uncertainties. Looking at her now he wonders if she is truly happy with him or is it just an escape, a salve for the wounds Kaplan has inflicted. He fears the answer and so he only says, "I'm sorry," and despises the weak sound in his own voice.

Ana looks around as though uncertain how to proceed, but he can see her rally her anger. "I'm sorry as well," she says but holds her resolve. She gathers herself, picks up her purse. "I should go."

"Don't," he says, but he is not sure if the words are lost in the scrape of her chair as she rises, or if she chooses to ignore them.

She stops briefly before leaving, forces herself to meet his eyes. She seems to begin to concede something but stops. "I have to go." She turns and walks away.

He sits in the shadow and watches her go.

—

He has no particular love of churches, but this is a beautiful old structure out of a tourism brochure; large grey blocks and old stained-glass that still show brilliant blue and red. He walks up the sparsely grassed lawn and through the arc of the doorway.

The mourners stand, sit or kneel, as it is called for. The church imbues the proper grandeur, but everything else is constricted by the feel of mysticism and ritual. He is aware of the fat calves of the woman two rows in front of him, the incense swinging from a chain like a mace before battle. The congregation chants, their rites vibrating. The priest drones. So much ritual, Porter thinks, it would be peaceful if not for all of this. He can do without these people's murmurings, the stories of unknown promises, the spells of hope. He knows of words and the tales people weave. This is the suspension of disbelief, to ease the living and bridge the gap with mesmeric spells, the gap between the world where the loved one resides here with you and a world where they are deceased and you are alone.

Porter looks at the image of the man on the cross, sees the devotion in faces around him. He recalls his wife's funeral and the emptiness he felt. For all of that, he cannot believe. He wishes he could, envies these people their faith and their solace which eludes him. To commit to an ideal that ultimately relies on blind belief. It is like a trapeze artist relying on a net he cannot see and may as well assume is not there. He looks to the head of the church and the casket which he knows contains Stellan's body, although it is not visible from where he stands. Porter wonders what net if any has caught him.

The artistry of architecture becomes enough for him. He takes in the vaulted ceilings, the high, still air and he does begin to feel placid. He thinks of his own rituals, his morning perch with his coffee and paper and feels the calm in the repetition.

At the end of the service Coraline files passed with her family. She looks young and demure in a white cotton dress, as though bound for first communion. She moves as an apparition in the darker colours of mourning, a part of the flowers, or light from the stained-glass. Her eyes meet Porter's and she gives a slight and fleeting smile before turning her eyes down to the coloured orchids in her hands.

She tells him later that Stellan had asked her to wear this dress for him at his funeral. He had made her promise. "You'll be a star when I look down, he said. I almost didn't wear it," she tells Porter. "I thought it would be embarrassing . . . embarrassing for me." She is squinting up at him against the sun behind him. "But I thought then that I promised him, and he believed me. I know he believed me. Somehow that part is important. He always believed me."

Porter smiles gently, "Some faith is rewarded."

Twenty-four

Porter sits and orders his notes, crossing out and adding passages. He is finally making progress, cobbling together the beginnings of something, discovering lines to draw meaning and occasionally the magic of meaning evolving from the lines. His mind shifts repeatedly to Anais, stepping to the side out of the stream of thoughts. He forces himself to not follow her and returns to the tumult of image and sound of his imagination.

He is sitting on the floor in the open doorway of the balcony, papers spread around him, his cup of coffee off to one side, ashtray to the other, both doubling as paperweights. There is the sound of the street and the empty silence of his apartment. Porter sits between two worlds.

A woman and her daughter, the daughter representing earth and the natural state, travel to a remote island. The woman has been through a trauma and carries the scars. She has come to the island to escape, but she cannot escape her fear. It is of everything. Her daughter is the victim, dragged along. Her mother smothers her in her attempt to protect her and the inevitable backlash is the daughter's revolt, a revolt which leads to . . .

He sips his coffee. He has not quite decided the mother and daughter's fates as yet. He lights a cigarette as he contemplates before picking up the pen again.

It will be set against the backdrop of an island at a time of uprising. The woman who fears everything will be persecuted for beliefs she does not possess (an illustration of the inability to control everything, the inability to escape suffering). The daughter will fall into the revolution, one she does not fully understand, her political revolt merely a stand-in for her maternal one.

He gathers his pages and stands feeling the stiffness in his joints. It has been a week since their meeting and he has not heard from her. He knows how this goes. Time elapses, those first few days being the most difficult, but things become easier. The senses fade, the feel of her in his arms while dancing, the softness of her cheek, her taste and scent, these things will lose their immediacy and be relegated to 'memories' robbed of their passion like pressed flowers. The longer he is away from her, he knows, the more he will dim in her mind and once these lights blink out it is almost impossible to rekindle, because now the lovers will know that they can live without each other. It is what holds him back from asking questions; this fear that if he missteps she will turn and run back to the world she knows.

He closes his eyes and can feel her breath on his cheek, the tip of her nose brushes against it and her lips press there momentarily. No, she is not gone for him. As much as he has tried not to think about her, she is still there waiting in the back of his mind, and he has been aware of her as though she were sleeping in his bed as he wrote. His writer's imagination makes it more difficult, having honed the habit of etching these sensations into one's mind. Infatuation for Porter is an occupational hazard.

—

Anais' voice is quiet on the other end of the phone. "Are you alright?" she asks. "I saw your friend's obituary the other day, in the papers. I thought of calling you, but I didn't know."

She does not state what she didn't know and he wonders what it could be. Could she doubt that he would want to hear from her, that any pretext for a call, for some form of contact with her, he would grasp at with the strength of a drowning man?

"I'm okay," he says. "How are you? Are you alright?"

Her voice sounds uncertain, "Yes." She hesitates before making-up her mind. "I'm sorry," she says quickly, awkwardly, "about our last meeting. I . . . I'm very confused right now. I'm not used to this sort of thing . . . Everything is just . . . I'm just . . . I don't know. I'm overwhelmed, I guess. It's just . . . ."

She is floundering and he feels that urge to protect her, to spare her hurt, even as he knows he is the source of part of her confusion, or at least a lens which has magnified it. "Don't, don't apologize," he says. "Don't even think about it. Just let me see you." There is quiet on the line and the twinge he feels in that moment escapes in his words, "I need to see you."

"I'll try," she concedes. "I'll call you. I should go now."

"Please try. I can't get you out of my mind."

"I will," she says, almost a whisper. "I'll call you."

He holds the receiver until that empty canteen spills its final drops of sustenance. "I think of you too," she says. "Goodbye, Cristobal."

—

He works haphazardly now between the distraction of competing passions, losing himself in the story, in the words and also surfacing occasionally to be swept in the separate sea of missing her, wondering if he will see her. The headiest moments occur where the two overlap, where the emotions of the story connect with his feelings for her. He is able to stand in the two worlds as they compete for his devotion, then slowly he will feel himself won by one or the other. Usually it is by the thoughts of Anais — the more real of the competing fantasies. Occasionally he will give in to these thoughts, a cigarette becoming a measurement of time, as he allows himself to enjoy potential scenarios before forcing his mind clear and returning to the page.

His head is down, mind focused on the scene where his competition with God in creation takes place, when the phone rings. He rises from under the waters of his subconscious, blinks and raises the receiver.

"Tobey." Peter's voice is a jarring disappointment. "Hi Tobey, tell me you have something. I know it's been a rough time, what with Nadia and all, but I really need to get something to hold over here."

"I have the pages here now, Peter. I'm just typing them up and I'll have them off to you tonight."

"Great, Tobey, great, just make sure I get them tonight. How far along are we?"

"Well you know it's hard to tell, written to typed, but it's a good start." He recognizes the silence and hastens to add, "And it's coming fast, Peter. I've finally got it nailed down. I really think you'll be pleased."

"Alright, just make sure to get it off to me tonight."

"Will do, Peter. Working on it as we speak."

They chat a moment longer, Peter trying to be sociable, Porter being guarded, unable to tell him how his time here is really being spent. He tells him about his meeting with Kadeem, about Stellan. It is a combination which buys him a little more sympathy. Porter hangs up the phone and stands in the silence, a weight settling down through his stomach into his legs, rooting him to the ground (remnants of Ovid), his eyes fixed on the phone. It is a hollow fear which takes him now that he has been drawn back to the shore of reality.

He stands there a moment and all is still. Slowly he turns his head, turns his mind and moves his feet one by one back to the desk where his laptop lies open. A mother and her daughter require him to complete their stories — as does an agent a thousand miles away.

—

He is submersed in the world of his book and so the first ring of the phone barely registers. When he answers the voice like dry crumpled paper on the other end is unmistakably that of a bleary eyed King George. He is in the bar downstairs, "Come have one, Porter. It'll do you good."

Porter removes his glasses and rubs his eyes. The laptop shows no testament to the seventy-odd pages he has accumulated — rough copy to be sure, but still something considering the two weeks it has taken to compile from scattered notes. "Okay, George old boy. I'll be down in a second."

So he finds himself in the dim light of the guesthouse bar once again, propped on a seat and shielding a scotch on ice. He listens to Clarkson and watches the ghosts of Cristobal and Anais sway in each other's arms on the dance floor.

"It's fermenting, my dear boy," George is saying. "Sure as hell it's fermenting. You can smell it in the air. This place is going to erupt sooner rather than later. Nothing good can come of it, I'll tell you that much." He gulps from his glass.

Porter says nothing, just listens and notes that the Old King's white suit jacket has gone grey, as though the old writer had been sat up on a shelf and the dust had settled into the pores. The salt and pepper hair protruding from his ears might as well be cobwebs.

"The fuse is already lit. You can see it sparkling in the streets. It's going to trace its way to the governmental powder keg."

Porter is already feeling tired. The table where they sat is in the corner of his sight, the ghost of Anais touching Cristobal's ghost hand. "You should be a writer," the flesh-and-bone Porter says drily.

King snorts a sort of laugh at the quip, "Once upon a time, my boy, in another life. Speaking of which, how's your own writing coming along?"

Porter is hesitant to say well, at a stage where he is fearful of any unknown blight, not quite superstition, but the atheist's fleeting concern for what god they might be offending if they are wrong. "It's coming along," he says. "Bits at a time, you know how it is. Never fast enough for Peter."

"No, no, of course not. The moneylenders, they rush the art for the sake of commerce, then complain that the strokes aren't refined enough."

Porter feels a twinge of guilt for the aspersion upon Peter. Peter who, he knows has been more than patient with him. "I'm to send the pages off tonight. Well, what I have so far. How I long for the days before the internet. I could blame the shoddy postal service and gain a few days, if it weren't for e-mail."

"Agreed on that. The computer age is destroying literature from the inside out. Don't even get me started on these so called 'blaggers'."

It takes Porter a moment, "I think you mean 'bloggers'."

"Same bloody thing," King blusters and drowns his top lip, its thin pink coming up glistening. "Couldn't you just say they don't have it? It's a third-world country after all."

"Everyone has it," Porter says. "Besides Peter went so far as to ensure this place had wireless before booking."

"Bloody hell. The Maltese Jew!"

They drift into silence, sitting and drinking, Porter with his ghosts and King with his demons. Slowly they raise brief questions of past acquaintances, exchanged for one word answers to maintain the tentative semblance of society. Eventually Porter decides that he is on that fine line. Reminded of his deadline he pushes away his glass and waves King's order of another round away. He stands and claps his acquaintance on the back. "Until next time," Porter says.

"Indeed," King stammers, "but it won't be here. I'm headed out tomorrow. All rhetoric aside, Porter, you should really take a look at making a move on. Things are going to get pretty sticky here pretty quickly. You need to leave before there is no leaving."

"Before the fuse burns down?" Porter smiles. King looks like a drawing of a man, Porter thinks, one that has been smudged and half-erased. "I won't be long again."

King turns back to his drink with a dismissive wave. "Don't get caught in the fire, my friend."

———

He can hear the rain as he passes the front landing and goes up the stairs. It fades and is present again as he enters the apartment, hissing its rush and cold air through the open French doors. He splashes water on his face which soaks some into the collar of his shirt. He stands in the doorway a while and enjoys the breeze and the black night outside, the ochre-cast streets in yellow lamplight.

A knock on the door makes him turn, the sound foreign in his stay here, so that the person on the other side has to knock again to reassure him that it is not just a trick of the rain and wind. When he opens the door Ana is turned sideways, one heel up as she adjusts her shoe strap shakily. Opening the door he appears to have caught her by as much surprise as she has caught him. She is damp from the rain, her hair tousled, a touch out of breath, but they smile at each other as he ushers her in.

"Let me get you a towel."

"I'm sorry. I hope it's okay that I'm here."

He returns from the bathroom, wraps the towel around her, holds it there so as to enjoy the cautious embrace a moment before stepping back. "Of course," he says.

"It's just that, well I did call, but there was no answer."

He gives a chastising glance to the phone, which appears to grin back with its rotary dial.

"So you came?"

She seems embarrassed now. She tilts her head to the side, dabbing her hair with the towel. "Well, yes."

Her awkwardness is like a vulnerability. He moves closer to her. "You came to find me?"

"Yes."

He is in her space now. She does not meet his eyes, but her hand rises to rest against his chest as he holds her. "Why?"

"I don't know . . ."

"You don't?"

"No. I mean . . . I wanted to see you." She says it like a confession and then laughs a short skip, as though the confession has freed her.

He touches her face and she raises it to smile at him, her eyes searching his face, as he is certain his search hers. "Was that so difficult to say?" he whispers.

"No," she says. "No, not difficult at all."

He puts his arms around her, but there is still a nervous line coiled in his stomach, something that makes her foreign in his arms. It is a fear that has frozen his heart, the awareness of the space where they cannot yet meet, their falling out where she could get up and walk away from him, the sentiments that can be drowned by the scrape of a chair.

Perhaps to never know the other may be the solution to everything. When there is the unlimited potential of the new, there is boundless hope — and how could anything live up to that? It is knowledge that brings to light the flaws, experience that teaches of the frailties. The Garden was paradise until Adam and Eve ate of the fruit of the Tree of Knowledge and then they knew their flaws and hid in shame. Had they remained in ignorance, perhaps they would, could, love more easily, eternally.

The question that haunts Porter now is whether one can love the flaws for how they informed the whole, much like appreciating a Shakespearian Tragedy. Was that not a celebration of man's weakness? Could not the flaws then be celebrated in some way? Not to be strived for but as scars of a battle won, worn with some pride for having survived.

If he could only close his eyes and believe in God, have faith in some order in the universe. But instead he closes his eyes and sees Anais, perfect and flawed. His teeth pierce the skin and pulp of the fruit, tongue tastes sweet juices, and it is worth damnation. It is what he thinks as he holds her and slowly feels that coil loosen, feels once again that he will let himself fall.

"I'm sorry," she whispers.

They do not make love but stand for a long time, hands touching each other. He kisses her face, her neck, her shoulder and her own lips find his. She is crying silently and he kisses her cheek, softer beneath the tears. They kiss in absolution.

Their conversation is stilted and they soon abandon it as unnecessary convention. They recline in each other's arms, touching lightly and kissing until eventually she seems to wake. She has to go. He walks her to the door where they kiss a reluctant farewell.

"Wait. I have something for you," he says. He brings her the Fibonacci Shell and she smiles as she runs her finger over it. He explains to her about the ratio of the Fibonacci sequence in its spiral, echoed throughout nature, the golden ratio.

"I know about the golden ratio," she says. "We learned about it in Art and Architecture." She smiles, "You're bringing back some ancient memories. Thank you."

He kisses her and lets her leave, having inadvertently touched her history. The room is once again made dull by her absence, but the hope woken in him counters it. He looks at the pages on his desk and thinks of Peter's deadline. The concern is wiped away by the thought of her warm against him. And the pages are coming. He sits before the laptop, peers through his glasses as he taps out words letter by letter, thoughts continuously interrupted by the memory of her lips, her taste. After an hour he surrenders to it. He e-mails what he has so far to Peter with a brief note that there is more, but he has been unable to transcribe it from his notes to the computer. The 'more' in reality consists of three rough paragraphs, each less than half a page, and the untapped flurry still swirling in his mind.

He lies in bed with the lights out and allows her image to wash over him. The moments of fear for their future creep to the edges with that cold twist to the gut, but he pushes them aside. Tonight they are happy, he thinks. It is only to keep those moments strung together in a never ending charm bracelet. He is willing to trust in it. He wonders if she can. He hopes she can. He will choose to believe in that too.

Twenty-five

In the streets, in broad daylight he begins to see what Clarkson was talking about; the scent of tension, the fire in eyes, the dwindling of smiles. People move a little more briskly. It is barely noticeable, but for the foreigner attuned to the differences, someone aware of the pace normally so much slower than London streets, he can feel the slight shift in the air. Suddenly people are not so keen to stay outdoors, not so easily swayed to stand and discuss. Everywhere he goes, Porter garners one of two looks: either reviled or feared for.

As he sits in his cafe, drinking his coffee and smoking a cigarette, he ignores the passing glances and somehow cannot feel himself in danger of any harm. Fear works that way, it is irrational. He is non-political, disinterested in their fight one way or the other. But he cannot leave, because of Anais.

Pasiphae, shares Porter's lack of concern, though she is somewhat more interested in the strangers who pass by. She sits patiently with alert ears until he throws her the expected bit of pastry. The shop-keeper accepts Pasiphae's presence now without the dour looks previously doled out. Porter assumes that it is tolerated since the mongrel arrives and leaves with him and does not linger to harass any other customers. His mind wonders on Coraline and how she is managing.

After his morning coffee and paper, he has taken to walking the sidewalks, simply absorbing the atmosphere, eavesdropping on occasional conversations. He has found a park and a bench, a comfortable vantage point, where he finds himself by midmorning and sits with a notebook and pen and works in the rough. Just before midday he walks back to the guest house, picking up a light lunch on the way. He sits and eats, has another cup of coffee and a cigarette and then spends the afternoon labouring over the laptop.

He spends his nights waiting for her. He does not wait long.

—

"I thought I'd surprise you. Would you prefer if I called first?"

"No," He takes her wrist and eases her across the threshold, into his embrace. "No, you are a perfect surprise."

She comes in and he offers her a drink. They are working their way back to comfort. He wants her, but there is not the burning passion of desperation. She is here now and he would enjoy her company, her presence. Their passion is evolving.

She sits on the edge of the bed, her eyes on him. He watches her. She slides her hand down to slip the shoe strap from one heel and then the next, slides them off. He comes to stand before her and she takes the two glasses of wine from his hands and rests them on the side table.

She pulls lightly at his shirt, urges him towards her and they kiss. He eases in beside her, back over her.

His hand feels the warm rise of her ribcage. When they stop kissing they gaze at each other, her eyes studying upwards, his absorbing downwards. They are like this for a while, kissing and admiring, renewing comfort but going no further. Eventually they sit up and take up their wine.

Rain begins to fall outside, gathering in intensity. They find little things to talk about, casual conversation of bits of their days, investing those inner impressions and experience in each other. Eventually, wine drunk, they kiss again, slowly undress each other and make love to the backdrop of the rushing downpour.

—

He feels he is coming to know Anais. She manages to come to his room several times over the next few weeks. For the first time he feels that she fully wants to be there, that she has finally made a choice to give herself to him. It brings a sense of relief he did not know was missing. Something unwinds in his shoulders and eases in the pit of his stomach. When she leaves she seems hesitant to go. As he stands and watches her descend the stairs she turns, stops to look back at him and smiles. He is a man cleared of a life-threatening ailment. He can think for the first time of a future.

—

Porter rents a car. He would avoid the added notice of driving in hers and does not wish Joseph to chaperone. The car is a stubby white vehicle that he sits in like an un-hatched chick, but it is suitably unremarkable and gets them from place to place. They go to the beach for the sake of simplicity and to fill the necessary gap in Porter's experience; to be able to say that he spent time on the beach, obligatory when visiting the tropics.

She wears a one-piece suit with cut out sides showing the corners of her hips and Porter admires her figure, the bronze of her skin everywhere. The sand burns the feet and they find a place beneath a palm's shadow, unfurl towels and recline. He watches the sea churn, the clean distant line of the horizon and the bleached sky, everything permeated by the sun which has dominion here. He studies Anais' profile beneath the shadow of her hat, that close-to-caricature of her sharpened nose, full lips. He resists kissing her lips knowing she would be self-conscious, but he enjoys stealing an occasional kiss of her smooth shoulder, salted and warm.

They buy coconuts from a vendor, a lean muscled Rasta with thick matted locks like the roots of the mangroves Porter witnessed in their sailing. The man's dark skin glistens with sweat. He hefts the coconut in one hand positioning it with small tosses and wields his machete with the other. Quick controlled and powerful strokes slice wedges from the husk revealing the top of the protected nut. Then with a brisk stroke he slices the top, stabs the machete into the ground and inserts a straw into the hole like a flower into a vase. He hands one over and repeats the process, an easy practiced violence carried out with assembly line efficiency.

They drain their drinks quickly under the vendor's watchful gaze. As they finish, the vendor reaches out his hand and takes the nut and still holding it cleaves it almost completely in half. "You want jelly?" he asks with a grin stretched around broad teeth. He seems genuinely pleased, an attitude Porter has recognized, the pleasure taken from the foreigner's experience. The vendor hands over the coconut now open like a book with a small wedge cut from the husk to act as a spoon. Porter hands the first to Ana, then takes the second and begins scraping the thin film from inside the shell. "You like the jelly," the man states cheerfully. Porter smiles reassuringly with a mouthful. The vendor looks over Ana, "I know the lady like the jelly." Porter is taken aback. The vendor continues to smile like a clever child his eyes meeting Porter's then roaming over Ana blatantly. She turns her back, rolls her eyes for Porter to see and laughs.

As they toss aside their empty husks, her shoulder brushing his chest, she turns and startles him with a daring kiss. It is brief, sweetened with coconut water, the salt of the sea and the taste of her.

—

His writing continues to progress. It is not the best he has written, he knows that, but he is also aware that it is just begun. The foundation holds promise and he can build upon it, further intricacies of plot and character, the architecture of a humble but lofty cathedral. His work is broken by her visits, during which he is replenished.

They lie in bed and speak for hours. He is learning her life, her history, even as he learns of her caginess, that habit of hiding or protecting herself from the world, of convincing herself that she is completely self-reliant. He feels that she is exploring herself as she is with him and he is discovering her in watching the process. She smokes more frequently, studying the cigarette and the fingers holding it as though seeing them for the first time, brow furrowed as she talks about other things.

"I remember wanting to travel," she says. "I always wanted to travel, but I was afraid; afraid of planes, afraid of boats . . . God, I hated boats. I used to have to be forced onto boats. Jack would get so angry." She laughs a strange laugh, as though she were drunk, as though the cigarette were a joint. "He would say I was embarrassing him, because I couldn't walk up a gangplank straight." She begins laughing in between her words, lying there on her back. He can't help smiling as he watches her, lying on his side, head propped up, engaged as much by how she tells these stories as by the stories themselves. "I'd be hunched over, clinging to the rail. I looked like an old woman with a walker. Inching along, inching along. Jack would get furious. He'd be trying to hide it in front of whoever, but he'd be turning red."

Porter prefers not to hear Kaplan's name, prefers the stories from her life before. But she has been with her husband for the last fifteen years, so it is natural. It is the only way Porter knows to understand her, her relationship with her husband integral to who she is now. She does not speak wistfully. Most of her stories that include Jack Kaplan are not about Kaplan, but about her. They are as though she were speaking to herself, looking back on herself in wonder at what she has endured, how far she has come, how foolish she has been. Anais critiques Ana, both her weaknesses and her strengths. She has these moments, as though talking to herself, as though he were not there. He does not feel neglected though, because he is allowed to be here, and because her comfort has grown to where he is a natural extension of her. This is the way he sees it.

Her laughing subsides. She draws on the cigarette and exhales. She turns, to out the cigarette in the ashtray on the side table and he sees her scar twisting its way between her shoulder-blades. He wants to ask her about it, but he holds back.

"But you're not afraid of boats anymore." he says instead.

"No," she says. "Well, there are moments; when I first step on board, or as the boat pulls away. On flights, I'm terrible on take-off. I feel I'm going to break my armrest." She smiles at him and he smiles back reassuringly.

He pictures her seated next to him on a plane, her hand squeezing his tightly as the aircraft rises with that elevator pull of gravity. In his vision he sees her smile at him — a smile at once nervous, apprehensive and at the same time excited. Beyond her, light through the window diffuses her profile and he can see the island grow smaller below them, green fading to blue ocean as they ascend and the world falls away and they escape to a new life.

In the now she smiles up at him, white sheets behind her and he gives in to the ever-present urge and kisses her deeply. For now her departures are solitary. He will watch her dress and shortly thereafter watch as she descends the stairway and vanishes.

—

263

The politics of the heart is that the mind governs, but when the heart truly decides then if denied there is revolution, sometimes violent.

—

Porter starts from sleep. His heart is racing to the pouring rain slicking the black night. He grabs the receiver more to silence the bell than from any comprehension or need to speak. Sense is not helped by the sobbing at the other end.

"Chris . . . Chris . . . ?"

He hesitates to say her name. To do so if he is wrong is to give them away, but it is difficult to decipher the voice amidst the rainfall and the tears, difficult to be sure. "Ana? Anais, is that you?" he eventually asks.

"I need your help. I'm sorry . . . it's . . . I'm sorry, it's my fault. I need you."

The words cut in and take hold beyond any intention. "Where are you? I'm coming for you. Just tell me where you are." He has not seen her for three days. Only three days and they have hatched something to terrify and unhinge her.

Her car is pulled at an angle in the parking lot of the bar. It is almost impossible for Porter in his drowsy and shaken state to understand so many others being out drinking and revelling at this midnight hour in the pouring rain, but the lot is near full still. He circles twice in his rental egg before he is able to distinguish her car, windows frosted and tear-stained by the rain. He finds a park in the aisle opposite.

He steps out into the torrent, soaked by the time he reaches her window. She is in a posture of prayer, hair bedraggled and wet, hands clenched in her lap as she crouches forward. She appears to be trembling. He tries to knock lightly against the glass, but she still starts, looks at him terrified before comprehension, before she leans across and fumbles with the lock on the passenger side.

He ducks in out of the rain, his hair in wet locks that stick to his forehead and stream water down his cheeks, his shirt sticking to his back. She looks at him briefly, tries to smile and fails miserably. Her eyes are red from crying, her cheeks still stained. She is trembling and he reaches over and turns down the air condition. He is not sure where to start so he waits. When she says nothing, he eventually reaches over gently and puts his hand over hers. Her hands are cold, they tremble.

"What happened?" he whispers, and the whisper is caught and drowned in the rush of the rain so that he must repeat the question. "What happened?" She does not react, stares straight ahead. "Anais."

It is the talisman. She turns her face to him, only briefly able to meet his eyes and then she slumps against him, buries her face against his shoulder and he holds her there. He strokes her back, tries to offer her some warmth but he himself is soaked through to bone. Her body feels frail and tense and he cannot tell if she is crying. When she looks up it is still difficult to tell, her cheeks dampened by his shirt, but her eyes are rimmed red.

"Come home with me," he whispers. Then, "Come home."

She smiles weakly, "I'll follow you."

"No, better I follow you."

He follows the glow of her tail-lights diffused in the diamond fall strewn over black asphalt. It is a silent walk up the stairs into the room with its mugginess turned welcome warmth. He fetches her towels, sets the kettle on. She stands still and dazed in the centre of the room and is attended, a ghost devoid of spirit. Her green dress clings to her, her hair in limp medusa locks. He does not ask her questions. He traces her outline with towels, works as best he can so as not to disturb her, even as he is aware of his desire for her. He kneels before her, dries her feet, her legs with a curators reverence. He does his best but the dress still clings to her shivering body. He feels cold himself.

"You need to change these clothes."

She clings to him then, holds him fiercely and he can only return the embrace, protect her from the unknown. She turns her face slowly upwards and he kisses her mouth soft and tender from the moisture of tears and rain. She looks at him with searching burnt eyes. A lock curled is stuck to her cheek and absently his finger touches her brow, traces down and slides it gently aside. She flinches and lowers her head, but not before he sees the bruise. He holds her closer and kisses her temple, until the kettle calls. "Come, we need to get you dry."

She seems to find herself. She takes the towels from him and walks to the bathroom, closes the door in behind her but does not push it to. He hears the shower come on as he removes the kettle from the stove and puts tea to brew. He changes his shirt and steps out into the cold night air off the balcony, lights a cigarette and watches the rain-obscured night. His nerves feel shaken, a cold dread of exhilaration.

He hears the door open and feels a draft of warm air from the bathroom. She comes out lightly still drying her hair, still considering what to say. He imagines she is also trying to decipher what he may be thinking. Their eyes meet briefly but she is not ready, not collected, looks away. She summons herself, looks at him and smiles as though it were all funny. She has pulled the damp locks of her hair over her right shoulder as though to shield the mark, but the line still peeks, playing with the light, there and not.

He moves closer to her and she receives him. He kisses her forehead, her lips, once each gently but his eyes will not return the playful look hers goad.

"What happened?" he asks.

She is disappointed that the pretence will not stand, looks away almost irritated, only briefly though.

"We argued . . ."

"You and Jack."

"Yes, but it's not what you think, it's not what it appears."

"It never is."

Her eyes flash, "No, it's not like that. He didn't hit me. What do you think I am? You don't understand him . . ." He reaches a hand up to her cheek but she pulls away. "He got very angry. He was angry from the time he came in. He was looking for a fight and I guess I was in no mood to deny him." She is looking away, seeing it. "He was drunk and screaming and shouting . . . horrible things." She softens looking at him, slowly subduing her rage so momentarily transferred to him. "We argued. It got heated. He grabbed my shoulders and shook me and when he let go I stepped back, I tripped and fell and hit my face on a side table . . . a stupid side table."

He does not know if to believe her, but there is something in the shape of the bruise, the thinness of the crescent and something in her words, the thinness of her voice that beg him to believe her. He steps closer and takes her in his arms. "Are you okay now?"

"Yes," she whispers against his chest. "I'm okay now. I'm safe. I'm with you."

—

They take their time making their way towards passion, kissing for a long time, undressing each other slowly. Unlike before she seems to take the lead. He is gentle with her, she is fragile he feels, but for her it would seem that she would be the devourer. It is not until they are lying spent, have dozed off and re-awoken to the touch and taste of each other that she tells him about the gun.

"Jack has a gun," she says, holding him as they lie in the shadows. "He took it out tonight." Porter is silent in the moonlight of their confessional. He cannot see her face. "He was very drunk," she says. "I think she left him. Nadia. He was crazy. But I know I could never make him that crazy. I never felt threatened. If he was going to hurt me he would have done it before . . ." She seems to halt suddenly. He can feel the blink of her eyelashes against his rib. "I've given him reason," her voice is broken, almost inaudible. She is alone in her mind now, he realizes and he has almost halted his breath. "I've hurt him too, you know," she says. "It's not so simple. If you knew, Cristobal . . ."

She falls silent as though affording him time with his unknowing. When she speaks again her mind has moved on. "I felt like a witness, some sort of non-entity . . . maybe a camera watching things unfold . . . I realised, I think, that I've felt like that so often in my life; just a spectator, there to take a role, to bear witness to someone else's life, someone else's passions . . . I don't know."

He lies in the dark, stroking her tangled hair, not knowing what to say. He thinks of the ancient tribes with their demigods and oracles, the old Indian shaman sitting stone-still on his timber chair, to be their light, to be their idol. He thinks of Coraline's words, ". . . the loneliest person in the world."

—

We are all of us just ideas.

—

It is still dark. They have made love again and she sits cross-legged in the bed wearing his shirt as they pass a bottle of wine and cigarettes between them. She puts the bottle to her lips and tilts it back using both hands. It is something childlike, a vision of some Alice shrunken by the size of the bottle and the oversized shirt, here in this wonderland. She grins as she wipes the corner of her lips with her hand. "I must look a mess."

He laughs as he takes the bottle. "Why do women always say that when they're at their best?"

"I'm hardly at my best," she says. The smile and the gleam in her eyes seem to slowly fade. He rises and kisses her cheek. She smiles back gratefully but her playfulness is not recovered. "I tried to draw again," she says.

"Really?"

"Yes," she grants him a brief smile but her eyes return, studying the bottle as she turns it in her hands. "It was horrible."

"Well, you're just out of practice."

"No. It was completely foreign. I took forever just to decide what I should draw. Then, when I started, I made these . . . strokes. But it was like I couldn't control my hand, I couldn't get a single line to come out right . . ."

He can see her becoming visibly upset. He moves close to her, holds her. "It's not important," he says. "You can try again. You're just out of practice."

"No," she says quietly. "No, I didn't enjoy it. I felt like I was the dying remnants of what I used to be. Does that make any sense to you?" She looks at him with intense curiosity. "It was like dressing up a corpse, or playing with someone's ashes. Like you're trying to fool yourself there's something or someone there when they're dead, gone, never to return. Do you understand what I mean?"

"Yes," he says quietly, stroking her hair. "Yes, I do."

She raises the bottle again to drink then rests it on the floor beside the bed. She eases him back, taking the smouldering cigarette from his hand, taking a pull and then pressing it into the tray on the nightstand.

"Anais?"

He wants to ask her if she is okay but she places a finger against his lips. She climbs over him, her hand sliding down between them. "I'm here," she whispers, kissing him, taking hold of him. She lowers herself onto him, as he feels her warmth and she looks into his eyes. "I'm here."

—

She rises late in the morning. He sits back and watches her dress and then she comes back to sit on the edge of the bed. There is a space between them, even as a new intimacy has developed, a wall having fallen. So many walls.

"Thank you," she leans in and kisses him.

"Stay," he says softly. He knows she won't, knows that she can't. She just smiles and kisses him again. He holds her for a while and then they rise and he walks her to the door.

"Will you come again soon? Perhaps we could have lunch."

She looks away. "I don't know. I need to figure a lot of things out."

"Figure it out here." He knows he is being childish, but he needs to say it, needs to try just in case.

She seems to recognize this. She smiles and he smiles back and she puts her hand against his cheek, kisses him but leaves her hand there a moment longer as she studies his eyes warmly. "I'll call you. Just give me a little time."

No false promises, he thinks. It is better that way.

They prolong their parting, studying each other, each farewell kiss extending and keeping them there moments longer until another is required. Eventually she goes, disappears as always leaving as well as taking a lingering veil of sadness.

Twenty-six

When she calls he is not surprised by her words. He has been expecting it in the days leading up, the worrying fingernail in the back of his mind. Her words are halting but although he has already decided that he will not fight her, he cannot make it completely easy for her. Time, she says. It is such a vague word — a concept that science itself cannot pin down yet we use so freely in determining the flux of our lives. She needs time to sort things out, she says. She is going away. Kaplan, "Jack," is going away too, but she is not going with him. They will leave together for the sake of appearances, take a flight up the island chain and then she will take a separate connecting flight from there. She is going home for a week. "Where I am . . . I'm seeing so many things . . . I can't make you any promises, but right now I think I need to get away from everything. I need to just clear my head, away from everything. I need to figure out my feelings, what I want. And decide from there."

"I understand," he says.

"I'll just be a week . . . Will you still be here?"

"I'll be here," he says.

There is a long moment of silence where he hears her worrying at the other end of the line. He can picture her sharp nose, downturned eyes and her fingers in the cord. He pictures the curl of her lip in the static vibration of each breath. "I'm thinking of leaving my husband. I'm thinking of leaving Jack."

She is wanting of some kind of reassurance. He only knows what he feels and feelings have no guarantee of surviving the mystical concept of Time, no matter how strongly they may argue their resilience in the beginning. Porter has experienced enough to know this. There are all the things he wants to tell her, all the assurances he cannot give. He wants to tell her to leave her husband, but she needs to do it for herself, because it is what is best for her. It should not be for his sake. Not to replace one with the other. This is what he tells himself, even as he questions his own motives.

"I understand," is all he can manage and hopes that she will do the same. "I'll be here."

They talk for some time, working the conversation to lighter fare. She asks him about his writing, about Coraline (his "young friend" is how she refers to her). She offers him use of the house off coast. "It would be fine. I'm sure it would be a great place for writing. You should take your young friend too. It would be good for her to get away after her uncle's passing. A change of scene, sunshine and the ocean, it could cheer her up a bit."

"Thank you."

"It would do me good to know there was something good happening there. And then too I could picture you working. It'll be nice to have that tie to you."

He smiles. "It would be, yes. I can picture you in that space."

He hears her smile across the wire, across the line, where understanding occasionally meets.

"Okay, I'll arrange it," she says. "Well I should go. But I'll call you before I leave."

"Okay."

And she does call him before she leaves. She is at the airport and they speak briefly. "I have to go. You got the keys though, right?"

"I got them," he says. "Thank you."

"I'll call you when I come back," she promises.

"Okay."

"And I'll see you when I come back?"

"Most definitely."

"Okay." She hesitates. "Well, goodbye then."

"Anais."

"Yes?"

"Just that," he says. "Anais."

Her smile unfolds. "Goodbye, Cristobal."

—

"My friend has a house on the islands." She had laughed at how he had said this. "Would you like to come?"

He was surprised that she agreed. Now as they walk along the jetty he is aware of the looks the men give. He tries to ignore them, but it makes him angry; at first for her sake, their wondering eyes, and assumptions, then for the way their eyes take her in, for part of him admits his own wishes to do so, even as he feels the thought is a betrayal of her. Coraline seems oblivious of the suggestive smiles and he is surprised when on the boat and part way out she suddenly smiles at him and says, "Those men probably think we're lovers."

The words embarrass him. He tries to smile, looks away from her glowing calves. "I suppose so," he chuckles. He keeps his eyes out to sea, trying to let the surf drown out her voice echoing in his ears, ". . . we are lovers."

He thinks of Nadia, of walking with her, where he received those looks before of the older man with his young lover. He never enjoyed them. They made him feel vulnerable, as though he were provoking a violence he were not equipped to deal with. But Nadia was different than Coraline. Where Coraline had affected complete indifference, Nadia would soak in the attention. He could imagine Nadia striding down that jetty like a runway, could see her eyes flash, sense the sex heighten in her movements, as though she too would have the provocation move to some form of violence, spoils to the victor.

The thoughts are the brief wrestle of serpents in his mind then gone as they are replaced with Anais, her image, her memory, moments to come and some never to come. The uncertainty is still there, the serpents' aggravated twist in the background. He fears she will forget him while she is gone. People are creatures of habit and a habit of his absence can be as convincing as the habit of her marriage. She has built a lifetime without him and there is no necessity in her life for him now — except for this: he is hers and she is his. It is all the poetry of a twelve year old. It is all the honesty of a child.

—

The problem with poetry these days is that nobody believes it. Then years from now we'll pull a quote from a book and say that it has captured exactly what we feel. Why are the words safe in the cage of their inverted commas? Why can't I speak them to you face to face without the artifice of it creating distrust? Something beautiful can be expressed beautifully the first time — we need just for our insecurities to step aside for the moment it takes our hearts to speak.

———

They sit in lounge chairs with drinks looking out at the water.

"Do you think I'm pretty?" Coraline asks, the ocean shimmering behind her.

He smiles. "Of course."

She studies him, a wrinkle appearing between her eyebrows, "Really?"

He laughs but feels the rush rise to his cheeks. "I'm old enough to be your father," he tries to sound offhand.

She grins, relaxing. She arcs one eyebrow, "But you're not my father," she says mischievously, somewhere between teasing and a statement of understanding. She looks out to sea, growing quiet again, looks down at her hands in her lap. "I feel so out of place sometimes. Sometimes I feel like a monster," she confesses solemnly.

The wind ruffles softly the whisper of waves. He is in a good mood.

"When I first saw you," he says seriously, "there in the shop, everything went still." He looks out as though seeing the image on the horizon, but really embarrassed to be under her eyes which he can feel turned on him. "It was like catching sight of a deer in the wilderness."

She looks at him somewhat suspiciously and he meets her eyes now and her face recalls the sensation. He is able to meet her gaze honestly. "In my life, you were one of the most beautiful things I'd ever seen."

He feels comfortable saying it, for in her question is the confusion and insecurity of youth and their conversation is somehow cleansed of sexuality. Still she looks away, her turn to blush and he watches her smile slowly catch fire. She gives a small nervous laugh and he laughs as well and the weight of the moment shifts. He sips his drink and they look out at the water.

—

Anais is everywhere here; in the outer reaches of the house, in the horizon view from the balcony. He waits a couple of days before finding himself in their basement room. Here in the shadow and scent of books, in the musty smell of history kept in boxes, is where Anais' past dwells. The curled skin of her abandoned sketchpad speaks of her personal past. It is a record of her at a time, an expression of internal moments, before resisted, but now too tempting. He lifts it knowing that if there are nothing but stickmen in the pages it will no longer matter because they will be hers, precious cave drawings of the ancient tribe Anais; tribe of one, she her own shaman.

He pauses before opening it, his only uncertainty now for the possible invasion of her privacy. Would she be opposed to him knowing its contents? He thinks of lying with her, the smell and taste of her and he cannot help smile to himself. He knows her body, has seen her naked and wounded, yet the strangest thing in all this intimacy; that there are secrets still in written pages, that there is more.

The first few pages are lightly drawn sketches, incomplete human forms made of the half-cracked shells of lines half-shaded. He is relieved to find that she has talent, or once did, this other Anais of once upon a time.

One gets older and in looking back it is less the seamless evolution of one being than a life of experiences handed off like a baton in a relay race from yourself at one remembered age to yourself at another.

After the pages of neat and controlled drawings, their lines cleanly erased and redrawn meticulously, he moves on to images done in pastels. These have not fared as well from time, like old women's lipstick smudges, but he can still imagine the original image intended. There are a number of pictures of dancers as well as musicians. The images become looser as they progress, the perspectives more intriguing. They do not all work, but he can imagine her becoming more assured, experimenting, trying different things. There is something manic in a few of the pieces. Most are unfinished, some are crossed out, and he reads her frustration in the black scrawl of charcoal that winds its way over the page, a devouring hairball.

He comes away from the pages with nothing definite. Still there is a sense of having learned more about her, the history adding dimension to her. It is the tangled rope of the past that cannot be severed, influencing our actions however subtly. He closes the cover having had this brief introduction to her younger self and his fingers press it lightly in a tender farewell to history.

—

He spends his days writing and speaking with Coraline, looking out at the sun over glittering scales of sea. He cannot say that his feelings for Coraline are purely filial. He is too aware of her beauty. He feels that surge flare on occasion, Oedipus' bane that serves only form and ego. It comes unbidden and he must tune it out. Afterwards there still lingers something palpable. Though he would shy from calling it simply affection, he makes peace with it, is able to enjoy the comfort between them, their conversations and the ease with which it all unfolds.

"The King on his deathbed surrounded himself with his wealth." She reads from a medium-sized notebook with a suede cover, "His gold coins, cold and unyielding, stole any warmth that remained, offering no comfort."

"You're writing is very perceptive," he says, his eyes closed behind dark glasses.

She looks across at him, her eyes narrowed against the sun which gives her a look of deep penetration. "I just observe. And think too much." Then she smiles, "Perhaps I should be a writer."

"I think you're an excellent writer."

"As good as you?" she asks playfully.

"Better."

She sits up still smiling, "Why better?"

Because you are alive, he wants to say. "Youth," he says instead, closing his eyes behind the dark lenses, soaking in the sun and her vibrancy. "Because the longer you live the more you believe the world's lies, what it tries to tell you it is. It happens. It can't be helped.

You accept too much. 'The world is too much with us.' But when you're young you still see it for yourself, see potential and possibility. You see what's under the stone, and not only that, but you make it matter."

"Make it matter?" She looks out, eyes still narrowed, a thoughtful pout. "Like faith," she says eventually, watching the sea. "Thinking makes it so?"

"Exactly."

She considers this a moment again, still puzzling. He cannot help but smile.

"You see?" he says. "You'll figure it out. That's what makes you such a good writer."

—

The folly of youth?

The genius of age only comes in recognizing the truths we took for granted when young. Our world becomes contorted, corrupted, to yield to a society seeking safety, comfort, security in our old age — a society that has nothing to do with real life, nothing to do with the passion of new ideas. Burning, unsafe, passionate ideas and concepts; like the conquer and surrender of love. We get old and we fear the fight, fear the leap. We make excuses as to why we should settle here on this side of the gorge. We tell ourselves and others there is nothing worth it on the other side, when life itself is there, not on the other side but in the crossing, in the leap. We sit and nurse our scars, remember what earned them, and live life only in the occasional heat of blood which pumps below the tender skin.

It is when Cain murdered Abel that he became truly old.

—

Time passes and he is able to release the world that waits. All except for his own waiting. There is a pleasurable feeling in the thought of her, the memories they have and in the hope of possibility. Though the worrying seed like a stone in his gut comes and goes with it.

He thinks of her as Anais, in their quiet room, against his hand, holding him. He loses himself in the memory and finds himself seduced. He tries to save the memory as much as he savours it. Mostly though he thinks of her, bronze and relaxed, book in hand on the patio there as he sits and writes. He imagines her lounging lean, imagines her holding one of his books, stopping to re-read lines half-aloud. And he would pause and take a sip of his drink and take pleasure in her pleasure in his words. His words made potent by the richness of her voice, her tongue, her lips . . . the word made flesh.

—

The day comes to leave and he is sorry for the time to end. Coraline has fed his need for discussing literary ideas and philosophy and the ghost of Anais has kept him company and kept him warm. It seems as though across the water lies uncertainty and as the boat grinds and bobs its way back to the other shore the feeling in his stomach seems to awaken and throb, pulled with a loadstone's magnetism.

Coraline climbs to the jetty, rosy smooth from the trip. For his own part Porter has taken on a reddish tint in highlights on his nose and cheeks, like a drinker's blemish or a bulimic Santa Clause. They gather their bags and walk the sun-drained casual pace to where Joseph is waiting.

"Thank you so much," Coraline says when they drop her off outside her apartment. "And thank Ana for me too."

Even in his drowsy state the sound of her name spoken aloud seems to pluck a chord at his centre. "I will," he says. "Goodbye."

He settles into the warm leather which reminds him with ginger scratches of the soreness of sunburn across his shoulders and the back of his neck. He is in a partial state of sleep and grateful for Joseph's silence. He is reminded of his arrival briefly, then nods off perhaps for a moment or two before they pull up to the guest house in the fading evening light.

"Home," Joseph says cheerfully.

Porter studies the cracked and dusted building with glazed eyes. "Home," he recites, even as he is thinking that there is no such thing.

Back in his room everything left for the week has reclaimed itself and he is once again an outsider, a friend who has moved abroad and returned and must be reacquainted. He starts with the kettle, the ceiling fan, the spider in its web in the corner. The spider has not taken advantage of his absence to expand but seems a comfortable cohabitant. Outside the setting sun bathes everything in a whiskey gold.

Twenty-seven

Coffee and ink — the pages add up. Most are in an invisible stack in his mind, where the real weight is, the extension of those white sheets in his laptop. He has the information he requires. He need not stay, not for the sake of the book. Yet he has to stay, for the sake of everything else.

A conversation with Peter takes place, a stage play of two men in either compartment of a confessional; the sinning writer and his agent priest. "I have to stay, Peter. I've met someone."

Silence briefly, "That didn't take you long. Nadia only just left."

"Nadia left ages ago. Or I left her. The fact that we were in the same room is irrelevant."

"And this new one?"

"Something completely different," Porter tries to explain. "Something real."

"They're all different, Tobey."

"That's not true." he tries to object, but Peter will make his point.

"It is true, old boy. I've known you for how many years now?"

Silence. Porter does not need to do the calculations.

"Almost thirty? That's three decades. It's a long time, Toby, and they're always different."

"It's not like that . . ."

"You've always been Don Juan. And it's not that you don't care, or have these feelings. That's just the thing. You can convince these women that they're the first of their kind exactly because you truly do believe it yourself. But how long is that for though? The question is whether you're fooling yourself, or is there something real to explore?"

Porter is silent. He believes and yet he asks himself now; how would he know? Isn't so much of life the decision we make as to what to believe, what feelings to trust and nurture and which to grind beneath our heel? Is love any different? Faith is powerful whether it is a lie or not, as long as we believe in it. If he has fooled himself, he thinks, the trick is simply to never see through the ruse.

Peter softens his approach, "Look, I'm sorry. I'm happy for you, I really am. I hope it is something different, something serious. I think you need that, think it would even be good for you. Just be sure before you complicate another life."

"I've never been so certain," he says, and he believes and doubts at once.

"I hope so, Tobey. I really hope so."

—

He works away like a sculptor or perhaps more like a carpenter whittling words, creating the arcs of sentences, paragraphs as blocks that interconnect, their carved faces weaving patterns joining, building histories, futures and imaginary lives unfolding. He tries to say what needs to be said, to imply subtleties of pasts for his characters, reminders of the shavings scraped away, the bare shoulder of wood that remembers the edge of the blade.

She invades the world of his creation constantly, wrestling for dominancy of his attention, but he has chosen to try to press on, to push her back or more rightly to coax her into patient recline as he would not offend her, even in thought. She will not go and he will not allow it and it is all a matter of will, like the right and left hand wrestling, it is not about a victor but about the choice of consciousness.

He sees the need to dismantle the blocks, rebuild the whole thing in structure, but the story is there. He feels the story is coming along, is beginning to have faith in it, beginning to feel his characters' and the cloaks of their tragedies carried over their shoulders. In the same breaths as though one were dependant on the other, he begins to fear for the possibility of a future with Anais, as though the hope for one were drained from the pool of the other. He tells himself not to think about it, to focus on the story, focus on the words. He steers his craft.

Dear Sheherezad, I would write a book that I would call my tomb.

—

In the streets the air seems darker. He sits in his cafe and the sun seems cruel, the sidewalks seem bare. When the news comes of Kadeem's arrest there is a tension on the street that is palpable. To Porter's eye it seems that the everyday activity continues but there is the sense of necessity that exists in a big city and not the languor that is usual to the island. Added is the threat of violence. He has heard of clashes between protestors and police in some rural areas. On occasion when he sits on his park bench correcting his notes he will glance up and see a dark figure moving through the crowd. He will grow alert with the fierceness of the features, partly expecting the man to draw a weapon and take some violent action upon the pedestrians. He will watch until the figure disappears and then realize the tension that has drawn up in his muscles. He thinks again of what Clarkson had said. But he cannot leave. Not yet.

—

Walking, he slows to watch a shaggy, dark figure seated on a flattened cardboard box on the sidewalk. An old vagrant plays a soundless piano, depressing the keys with a dull 'plunk'. The piano is an upright box-piano made for a child or a dwarf in a carnival. That the man would be playing with the discarded instrument of a sideshow circus lends his hollow concerto further air of the pathetic. The paint flakes in mottled chips. Pasiphae risks a pass of her ribcage against Porter's calf and then bolts forward with a happy skip. Grinning, she waves her whiptail like a child dared to poke a sleeping stranger. Porter looks at her and her ears shoot up, awaiting the rebuke which does not come. The beggar continues, seated on the floor and hunched over like a Shultz cartoon.

Porter notices that one of the man's fingers is missing, the right index gone from the knuckle; the punishment of the false accuser, or one denied the power to condemn. As the beggar plays, the stump splays occasionally, as though to take part, pressing down with its spirit, to partake in the soundless melody. It is denied the physical 'plunk' but rewarded by the same music of silence.

Something in the performance captivates Porter. He finds himself standing still, watching this man making his shadow music, the spectre-finger contributing its verse. Porter remains standing there with his mongrel jester, serenaded by the notes of an absent accusation. The man never looks up and Porter eventually pulls himself away, the dull clack of keys quickly fading.

—

He has memorized the date of her return, but he does not know the time of the flight. The day passes over an eternity, the sun unmoving where it clings in the corner of the doorframe. The world of his story has gone silent, as much as he tries to move them his characters all stand still, stare at the sky and wait for it to rain.

She does not call and he lies awake in the night in case her arrival was a late one, then tosses and turns when he tries to sleep, tries to quiet the scenarios of the overactive imagination of the writer.

Does anything end well? At the end of every journey there is the inevitable destination of the grave. Hope is a doorman for disappointment and anything of value is burdened by the fear of its loss. Yet we must try. It is the only thing left to us. Built into our DNA is this need to try to achieve, to be at least acknowledged in the now before the tide of time swallows us. We must seek out someone to look upon us, understand us in some small way and say that we left a fingerprint, a smudge on

*the face of the world. Someone whose eyes will bear
witness to the idea that we existed — that we existed
and, if we are lucky, to say that we mattered.*

Porter lies in bed, sand in his eyes as the sun rises.
He has possibly slept a scattered total of three hours
for the night. It has always been this way though, a
mind that finds its own moments, bursts of energy
(perhaps storing the caffeine which generally produces
little effect, for these sudden bursts). The thoughts rush
as though pushed from some machine that throttles
forward at a gallop, unstoppable. And as he tries to
close each one, to lose himself in the obliviousness of
blackness, more and more spit forth, unfold, unravel
a million scenarios generally spinning darker and
darker. He has taken to consoling himself only with
the fact that no matter how many variations he plays on
these scenarios, the Grand Author of life, will never be
outdone, will never be anticipated, and the reality will
always be unexpected.

He tries to go through his day without wondering
where she is, what she may be doing. She should be
back on the island by now. He cuts his cafe stay short
when the thought occurs to him that she might decide
to show up at the guesthouse. When he arrives she
is not there, no one has been there according to the
girl at the front desk. Porter goes up to his room, not
surprised because he has envisioned it; her arriving at
the door, taking her into his arms and kissing her, she
kissing back without restraint as she says, "It's done.
I'm free."

He has envisioned it and so the Grand Author has
struck it from the list of possibilities and will write him

something new, something less glorious or perhaps something terrible.

A week passes without word and does not dull the sense of anticipation though it gathers a foreboding. Conversations have inevitably become annoying as his mind drifts in mid-topic, unable to sustain focus. On the street, the glimpse of the back of a head, a shoulder of the same burnt honey and he is momentarily terrified.

Twenty-eight

Walking in the market his veins suddenly fill with freezing water. Kaplan is in a light-coloured suit and beside him is Ana in a loose green dress wearing a wide-brimmed hat. Porter considers walking away before they see him, but some sick need propels him forward. Perhaps it is the need to make her uncomfortable, to share his torture, to hurt her with the image of her handiwork simply to prove that she can still feel something for him, even as he hopes the reminder will bend her will. Or perhaps it is simply the need for closure.

As he comes closer though, he sees her smile at a vendor and his conviction falters. Her hand is on Kaplan's elbow, something colonial and quaint about them. Then he sees her eyes. She is distant, her face the mask he has seen before. Still there is a calm about her he has not seen in some time, a tranquillity in that numbness. He stops in his tracks, considers leaving once again and then she sees him. The mask slips and she goes pale for a moment, as the black hole in him takes a deep gulp.

Just then Kaplan turns, spotting him as well. There is a quick beat where everything stops, the length of time for a quick inhalation, a skip in music of the band where the world stops and restarts, and then they are all playing their roles. Porter smiles, difficult creases in the resisting rubber of his cheeks. Kaplan's smile is less forced but tight and disapproving.

"Porter." They do not shake hands. He is certain now that Kaplan knows, but they uphold pretences to avoid further unpleasantness, enact the white lie.

Ana smiles and leans up with affected casualness to kiss his cheek in greeting, a hand in place to secure her hat. There, eclipsed below the brim for the briefest of moments, Porter's heart seems to leap and then crash. He is enveloped by her and then she is gone and his skin burns at the stranger's kiss from a lover's lips. "Chris, how are you?"

"I'm not bad. Making progress." Porter tries to avoid looking at her, to avoid falling into her eyes. He tries to focus on Kaplan though it takes actual willpower. However, to maintain the appearance of normalcy he must address her occasionally and each time he does she seems to grow nervous, her eyes fluttering back to her husband or beyond his shoulder. "I understand you were travelling," he says. "How was your trip?"

He points the question at Ana, but Kaplan answers, "It was good. Laying the groundwork for a new post. We'll be going back to the States for a while. Back to civilization."

"You must be looking forward to it."

"We are," Kaplan speaks for them both. His role is the gatekeeper, denying Porter any access. "Speaking of which, weren't you supposed to be back in London by now?" Kaplan is a diplomat but the implication in the question is apparent.

"Yes, well I had got an extension, but I think I've done all I can here. I should be heading back shortly."

"Good," is all Kaplan says.

They regard each other a moment and then Porter relieves the awkwardness. "Well, in case I don't see you, thank you for everything." They are two against one, he is the intruder. He shakes Kaplan's hand, smiles at Ana and gives an awkward wave. Her mouth tweaks back in an equally awkward smile and then he turns and walks away, the exiled retreating into the wastelands.

He feels hollowed out, gutted, as he walks back to the guesthouse. Pasiphae runs out to greet him and he is moved by a shining star of gratitude, even as he has the desire to kick her for reminding him of any hint of the acceptance which he has been denied from Ana. The mongrel presses her flank against his leg and he pats her side guiltily. "If only I were born a dog, ol' girl, you and I with only the fleas to come between us." She smiles up with lolling tongue and then he leaves her, rolling back his cave door to be alone in the dark.

He sits on the edge of his bed and closes his eyes, feels the outside world tip and sway as though he were on a boat in rough waters and seasick. A man is not supposed to feel this way, he thinks. What is it about him that makes his emotions reside so close to the surface, makes him so weak? It is a whole history that he must wade through, psychological puzzle-pieces that have built him up to this moment. In this moment he curses it all, all of the gentleness of his childhood, the mother's loving cradle, all that shaped him. It is one further step in his abandonment of history, his wish to set himself free of only the present, to lose those traits of his that make him susceptible to these feeling. He feels the ball in his throat sting his eyes and recede as he pictures her Judas stare. He will not allow it.

But he knows he cannot abandon who he has become, as much as he may wish it and it twists his bones with futility. So he curses it all, his family, his life and everything that is in him. He curses the words that have no power over the sword, curses his heart with its faulty lock and key, he curses fate, Kaplan, this island, God. He curses it all but stops short at cursing her. Even now in the depths of it all, with the black hole stretching outwards and devouring him, spreading into the room and swallowing his everything, he will not curse her.

She is Anais, with her scars, with her pain and the faults and weaknesses that make her whole.

And she is perfect.

Twenty-nine

When Kadeem speaks in public, God is universal. "Our Heavenly Father," he says, "He who only wants the best for his subjects."

Porter muses on the word "subjects." God as monarchical, an absent king who still demands his taxes be paid. And humankind is communally responsible or the punishment is meted out in death and pestilence to the just and unjust alike. A man's very being is exposed to ridicule.

When the authorities announce the various criminal charges against Kadeem, including 'conspiracy to commit treason,' it is the tear in the wall of unrest and it eventually does spill violence. Porter is at his bench and sees the protesters brandishing placards and fury, signs painted on cardboard squares and stapled to wooden poles and fists tight on upraised wrists. It seems to go on for a long time without boiling over or cooling.

Porter surrenders his vigil and returns to his room. He is sitting on his bed unable to concentrate on the words of a book when he hears the explosion, feels it like a grumble in the belly of the world. The ceiling fan rocks, the spider's web vibrates. He looks out of the open doors and sees smoke slowly billowing from the direction of the square. He hears screams and feeble pops. It is a thick gray and powdered cloud, cement returned to its original state and tossed into the sky. He turns on the television but there is nothing. He hears more pops of gunfire and retrieves his camera, going to the French doors to attempt a closer view through its lens, but the zoom is not powerful and the smoke and buildings from this angle offer him no clear view.

He keeps the camera slung around his neck and heads down into the streets, jogging towards the rising commotion. The gunfire resumes; three shots followed by several answering reports, overlapping, multiple shooters opening up on one. He stops a moment before deciding and pressing forward. As he gets closer there is the growing feeling of panic, disorientation. Figures run in both directions, a few away, more towards, curiously. Porter moves towards the smoke, finds a position at the corner of a building and peers from behind.

It is impossible to tell what is taking place at first. The shadow of one shooter fires and Porter ducks slightly, reflexively, though the man is not pointing in his direction and is a good distance away. A car is on fire off to his left, and then he sees the burnt out shop front, flames still licking from its charred mouth and jagged black glass teeth gaping. There is the sudden rippling of automatic gunfire, like firecrackers. Porter does not see the man hit, only sees him on the ground beyond the smoke. The bench where he normally sits is charred in spots and he snaps a picture of this symbol of his commonplace ritual scorched by violence.

Suddenly he feels a powerful hand grip his wrist, twist and pull hard. He feels real terror at the swirl of dark sweaty skin that he smells but cannot define. He feels a blow glance off his shoulder and loses his footing and feels the camera pulled from his hand, feels the strap dig in and rake the skin of his neck.

"Press! I'm with the press!" he cries, in his muddled mind seeking some words to satiate his attacker — one, now two attackers. He is hit and falls, the camera eventually pulled free, his ear left burning, and then there is a rain of blows, heavy boots to his midsection. One of the figures stands over him, a foot on each side of his body where it lies curled into a foetal position, either to protect his vitals or from some regression to prenatal protection. The man's hand shoves Porter's head down, jarring cheek to pavement, riffles in his pockets turning them inside out, finding nothing, flipping him over to search the other side and still no sign of the wallet left absently back in his room.

'Fight!' his mind screams. *'Fight!'* But his body receives no clear instruction.

Then he is punched again in the side of the head with the frustration of disappointment, followed by a parting solid kick to his spine that makes him cry out for the first time he can recall in the attack.

Porter is vaguely aware of the retreating footfalls beyond his own laboured breathing. A ball of pain rolls around in the small of his back and a sharp sting informs him of a cut at the side of his left eye being traced by sweat. He is burning in the sun. He somehow registers the fallen body of the gunman a distance off. Beyond the moving smoke he makes out the strange curl of an ear. It somehow provides the impetus. Porter drags himself to a seated position against the wall, feels the pain in his ribs now. He sits there squinting in the bright light, the heat, the dust and feels the grit in the dull breeze sticking to his cheek. He feels vulnerable, flinches as strange figures run by. Slowly he becomes reoriented to his surroundings. He pulls himself up and makes his way as quickly as possible, a slow hobble back towards the guesthouse.

It seems forever away. Things tilt in his vision and sound seems off, distorted somehow, backed by a solid ringing. His neck strains to support the weight of his head and he feels exhausted, thirsty and the pain asserts its dominance around his back and left side of his ribcage. He is almost to the guest house when he sees a man near the entrance on the sidewalk. The man is dark with broad spread features. His hair is cut like an arrow at his ears in thin corkscrew curls. He wears a red shirt with faded orange flowers. Porter tries to recall; is it possible he saw a flash of those colours in his attack? The man stares at him with a look of blank hostility, his dark eyes piercing with their outlining whites in that pitch face.

Porter looks at the man, looks away again, glances back. The man's eyes remain locked. Porter slows to a standstill, fears passing the man to get to the entrance. There seems to be no life beyond the two of them. Porter knows he would be unable to run, unable to defend himself. He wonders what more the man could want knowing that he has no valuables, but the fierce look threatens the worst, it speaks of some ancient hatred, something primal.

A loud, sharp report in front of him makes Porter start visibly. Pasiphae repeats her shrill but edgy bark. She faces the stranger in the flowered shirt, legs set firmly, ears forward, repeats her complaint in his direction. The man seems momentarily confused. He contemplates the dog, then Porter. He seems to hesitate. Porter feels for the first time that he is not alone in his ordeal and tears of gratitude sting his sore eyelids, a gratitude that balls uncomfortably in his throat. He ventures a step closer. Pasiphae takes up a more forceful tone, advances a couple of steps on the would-be attacker, baring small sharp teeth. She growls menacingly in between her barks. The man seems to focus his fierce look on the mongrel and Porter momentarily fears for his protector. But then the stranger seems to think better of it. With a last disdainful look at Porter he backs off and begins a brisk walk up the street. Pasiphae gives a succession of barks skipping forward a way before turning proudly to Porter.

Porter moves briskly up the path, collapses on the stairs and embraces the dirty mongrel, her tail whipping wildly. Her small slick tongue darts across his cheek, strangely soothing as it flicks quickly with the racing of his pulse. "I owe you a fine meal my friend," he says and drags himself for fear inside. He holds the door, intent to reward his saviour with the shelter of his room, but she stands and watches him dumbly grinning, tail pumping from the stoop, unwilling to attempt entry. He slowly closes the door on her and stumbles upstairs. He can feel Pasiphae's spit solidifying on his cheek with the grime of the sidewalk, bloody scab tightening at the corner of his eyebrow. He tears clothes from his body and seems to use his last strength to turn the shower handles, get a cool stream going. Then he collapses, the cold tiles soothing against his aching skin as the water soaks through. He cups his hands and drinks greedily. He shudders from the adrenaline in his system and watches the water from off of him swirl down the drain, serpentine dark grey rivulets of dust laced with crimson blood.

———

He wakes shivering and cold beneath the falling water in the dark of the shower. He reaches up to turn the handles shut and his side screams, his muscles knotted and stiff. He hears a stifled cry escape his lungs. He manages to pull himself to his feet and climb from the shower, wrapping a towel around himself and he makes his way out of the bathroom. Something clicks in the darkness, he turns his head too quickly and there is the explosion of a black star behind his left eye and the room tilts and then spins. He feels nothing as he is swallowed by darkness.

Thirty

It is a cliché thing, the waking to the brilliant white overhead light of the hospital room. And the truth is that there is consciousness before this, the swimming up from the darkness to the place where one recognizes you are asleep. Porter feels the tickle of a fly alighting on the back of his hand, feels his skin twitch and the eyelash tickle disappear. His consciousness pulls against his eyelids heavy and resistant, then slowly yielding. The light is soft and pale, the walls butter yellow.

He wakes from a solid, heavy, drug-induced slumber. Slowly his limbs check in and reconnect with the brain. His torso sobs mild complaints, then his side screams as he shifts upwards into a sitting position, drops back to a recline. His head is stuffed with cotton wool. His fingers brush the seam of stitches in a short arc extending from his eyebrow. He is a busted ragdoll. He sits there studying the blankness of the room, the IV drip in his arm. He feels naked beneath the hospital gown and empty inside, his stomach hungry but his mouth without appetite.

A door opens and a nurse comes in. She is a dark snowman carrying a tray. She shows no surprise that he is awake but smiles. "How are you feeling, Mr. Porter?"

He considers this a moment. "Like a piñata," he says.

She chuckles. "Well if your sense of humour isn't broken that's a good sign. Just relax now." She comes close beside him, feels his forehead with a bare palm easing him back into the pillow at the same time. Then she slips the needle from his arm in a smooth motion. "The doctor will be in with you shortly, okay."

She begins to leave when something occurs to Porter, his mind now noticing the void in its logic which needs to be filled. "Wait. Can you tell me how I got here?"

The nurse stops at the doorway, "Your lady friend, she found you in your room, called the ambulance for you. Don't worry, Mr. Porter, just rest up." She leaves him in mystery.

His mind goes immediately to Ana. Had she come looking for him? Perhaps he had called her and does not remember. Or was it someone else. Perhaps it was the front desk clerk, the nurse's statement just poor wording. Could it have been Nadia, come back for something, a confrontation or reconciliation perhaps? Ana is the only sensible conclusion he can come to, but he has to doubt it, because if it was she who returned looking for him his mind must now wonder at the cause, and he dare not.

The doctor arrives, short balding with a moustache and tortoiseshell glasses that he peers down. His dark skin carries uniform creases, his forehead rising and falling like horizontal blinds being turned. He pokes and prods Porter in all of his tender bruises, then blinds him twice and checks his throat to see where his sight has retreated to. The man is a mechanic. After a while he prescribes some mild painkillers and pronounces that Porter can leave soon. "Just rest up until we get someone to take you home." He leaves and Porter never gets his name.

Porter lies there barely thinking. A small television in the corner shows footage of the carnage of the riot, debris and fire-trucks outside the burnt out shop. There is a shot of the man Porter saw killed, his body half-covered by a flapping tarp. The sound is down low to a bee's drone and as Porter watches it the image seems to grow indistinct until it is a blur of dancing dots of coloured static, his eyes sliding out of focus. With the hum in his ear and the dance of a million dots upon his retinas he falls into sleep.

—

When he opens his eyes she is seated quietly beside him past the horizon of his right hand, legs crossed, arms folded across her chest. She gazes to the side, lost in thought and he tries not to move, not to make a sound to just stretch this moment of peaceful togetherness. But slowly she becomes aware of his gaze and raises her eyes to him. Her smile is sad and concerned, as though she feared he would not wake, but she bottles any sense of joy. It finds only a small aura at the edges of her irises.

He pulls himself up into a seated position.

"No, it's okay," she says, then rises to help settle the pillows behind him.

He feels a mixed sense of frustration at being met as an invalid and gratitude for the opportunity of her closeness leaning in like this, even if only for a moment, "It was you," he says, his mouth sticky and dry. He wonders suddenly what he must look like, a broken old man in a hospital bed. He raises his hand reflexively to check his hair and a shooting pain bolts through his side and back and he tucks his arm back.

Anais, smiles softly and as though having read his thoughts, she touches his hair lightly rearranging and smoothing back. "Do you remember what happened?"

"I was robbed. There was the explosion, the riots. I went to see and some men — two, I think, I'm not sure — they attacked me, took my camera. I had forgotten my wallet in the room." Her eyes well up with tears. "Pasiphae saved me," he says, becoming rambling almost incoherent to his own ears as the events flood back to him. "I should have given her a better name." He squeezes his eyes against the fog, looks back at her.

She returns to her seat, leaning forward towards him to touch his hand with hers. "I was terrified when I found you."

"You came," he says and she looks away. "Why?"

She is quiet for a long time, seems to have to summon the courage to meet his eyes again.

"You must hate me."

It is his turn to study her, the curve of her nose and the smooth angle of her jaw. "I can't," he says hoarsely. "I wanted to," he admits. "But I can't."

They are both quiet. She fingers the Fibonacci shell at her throat. Porter sees something there that pushes the black hole back, makes it contract just a bit from where he had forgotten it. "You came back," he says, squeezing her fingers lightly.

Her eyes let go, find safe perch on his collarbone. "I just needed to talk to you." His gut seems to anticipate ahead of his mind. The black hole smiles. She looks up and pats his hand reassuringly, a hint of hopeful desperation in her eyes. "Not now though. You should rest."

"It's better we talk now," he says. "We're in a hospital afterall," he says with a smile, trying to add some charm, like throwing a rubber ball at the ocean's tide to chase it away. The smile slides away. "Please. We can't drag this out any longer. It will kill me."

"I didn't want to leave things the way they were."

"And how were they?"

She studies him a moment. "I just can't do this," she says.

"Do what?"

"I can't . . ." He sees the emotions torture her face, sees her fight to take hold. "I can't be having an affair. I can't be two things to two people at once."

"You said you felt empty when you're with him. Is that a person you want to be?"

"No."

"Then leave him."

"It's not that simple."

"Of course it is," he says unreasonably. And he knows that he is being unreasonable, but he cannot help himself. "Leave him. Leave him and start anew, start anew with me."

"You don't understand. There are things, Cristobal. These things . . . the past, my past . . . things you don't know . . . you don't know me . . ."

"I do."

"There are things . . . from before . . ."

"It doesn't matter. I won't leave you, Anais."

"Don't say that."

"I won't, if that's what you're afraid of. I won't leave you alone."

"You don't . . . you can't know that."

"I do," he says. And he does; as long as they believe it, as long as they never lose sight that this is what they want, this is what they have chosen to want. He thinks of Peter's words, of the past, of the ones before. "I love you," he says.

She looks at him fondly, "We're too old to believe in those fairytales."

"It is only if you think so that it doesn't work. Love is the real god of things. Faith makes it real, belief makes it live."

"Life can't be like a movie, Cristobal."

He smiles to hear his name from her lips, "Why? Why can't it?" He measures his voice to try to sound calm, to seem rational. "There would be arguments, of course. We would have disagreements. I'm not unrealistic, Anais. But those things wouldn't matter. They would be passing trivialities, because at the end of the day, if you wanted to be with me, we would just make it work — because we choose to. We would be the only two people in our world, the only two people who mattered, and we could make it work."

"Adam and Eve?" she says with a smirk, but there is a softening in her eyes, something warm.

He smiles and she looks away, but then slowly her mind pulls her features' mask. "It's not realistic," she says. "I . . . I . . . can't just leave everything and run away."

"What are you leaving behind, really, Anais? What?"

"I don't even know you that well. Please, don't make this so hard on me."

He feels as though a weight has dropped down on his chest. "You do know me, Anais. I've seen it in your eyes. I've felt it in your touch. Why do you think this is so difficult? You may not know how I take my coffee, but you do know who I am, better than anyone. Just as I know you. Why are you so afraid to admit it to yourself?"

She is struggling visibly now. She wraps her arms tightly around herself, squeezes her eyes shut, but the tears still seep through. "Your words," she says.

"Are true."

They are silent a moment as the tears well in her eyes, as he hangs in balance, wanting to comfort her, but needing her to make the required step.

She comes up as though for air, a deep breath and her features harden. "No," she says and he feels she is speaking as much for herself as for him. "No, it's too much."

"I love you, Anais."

"I can't do this. Things must change, but I can't do this. Not like this." She looks at him imploringly. "Please don't make this harder than it already is. Please don't say the things you say . . ."

"I'm only telling you how I feel. I'm speaking honestly. And you know it's true. Why won't you be honest with yourself?"

"Your words, they spin me around and confuse me. They're beautiful notions, but it's not enough. You don't understand."

"Does honesty count for nothing?" his hurt begins to show its teeth.

"Honesty?" The word is an accusation. "I'm a married woman, Chris." The shorthand stings more than the charge. She seems to turn the finger on herself as well. "I don't think either of us can bring honesty to our defence."

"You have me hanging on a string."

"And where do you think I am? I'm the knot between two weights." Her tears flow freely now, fiercely. "You both pulling at me, demanding my allegiance . . ."

"I'm sorry," he says, before he knows why. "I'm sorry, don't cry."

"I feel tortured, pulled in every direction, like I'm just being used by everyone, everyone around me. It's this constant drain and I'm empty, I'm already empty."

"I'm sorry, just please don't cry. I just . . . I love you. That's all, I just do."

She buries her face in her hands, her shoulders shake. When she looks up her eyes are red, she looks exhausted. He sees it for the first time, the lines around her eyes show. "I don't think," she says slowly, trying to piece it together, learning it for herself, "I don't think I could even love anymore, Cristobal . . . I mean anyone."

"You shouldn't think that. You shouldn't ever think that. You've just shut yourself off for a long time. But I've felt it, Anais."

She wipes her face.

"Tell me you don't then," he says softly. "Tell me you don't feel the same way about me."

She stands and he worries that she will walk out without another word, but she looks at him, then steps closer. "I don't know," she says.

His certainty flags, the elevator-drop of the earth beneath him sense of panic. "You do, Anais." She seems to shake her head slightly, almost imperceptibly, so that he is not sure if he imagines it. "I can make you happy, Anais. Just give me the chance to. I promise you, I can make you happy." It is pathetic even to his own ears.

"I have to go," she says.

"Promise me I'll see you again," he pleads and hates the sound, the break in his own voice, that weakness. "Promise me, please."

"Okay, I promise." She tries to smile and it looks pained. "I'll see you." She touches her hand to his cheek and in the tenderness he feels hope again, just the flicker but it is enough. He presses his hand over hers and she smiles with a genuine fondness, though the pain is not driven fully from her eyes.

"Believe in me, Anais. Just trust what you feel, I won't let you get hurt."

"Adam and Eve," and her smile twists playfully and he is allowed to smile, a natural, instinctive smile. "I want to, Cristobal. I would like to be able to hope for something again."

"You can. We will."

She kisses his forehead, then kisses his lips softly. "Goodbye," she says.

"We'll figure it out, Anais."

She smiles and walks to the door and as she steps across the threshold he immediately wants to bolt from the bed after her, to stop her from going back out to the world, keep her with him and prevent whatever is out there from cutting their tentative bond with doubt and disappointment. He wants to. He even sits up, but feels the drunken ache in his skull shift and the pain shoot along his back. He considers going further but decides it is too late and he lets her go.

He attempts to have faith.

Thirty-one

When they tell him that his transport has arrived, he finishes dressing in clean clothes that Anais has left for him. As he exits the hospital back into brilliant sunshine he sees Joseph leaning heavily against the side of his steel whale.

"Mr. Porter," he opens the back door for him like a true chauffeur, his hand poised to catch Porter's arm.

"Joseph." Porter smiles and pats him on the shoulder. He somehow feels grateful to Joseph as he feels grateful to every friendly face, grateful for the sunshine and clear air. "I'd like to ride up front if that's okay."

"Of course, of course."

He makes his way stiffly around before Joseph is able to open that door for him. He wants to shake the feeling of victim, of weakness. He sits inside in the scent of warm vinyl and nicotine. He suddenly craves a cigarette desperately.

The car rocks along, the warm wind blowing over them. He feels new to the world. Not in any glorious way, just as a stranger or an observer. He is a foreigner in a world that is neither good nor bad. He is indifferent but it melts away the previous shackles of his terror.

"We'll avoid town," Joseph says. "There's too much chance of trouble there. You shouldn't stay here much longer, Mr. Porter. If you can, if I was you, I would leave here as soon as I could. Lots of trouble happening and it not getting better soon."

He makes Joseph stop along the way and enters a butcher's shop. In the frigid air he selects a large rib-eye steak. The place smells of frozen flesh and blood, arctic meat. The butcher, thick and heavy like all butchers everywhere, wraps his steak in brown paper, ties it off, a neat gangster's Christmas parcel.

They reach back to the guesthouse and Joseph offers to accompany him upstairs but Porter declines. He reaches into his pocket to offer Joseph a tip and is reminded that his wallet is still in his room. Joseph does not wait though, he smiles and drops back into his seat. Porter leans in through the window.

"Thank you very much, Joseph."

"You take care, Mr. Porter. Not to sound bad, but I really hope the next place I'm takin' you is the airport." Porter pats the door and watches Joseph drive off.

He heads up the vacant stairway with his package underhand. The room is less foreign on this return; sheets tossed, he finds a spot of blood on a pillow. In the kitchen he rests down his parcel. He puts on the kettle then unties the parcel string and unwraps it carefully. He takes a knife and cuts the steak into sizeable chunks. Looking around he finds a paper plate and empties the meat and bone into it. He covers it over with a piece of foil. Then he washes his hands and prepares a cup of coffee.

He goes to the bathroom and examines himself in the mirror. To the left side of his eye is a dark crescent laced with blue stitches, it is slightly swollen giving his eye an even more brooding look. The white of his eye in that corner is also a dark red. There are freckles of scratches on his right cheekbone, probably where it scraped the sidewalk, he does not remember. There is also a sore square like a patch of sunburn on the side of his neck, edged on top and bottom by bruise lines from the drag of the camera strap. There is a large amoeba of purple ringed with yellow bruised along the entire left side of his ribcage. He looks like an aged prize-fighter. At his age it is barely one step better than appearing a falling down drunk.

He tries to neaten himself then collects his cup of coffee and his plate of diced meat and heads back downstairs. He settles on the stoop with his strange meal and waits. He begins to get concerned when he finishes his coffee and continues to wait. There is so much that could befall a wayward soul such as hers. It is just over an hour when she appears as though from nowhere, his shaggy mongrel saviour. She seems surprised to see him, uncertain. She stops and looks at him, ears forward and still. She wags her tail once tentatively, stops, tries again as though feeling him out, trying to confirm their relationship is still on positive footing.

He rises painfully and Pasiphae trots back playful and cautious in the same movement. She smiles at him and he uncovers the plate, now stained with grease, and places it out of the way beside the stairway. He backs away and she moves towards him seemingly oblivious of his offering before the scent finally reaches her and she moves towards it shyly. She keeps looking towards him trying to interpret his approval. Even as she begins to eat, gobbling the first bites, she looks to him while chewing. She eats so manically that she chokes at one point and must stop to cough.

"Thank you, my good Samaritan" he says.

She seems oblivious of the cause of this gift, seems to think only that he has not yet realised his error, or perhaps that these are his castoffs. Porter leaves her and heads back inside as Pasiphae continues eating greedily, lost in her banquet of a good turn repaid.

—

He spends the next couple of days in the apartment, trying to write, being drawn away by bouts of depression, thoughts of Anais and fears that he has already lost in her battle with obligation but is simply trying to fool himself that hope exists. He tries to distract himself.

He watches the news, Kadeem on trial. There are reports on it regularly though the court system seems to stall. They take Kadeem to the courtroom repeatedly and he is allowed to speak with reporters on the steps. He incites the "resistance" more like riots, that seems to round out the rest of the news broadcast but nothing seems to have occurred within the court halls. The riots are little more than acts of violence and looting. There is little to suggest a political or moral motivation to any of it. There is a protest organized with a handful of Kadeem's supporters. He recognizes some of the men from Kadeem's house, but the majority of the protesters are women, as though Kadeem had a vast harem. Still there is something Porter finds threatening in this, as though the men were preoccupied with other things, preparing for a more forceful form of protest couched in the manly art of violence.

Peter calls him four days after his release from the hospital. He has just received word. "I'm sending you a ticket," he says. "There's an advisory for all visiting foreign civilians. They expect an uprising. It's not safe."

"I can't leave," he says. "Not just yet."

"Tobey, be reasonable. You've already been attacked. You could've been killed."

"Reason has nothing to do with it," Porter saya calmly. "Reason means nothing. I have to stay, at least a little longer."

"You're in real danger there, Tobey. And, I'm sorry to bring it up, but you have obligations here that need attending to. I'm talking about your livelihood as well as your life here."

Porter is still calm, or perhaps just resigned. "I'm dead if I leave now," he says simply.

He does not bother to explain, cannot explain how a man can change, can find faith. How a jaded heart can become young and hopeful again, find a world beyond this one to live in. He cannot explain because it cannot be understood unless one has seen it themselves, seen it and believed it, something more than the real world.

Scientists have discovered dimensions that are unperceivable by the naked eye. String theory suggests that the nature of something may be determined by the vibrations of the smallest particles of matter, the rate at which they vibrate determining their nature. By this thinking we are all a cacophony of vibrating particles, walking symphonies. So much in the world is not how we perceive reality. Could not love also exist as an opening of one of these dimensions, as the harmony struck up between two such orchestras?

"I won't be long again, Peter. I'll purchase my own ticket. I'm sorry. You've been a good friend, but this is something I have to do. I'll talk to you soon." He has taken the monumental leap of faith across the chasm. One cannot turn in mid-air and go back.

"Tobey, please . . ." Peter protests.

"Goodbye, Peter." He hangs up the receiver and returns to his desk, to the words and the matter of that universe that he can control, though his characters seem to drive their own destiny towards peril and ultimate tragedy.

—

He measures time in increments of her silence. It has been eight days since her visit at the hospital and he sits in his cafe, attempting to reconnect to the real world in some small way, feeling so apart from it. He is not alone. Coraline has prompted him here, having heard of his attack through vague channels that seem to connect most likely to Joseph. He has told her the story of his wounds and she looks at him with childish over-affected pity. "I'm alright," he concludes, his emotional injuries aching more than his bruised ribs. "Tell me, how have you been?"

"I'm okay. I've been thinking about Uncle a lot, especially with everything that's been going on. I know he would have opinions on it. I imagine the things he might say."

"He was a very interesting man," Porter says fondly.

"I'm going to dedicate my book to him," she says.

"And have you been writing?"

"Some. Not as much as I would like, but pretty regularly. I'm making progress."

"Well that's the important thing."

They fall silent a moment. Porter is suddenly aware of the cold ball rolling in his stomach, the monster reminder of a sense of loss coupled with the roiling disgust of rejection.

Coraline seems to read something in his face, "How is your lady friend?" she asks.

Porter forces a smile back, drawn to the present and the mundane blankness of its slate. "I'm not sure. Things are very complicated for her right now. I know she's having a difficult time."

"Does she love you?" Coraline asks the question shyly, but she seems to sense that he is not all there, as though he has been hypnotized and it is okay therefore to ask this question, that he wants to talk about her to live her in some form or fashion, even if it is so far removed, even if it pains.

"I don't know," he searches his mind, searches the image of her face. "I think she does," he decides. "But I think she doesn't know how to trust that anymore. I think she feels that it would require too much, because of where she's been before. I think she's afraid to."

"And you? Do you love her?"

"I do," he says like a vow.

"And you're not afraid to?"

"I am," he admits. "I am because one becomes vulnerable. I know there could be hurt involved. But, I guess I believe we can move beyond it."

"No matter what?"

"No matter what."

She smiles, enjoys this idea for a while as he does. "Have you ever felt like this before?" she asks.

He feels a twinge, that sadness of the no longer innocent, where nothing can be completely new and threatens to rob experiences of their novelty. "I did feel similarly once."

"And what happened?"

In his trance he tells her. He does not fear offending her youth, does not underestimate her intellect or feel that he needs to speak down to explain how life and emotions are. There is nothing in age that cannot be figured out by the young, he has decided. He tells her of his wife: "I was married. I loved her very much. We loved each other passionately. Then I became careless and lost sight of what mattered." He takes a deep breath then continues. "I had affairs. I became distracted by cheap thrills, chose that over what I had, what I had which was of real value." He watches a group of pigeons pecking lightly in the brilliance of the afternoon sun, brown and grey turtledoves. "Love needs nurturing. It takes work. Love alone is not enough even. It takes will and commitment. You have to be willing to take a lot, to compromise a lot, to work at it. But it's worth it. It's work you don't mind doing, because nothing else will pay such dividends. You have to keep reminding yourself though; it's worth it. That it's what you want. I forgot that. I got distracted by trivialities and stopped believing in what I had. I lost faith and I hurt her terribly as a result."

He pictures her face as he talks, sharp Asian features, black hair which would billow endlessly, waves of ink that would cascade against her cheeks, against his cheek, a raven's wing waterfall when she was over him.

"And what happened?" Coraline asks in a whisper, "in the end."

"She died," he says. His mind, somewhere else registers the emotion in his voice. His eyes feel dry and he blinks and lowers his eyes studying the stitching on his loafers. "I drove her away. It wasn't her fault, no one could blame her . . . She found a lover. She was with him, driving with him when their car crashed. She died. Not immediately, but after an hour in the hospital, she couldn't last any longer." He coughs, wipes at the threat in his eyes. He gathers himself, snaps to as though from a dream.

Coraline is sitting upright, studying her hands on the tabletop. He tries to smile to ease the moment. "I'm sorry," he says, "perhaps a bit more information than you were looking for."

"No," she says, "it's okay." She smiles, studies her hands again. She seems to want to ask something.

He senses it. "You're wondering why this time should be different?" he smiles.

She looks at him sheepishly but smiles back, shrugs lightly.

"Because," he says, "I've learned. Because this time I know better."

She smiles as though pleased with this response and settles back in her chair. They seem back to their casual selves when she speaks something suddenly occurring, a thought realised and escaped before fully considered, "Well, I hope that she does too."

They sit for a while, Porter having no response, Coraline seeming to expect none. The pigeons suddenly take flight, scattering the light.

Thirty-two

He stacks the papers on his desk. Page by page they have slowly gathered weight like a life of years. The fading evening seems muted, the air dull and empty. He moves around the room tidying items. He folds the pillowcase with the bloodstain and makes a note to pay the front desk to replace it. He finds a strand of Ana's blond hair attached to it and carefully pinches it free. He holds it in the light, coils it around his finger tip squeezing tight a white line below the red tip. He uncoils it and holds it between the finger and thumb of his left hand then goes onto the balcony and lights a cigarette. He is sliding his thumb over it, trying to capture its texture when it slips free, falls to the balcony tiles. He watches it coiled there a moment, before a gust of breeze brushes it over the edge.

Back inside he mixes a cup of coffee. He picks up the copy of his book, A Sceptic's Banquet, she had brought for him to sign. He flips the cover open, looks at his name imprinted there. On the next page is printed the dedication: "in loving memory of my wife, Charlotte." He closes the book and places it back.

When he removes the bundle of clothes and sees the teardrop earrings of Nadia's, that she had once used to weigh down a simple note, he cannot help but stare. They are a talisman, the subtle tendrils of history seeping out to hold him.

He lies back in bed, still feeling sore and smokes cigarette after cigarette until the light has faded and night taken over.

—

When Porter awakens to the ringing phone he is aware that he has only slept a couple of hours. He rolls over and snatches the receiver. It is morning but it is still dark. He rubs at his eyes and feels the burn of his cut.

She is crying.

"Anais," he tries to calm her, "Ana. Anias."

He can hear her breath catching at the other end. "Chris, I'm so sorry. Cristobal . . ."

"What is it? Tell me what happened. What's wrong?"

"I'm so sorry. Please, forget me and be happy, I want you to, I do . . . I just can't keep . . . Just promise me, please, don't remember me . . . differently . . ."

She is crying choking on her words. He feels a real sense of worry now, a physical fear for her.

"I was wrong. I never meant to . . ."

"Where are you?"

"No, Cristobal . . . No, I can't . . ."

"Anais, tell me where you are. It will be alright. I love you regardless. It will be alright. Now, tell me where you are."

She is quiet for a moment, he can hear her breathing heavily, hear her sniff against the tears. She gives him the address of the apartment. He does not recognize it, searches for a pen and scrawls it on the corner of a page as she begins to cry again, mumbled words turned to sobbing. He wants to get to her, to hold her in his arms and make sure she is alright, make sure she is protected and safe.

"I'm coming for you," he tells her, his mind already on calling Joseph. "You wait there and don't do anything until I come for you."

"No, please . . ."

"It'll be okay, Anais. I promise you. I'm coming."

"Cristobal . . ."

"It'll be okay."

—

Morning is breaking as they arrive at the apartment complex, a low block of rooms arranged like a motel, a pastel green faded like its lawn. It seemed to take an eternity; the wait for Joseph, the drive here in the morning dawn, the sky changing vibrant colours — pink, peach, orange.

He jogs up the short walkway now to the room and knocks, calls to her, "Anais."

There is no sound from inside. There is a white paned window beside the door but it is draped with thin orange curtains. Beyond them the room is mottled with shadow and light, but nothing is distinguishable. There appears to be no movement from inside. He wonders if she has left, if she has given up on his coming.

He bangs again, harder. "Anais!"

He looks around him in the half light growing, the quiet and early morning sounds stirring. He considers locating the main office, turns back to the door and rests his hand flat against it. The orange curtain drifts softly.

He leans against the door in exhaustion. Something telling him she is still there, just beyond it.

"Anais," he calls, softly now. "Anais, please let me in."

His hand tries the doorknob but it is locked. He peers through the glass cupping his hands on either side, imaginary shapes drawn in the shadows behind the curtain. The curtain shifts again on some current and he catches a glimpse of an ankle and foot lying on the ground. His stomach drops and chest tightens. He calls out to Joseph and convinces him to help, his mind racing with fear. Together they force the door on the third try.

The room is small, a bed against the wall to the right, small side-tables with nondescript lamps, the carpet a dull grey. He sees her legs first, the sole of her foot, one knee up slightly, her hips and her waist turned, something odd in the angle. As he steps forward, the upper part of her is revealed beyond the corner of the bed, a shaft of sunlight sliding beneath the curtain on that side to light her slender hand and beyond it he sees the red spray against the wall below the double windows and the gun lying heavily in the carpet just beyond her hand.

He hears his voice, an odd cry, something guttural as he rushes to her, three steps and then some instinct halts him, some remnant of unwanted logic forces him back a step and he hears a sickening crunch beneath his foot. He looks down at the shattered Fibonacci shell and falls to his knees, winded. Her body lies on the floor like a dropped marionette, strings cut, as though she has already crawled into some artist's chalk outline. Her hair cascades, but the dark ruby snake's greedy eye burrows into his memory and he can smell the brand burn its way there. He cannot breath.

He does not know how long he is like that. He does not hear the cars pull up, the police someone has called — most likely Joseph. When the strong hands take him he has a sudden jolt of panic that it is his attackers returned, the murderers of his Anais come for more blood, the man in the red shirt with tar skin. He is held by his arms and dragged out of the room as he struggles. He fights only to remain at her side, though he knows that what is her no longer remains. Still he would hold her again, hold her until their bones were one and they crumbled to dust.

He cannot speak, he has reverted, devolved. He hears his own voice in the grunts and bellows of a wounded animal. The arms drag him back out into a world broken off its hinges; pale sky changing places with lawn, fence, roofs, black shoes, all at angles as the horizon spins off of its axis. Joseph's voice somewhere far away speaks in tongues and then Porter chokes and his stomach closes, tightens to a fist. The arms ease him out to allow him to double over and puke at a comfortable distance, to save polished governmental boots. He wretches and spits, his stomach begins to ease then clenches again. He hangs like that, held at the elbows by his two captors, doubled over as the blood rushes to his face, tears and mucus flowing, spots running before his eyes. He spits again, wipes his face against his shoulder, and then his captors haul him into the backseat of a vehicle.

He sits there dazed, emptied, staring unseeing at the headrest before him, the bitter acid taste of bile in his mouth and then slowly images of her rise into his vision and he begins to cry. He sees it, the snapshot of her body lying so strangely, lifelessly. He sobs and tilts over onto his side in the pitted backseat. It is not a romantic weeping that overtakes him then, but the ugly twisted tears of a grown man broken.

Thirty-three

Somehow he is taken to the police station. He is placed in a small cell with a cracked plank of a wooden bench. He is unaware as to whether he has been arrested or is just being held. How he got here and whether he is ever seriously considered a suspect, are mysteries that will forever remain unanswered. They are mysteries that will never interest Porter. There are bigger mysteries that will haunt him.

He remains in a stupor, his thoughts incoherent, random images that flicker up and overlap. He flips through a picture-book of memories of her and goes through starbursts of hard emotion, firework pops of happiness, misery, hope and despair. It is all removed though. Something at his core has gone numb. He is aware of the black hole more concentrated at his centre, as though it had surged up and swallowed his insides and now shrunk back satisfied, the press of the contracted universe. So much of his life is lived in this sinking gut, and he fears it, fears this compression and the destruction and pain it will unleash. Around the void are organs, sinew and bone that function with the raw efficiency of machinery. At some point he curls onto his side uncomfortably on the rough wood. At some point he falls into a black sleep, dreams of nothing but cold and the aches in his bones.

He wakes, sits up painfully and after about an hour someone opens the cell and he is invited to step out. He walks uncertainly and when he sees Jack Kaplan waiting for him, Porter is still too numb to register surprise. Kaplan takes him by the arm and ushers him out of the police station. They stand on the sidewalk of a clear, cool day. Kaplan lights a cigarette and offers Porter one which he takes.

"These officials here are a bunch of fucking morons." Kaplan lights his own cigarette then Porter's.

Kaplan looks older. There are lines on his face, like misplaced pillow creases. His suit looks slept in, his hair sweat-slicked at the temples and his eyes blurry. Porter can only imagine that he himself looks aged. Porter pulls on the cigarette and the smoke grates through his throat, through his lungs and causes a sharp pain in his empty belly. He forces himself through three inhalations before dropping the cigarette to the ground and grinding it beneath his shoe.

"It was my gun," Kaplan says, not so much to Porter but to the physical world. "I should have kept it locked away."

Perhaps he is looking for absolution. He pulls greedily on the cigarette, one hand on his hip, the slight paunch showing beneath the twisted shirt. Porter says nothing, feels nothing.

Kaplan seems aware of him suddenly. "She tried to do it once before, you know. There was a history . . ." he trails off. His eyes touch on Porter and then look beyond him, around him. "I should've been more aware."

Porter feels alien to everything, to his own skin and watches Kaplan blankly. Kaplan outs his cigarette, rubs the back of his neck heavily.

"You should go," he says. "I don't just mean from here, I mean from the island. I can't say I'll be sorry to see you go, but it's for your own good. This island is about to fall apart. It can go to hell for all I care."

"We killed her." The words come up unbidden from somewhere inside Porter.

Kaplan turns on him angrily. "She killed herself!" he barks. He seems to consider saying more, but decides against it, seeing the deadness in Porter's eyes. "Just leave, Porter," he says. "Just go."

Porter suddenly realises that he is standing beside Joseph's vehicle. Kaplan opens the door for him and Porter obliges, steps inside and they drive away. Porter wonders at the clear day, at the universe that can go on so unblinkingly in the face of tragedy. He turns to see Jack Kaplan who simply stands there still on the sidewalk staring at a point in the sky as though trying to make sense of the scattered clouds, as though watching a departing plane that has become a point in the distance.

—

On the night he was awoken by her call, Porter had been dreaming of the word "idea". It was a strange dream, this dream of a word. The dream seemed imbued with hidden meaning, the word hanging there like a cipher, like the strange key to an unknown lock. He would try repeatedly for years to recall further details of the dream. He knew there was more, but as is the nature of dreams, it would always remain elusive; the word at the tip of the tongue never discovered, the word that may hold some answer or may be nothing more than the sound of another tongue of Babel.

—

There are a few days of staring at walls and the television. The looting is more widespread and frequent and there are rumours of a planned armed action by Kadeem's people. A State of Emergency is declared by the government, a curfew put in place. The army is present in the streets, but there is talk that many of them are sympathetic to Kadeem.

Peter calls and offers Porter condolences. He is gentle with Porter and in the end he is the one who arranges the ticket for Porter's return. Porter promises to repay him, says he is grateful, but he can feel little. It registers like a drop of water at the bottom of a very deep well.

Porter packs his things, finding traces, fragments of memories distilled into objects; the copy of his Ovid which she held and touched, the address he scrawled on the corner of his manuscript. He uncorks the almost empty bottle of wine from his fridge and touches the mouth of the bottle to his lips. He tries to capture any hint remaining from where she drank. There is the copy of his book as well that she had given him, its inscription still unwritten.

He stands in the doorway with his bags and takes one last look around. The French doors are pulled in, the fan rocks gently as it slows to a stop. In its corner the spider's web is draped dormant, no sign of its occupant to bid him farewell.

Joseph awaits him downstairs and he is surprised to see Coraline there as well. "Do you mind if I come with you to the airport?" she asks.

"Of course not," he smiles, and it is the first genuine hint of warmth he feels.

As they get into the car he sees Pasiphae lying near the stairs, chewing playfully on the dried and scratched dusty bone of the rib-eye. He smiles at her and she watches him with only a little curiosity.

Coraline does not attempt to make conversation as they drive. Joseph talks randomly, general topics of the impending confrontation, uprising or revolution — the term changing depending on who you ask. Porter watches the buildings grow sparse, the fields open and countryside grow.

At the airport Joseph takes the bags for Porter. Porter thanks him, presents him the remainder of his local dollars, a generous tip. "I appreciate everything," he says, shaking that leathery hand.

"I'm sorry it was a bad time for your coming, Mr. Porter. I'm sure things will work out."

Porter is not sure what 'things' Joseph is referring to but he does not ask. Joseph says he will wait at the car for Coraline and see her back safely. Coraline walks with him to his gate.

They stand awkwardly facing each other for a moment. "You'll be alright?" he asks her.

"Yes," she says. "We've been through this before. We're away from the trouble where we are. Our area is a good community, we watch out for each other. So we'll keep our heads down until it's settled. It's not about any extreme ideals. The people here, we don't get too extreme." She smiles momentarily and she has a vitality that moves him, like standing before a fire in the wintertime.

"And you?" she asks more cautiously. "Will you be okay?"

He considers this a long moment, considers the girl before him, the promise and hope she represents. There is a call for his flight.

"Thank you, Coraline," he says eventually. "Thank you for everything. It has been a blessing meeting you." He steps towards her and touches her head, the silken hair, smoothes it once fondly. "Goodbye."

She hesitates, then puts a hand on his shoulder to steady herself and leans up on tiptoes and kisses him briefly, gently on the cheek. Her fingers trail from his shoulder down his arm as she steps back and away. Their fingertips touch, perched, linger just a moment, then fall away. It all burns a trail of pins and needles in him. She backs away further, looking at him, smiling with a trace of sadness, she waves; the princess to the commoner beloved.

He wants to call out, "I love you, Coraline." In that moment it is true. But he already seems to be moving away, trudging towards his gate and the plane that will remove him. He looks back at her several times and she is there standing still and growing smaller in the sea of people, until eventually she is gone.

Thirty-four

In time questions creep in. There are rumours circulated that Ana was murdered by a local lover. It is an idea that appeals to the gossip; the foreigner who is seduced by the wild of the island and the primal islander, and eventually pays the price. It is a cautionary tale promoted, ironically enough, by the island people themselves. It is not given much credence and Porter knows it is nothing more than sensationalism.

Officially, Ana Kaplan was killed by an intruder. It was a story, Porter believes, that Kaplan put in place as a means to protect them; to protect Kaplan's career from rumours, to protect Ana from the stigma of a Catholic condemnation.

One thought that does occur to Porter is that Kaplan may have been responsible. He thinks of Anais the night he found her, soaked to the skin in the parking lot, her confession about the gun. He wonders if Kaplan's jealousy, his fear of rejection, could have pushed him that far. Part of him wants to believe this scenario.

But small moments stick in his mind and he feels more aware in retrospect of Ana's fragility — the damage, like shards of broken glass that cling to the frame of her psyche, the hairline fractures of a soul. Porter recognizes that Kaplan's culpability is the same as his; that they did not recognize the fragility of her state, her inability to bear the load of their demands, to be the source of the spring from which Porter drank so greedily. Not willing to be responsible for the disappointment of either's expectations, she escaped the only way she thought she could. Added to the weight of her disappointment in herself, it all proved too much. Porter will replay it all in his mind for years without resolution; this violent uprising, their failed revolt.

Much like Kadeem's failed uprising which took too long to manifest, built on too weak a foundation and plagued by too vague moralities. Kadeem was eventually sentenced to time served and returned to his estate. His followers were rounded up when their weapons stash was uncovered. Some property was destroyed and a few lives were lost, and the island's life went on as before.

It all ended in nothing.

Porter never finishes his book. Not that one anyway. He is unable to complete it and the powers that be decide (based on what is written so far) that it is not worth their while anyway. He eventually writes another. He writes a simple story, a novella, of people shipwrecked on an island, each dreaming of things they are missing, things they want to get back to civilization for, all unaware that their needs are there in each other. They are blinded and eventually turn on each other. It is a thin volume, another tale of another kind of revolution and it achieves more success than his previous novel. It is a tale of ideas and ideals gone awry.

He sometimes pictures her; Anais, sitting on the edge of the bed, alone in that apartment, weighing the silver .45 in her hand, weighing her life in her mind. He sees her crying, shaking violently, torn by her feelings of being trapped between two men, between two lives, the knot pulled taught, now unravelling. He sees her raise the gun, feels the cold muzzle bite the tender flesh of her temple, the tension of her finger against the trigger slowly tightening . . .

He can go no further. It is not real. Somewhere something breaks down for him. He cannot see her as he knows her coming to that point. He cannot see her as Ana or Anais pulling the trigger. There is someone else, another Her. There is something he has missed, something so integral that it has cost her a life and him some large part of his soul. It is this oversight that haunts him.

He thinks of her sketchbook, his feeling of excitement as he went through her drawings. But he wonders now what she saw when she had revisited those pages. Did they only serve to remind her of how far she had come from who she used to be? He remembers her that night, cross-legged Anais-in-Wonderland in his bed. That small crescent bruise seems to suggest the hint of the fracture, as does her finger on his lips and the words she breathed, as though feeling the necessity to remind, or perhaps to convince herself: "I'm here."

—

"Hello. Chris? It's Nadia."

"Nadia?"

"Yes. I'm in London, I was thinking we should meet up."

It is a little more than a year later when she calls. He agrees to meet her, at first telling himself that he does not know why, but really he knows that it is because it is a connection to that time and place, to Anais.

He meets her at a small cafe, one similar to where they had gone on their first date — perhaps it is the same place, but he cannot recall. They sit by the window. She wears a jacket and a light wool scarf, and she looks older, more mature, still beautiful though she has lost some of her softness. He tries to feel some of his old attraction for her but he cannot summon it. He wonders what it is he had felt, once upon a time at the beginning. They sit and talk with difficulty at first, trivialities and a lot of silences. At some point they begin talking about their time on the island. Porter begins to question her about her affair with Kaplan, and she answers openly. Then the talk turns to Ana.

"You were in love with her, weren't you?" Nadia asks.

"Yes."

Nadia leans forward, her elbows on the table shielding her bowl of cappuccino. Outside is dreary, overcast and cold and it emanates from the plate glass beside them. "Jack talked about her sometimes," she says. She hesitates a moment, studying him before venturing forward. "She had problems, Chris. She was a nice person, but she had problems."

"We all have problems," Porter says defensively. He resents Nadia talking about Anais this way, resents the thought of Anais being subject to dissection by her husband and his lover. All this time later and it is still fresh, the skin healed over the wound is paper-thin and aches.

"She tried to kill herself once before, crashed her car on purpose. That's why she had those scars."

"I know," he says. "I know all about her scars."

"I'm just saying; you shouldn't blame yourself. I think maybe you didn't know her as well as you think. An experience like that . . . it does something to someone."

He adds some sugar to his coffee and stirs, watching the light foam spiral.

"People have whole lifetimes of experiences," Nadia continues, "lives they've lived and all the little pieces of shit they collect . . . You knew her for how long? You can't ever be expected to know everything about someone." She is as gentle with her words as Nadia can be, trying to console but only cutting him in the process.

"I knew what mattered," he says, trying to sound unmoved.

She studies him, shakes her head. "You carry around your conviction like a shield."

"I should've been able to help her," he says eventually, his voice betraying emotion.

"You should have been a priest," she says.

"If only I believed in God."

"But you believe in love?" It sounds silly from her lips, the fairytale Anais saw as childish. "You think God is love?" Nadia leans in, still trying to be gentle but exasperated. She tries to catch his eyes where they are fixed low on his clasped hands on the tabletop. "God isn't love. God is Nature. And Nature is very often cruel. Beautiful, but also cruel." She leans back, says more gently, "Don't take it so personally."

He does not respond. He has grown cold as a stone, an image of resigned grief sculpted by Rodin.

"I'm just saying, there was only so much you could've done," she continues practically. "I mean, how does someone live with that? To know that you killed your own child? That you're responsible . . . I just can't imagine that."

Porter feels himself grow suddenly cold and nauseous. The ground drops and lurches up. He tries not to betray the fact, but Nadia seems to realize. He stares at his hands gone pale on the tabletop.

She had raised her cup but stops before drinking and rests it back down. She looks out the window. After a while she begins to speak. "They had a child. Jack and Ana had a boy. He was three." She talks as though thinking out loud, and he knows that she is explaining for his sake — explaining this way so that he will not have to admit his not knowing. "When she crashed the car, when she tried to kill herself, he was in the backseat. She was so distraught she didn't even think of what could happen to him, she forgot he was there. Her only thought was that she wanted to die. Only she lived and he didn't." He can feel her eyes study him, but he is numb, frozen in place. "Jack said she was prone to depression, she didn't really know what she was doing. He defended her. He stayed with her. He said he tried, but he couldn't make her happy. He said after that she could never look at herself without thinking about what she had done. It was like a constant weight."

He feels emotion choking him, his eyes burn moist.

"She was tormented by guilt, Chris. How can you even expect to know how that affected her, how that would feel?" She leans forward, and when she touches his hand he starts. She removes her hand, leans back.

"You should just appreciate that you made her happy for a time."

But he cannot. He cannot console himself with this now because he no longer feels certain of how happy she ever was. He believed it at the time, but when he looks back there are too many things he fears he has missed, things spoken in looks and pauses, in between the words.

He understands now the connection in sadness he had recognized that first meeting. She had lost her son and he his wife. But it was not having lost a loved one that was their bond, but the guilt of culpability they had in their own losses. Porter sees now how he has tied himself to his own past. He has bound himself to his own history, fixed himself to it, just as Anais had — their fates sealed in the crash of a car. Anais could not escape it, could not free herself from the tide. Could he? For some reason he thinks of Pasiphae watching him blankly with her dry and scratched bone.

His mind reels as he re-examines everything in the cast of this new light. And every misspoken word, every misstep is the crunch of the Fibonacci shell beneath his foot. The mysteries in these missed interpretations persist and perpetuate themselves, continuing to make him a stranger to her.

But he knows already that he cannot let it go. Because to let go would be to release her memory, it would be to fail her again.

Thirty-five

Ana is driving. Her son is asleep in the backseat.

She is crying, trying to stifle her sobs. Jack has betrayed her again. Every time the wound begins to heal over with its frail stitching of skin, he tears it anew, and she can feel it now, her heart raw and bleeding.

She is trembling and she is thinking of all that she has given up — her art, her friends, her career, everything — only to be humiliated by him, time and again. And how could she be so weak as to allow it? It is her own weakness that so shames her, the weakness in her that he reminds her of and magnifies with his infidelities. It is her weakness which has permeated her life.

She sees it even when she looks at their son: a sacrifice she has made, something given up for him. She has never told a soul of the despair she felt after giving birth. She looked upon their child and loved him, even as she saw in him the final surrender of her last self, the forfeiting of her freedom.

The night is dark and the road wet from recent rainfall. Streetlights and the headlights of oncoming cars haze and bleed in her wet vision. Her mind plays a tumult of images of past and present, all painful for what she has lost, for the shame she is trapped in.

She is aware of the grit that crunches beneath the tires, of the weight of the vehicle and the wheel in her hands. She is aware of the emptiness in her gut and the pain in the centre of her chest, clenching there like a fist, choking her. Her life rises up to cut her quick and sharp, again and again, and she wants to scream, but has no breath. She wants it to stop. She wants to disappear, to cease to be — because there is no other way, other than to live with this.

A light flashes and the road is a blur through the tears, a drowned painting of dark running colours. It is unreal, and she focuses on that darkness as her mind goes blank, and the pain gets dialed into the background. As long as she can empty her mind, lose herself in the dark ahead of her, it will hurt just a little bit less. Her foot grows heavy on the accelerator, pushing into the blackness and her hand loosens on the wheel.

She wants to disappear, to cease to be. She lets go, closes her eyes. She finds release.

Gravity takes her, sways her, lifts and tilts . . .

Then the universe explodes, and she is thrown, battered hard.

Only a split-second, and her life is left in wreckage . . .

—

Could this be how it was: A moment of release, for a lifetime of suffering?

—

Night is at the window. He looks up from his desk, cigarette poised in his naked hand, and looks out of the room. A world outside and he held at bay from it. For so long, trying to find the words, to define in words the connections people forge and fail to forge, emotions hidden, spun and revealed in some shadowed form. Now he looks up and sees only: a window (frame and glass), a building beyond (brick and steel). No mystery there, just a construction for practical purposes, constructed by practical methods, by practical people. And somewhere along the line he will become practical too, his emotions dried and shrunk, like a nut inside an iron shell.

He closes his eyes.

—

She stands calf-deep in the water looking back at him, the hem of her dress clutched in her hands. She smiles, then looks out to sea again and slowly begins wading out into the deep. He wants to rise and follow her, but he stays where he is and watches, letting her go. She becomes a silhouette growing smaller, sinking. And the pale sun flares up like a match head struck, and it is all swallowed up, everything, burns to white and ash and nothingness.

—

H. M. Blanc was born in Ontario, Canada and raised in the Caribbean Republic of Trinidad & Tobago. He studied Film and Creative Writing at York University. Over the years he has worked as a Telemarketer, Dish Washer, Sales Clerk, Handy Man, and Art Gallery Manager, among other things. Between Bodies Lie is his first novel.

Lightning Source UK Ltd.
Milton Keynes UK
UKOW040153010513

210019UK00001B/9/P